ALSO BY JUDITH A. BARRETT

DONUT LADY COZY MYSTERY SERIES

MAGGIE SLOAN THRILLER SERIES

RILEY MALLOY THRILLER SERIES

GRID DOWN SURVIVAL SERIES

Sweet and Sour Deal

Donut Lady Cozy Mystery
Book 6

Judith A. Barrett

SWEET AND SOUR DEAL

DONUT LADY COZY MYSTERY, BOOK 6

Published in the United States of America by Wobbly Creek, LLC

2021 Georgia, US

wobblycreek.com

SWEET AND SOUR DEAL is a work of fiction. Names, characters, businesses, places, events, locales, and incidents either are the products of the author's imagination or used in a fictitious manner. Any resemblance to actual persons, living or dead, or actual events is purely coincidental.

Edited by Judith Euen Davis

Cover by Wobbly Creek, LLC

ISBN 978-1-953870-24-7

Sweet and Sour Deal is dedicated to gold that glitters and to friends who laugh at our jokes.

PREVIOUSLY...

I'm Karen O'Brien, and I was in prison for twelve years for murdering my husband, which sounds a little startling, even to me. By no means do I recommend prison; I have haunting shadows and terrifying nightmares, and I still miss my dear, trusted prison friend who died a suspicious death.

After I served my sentence, I moved to Asbury, Georgia, my hometown, and against the advice of my old school friend, Shirley, bought a donut shop from a brilliant baker who insisted that his old German shepherd, Colonel, and sassy, gray cat, Mia, were included in the sale. Roxie, a beautiful collie, later joined our family. I never dreamed that when I solved my prison friend's murder and stopped a serial killer, I'd begun a side hustle, as they say, of solving crimes and exposing killers in our small town. I'd like to go on record that I certainly have never sought out trouble, despite what Sheriff Grady may think in light of the annoyingly recurrent deadly events.

The most recent complication started when Shirley discovered her real estate partner, Charlotte, covered with blood and with fatal stab wounds in her chest in a shower at a vacant house, but that was just the beginning of Shirley's woes as Charlotte's sister, ex-husband,

and a realtor from another town all laid claim to Charlotte's business. It took a lot of sleuthing on my part to straighten out the entire real estate mess that Charlotte had created, but the outcome was great for Shirley because she and Alfred, our local banker, became engaged. I didn't see that coming!

To add to the town's nervousness from the murder, the news spread that coyotes were overrunning Asbury. The sheriff asked an old mentor of his, Ned Burke, a retired wildlife officer, to come to town to investigate. At the same time, one of the local men contacted a wildlife expert, Rocco Marsh, to rid the town of the coyotes.

The sheriff did warn me that Ned Burke had rough edges, but rough-edges Ned was right: the phony Rocco Marsh did orchestrate the coyote rumors.

I had five potential suspects who could have murdered Charlotte. When I recognized one of them as an escaped convicted murderer from an old photo, I stopped him before he killed me; I was relieved Ned never knew about my wild theory that he was suspect number five.

CHAPTER ONE

"Ready to go to work?" I opened the back door and peered into the still-dark yard for the dogs. The crickets chirped a song of upcoming rain, and the birds were silent.

I paused as I listened. *There wasn't any rain in the forecast, but the crickets are usually right.*

Colonel dashed past me and trotted through the house to the front door, and Roxie zipped inside then danced around me while Mia marched to her cat carrier. When I grabbed my umbrella, the shadows slinked behind Mia until she flicked her tail, then they billowed and disappeared down the hallway.

That was odd. Are they worried about Mia?

I rubbed my forehead. *Can shadows worry? Should I be worried too?*

I shivered as a cold chill ran down my spine then shook off the creeping feeling of dread.

Colonel and Roxie crouched next to the minivan and quivered in anticipation; when I pushed the fob to open the minivan back door, they leapt inside. Roxie took her usual place in the third row of seats, and Colonel proudly perched on the seat behind the driver.

After I placed Mia's carrier on the back floorboard behind the passenger's seat, I started the engine and backed out of the driveway.

As I drove to the shop, the earlier thick fog was spotty, but the air was still damp, and the streetlights cast a warm amber glow that was a beacon in the dull gray of the fog.

The lights were on at the shop when I parked the minivan, and I sighed in relief. *Finally, something normal: Andrew is already here, as usual.*

After I opened the driver's side back door for Colonel and Roxie, I hurried around my vehicle and lifted out the carrier; the din of the cicadas confirmed my predicted rain. I grabbed my umbrella and stuck it under my arm then closed and locked all the doors before I walked inside.

Andrew was mixing his second batch of dough for the day's donuts while his first batch rose. He wore his *Donut Hole* apron over his favorite oversized black Bulldogs T-shirt. His *Got Sprinkles?* ballcap covered his cowlick, but his unruly brown hair spiked out around his ears. Andrew had his father's hair and his mother's smile. He was a "special education" student in school and had worked in the stockroom at his parents' hardware store since he graduated; Randy and Kim were surprised at how quickly Andrew picked up making donuts, and I've been privileged to watch his progress as he takes on more responsibility at the shop.

I smiled. *Now Randy brags about his son the talented baker to everyone who walks into the hardware store.*

After I released Mia, she waved her tail and held her head high as she marched to the storeroom. I followed her and tried to copy her regal walk.

Andrew snickered. "You've almost got it down, Miss Lady."

I smiled. "I'll keep practicing. Monday is the Methodist Men's group, right?"

Andrew had the weekly planner that Barbara had bought us on the counter in front of him, and even though he would have checked as soon as he came in, he squinted at the words as he read it again.

"The Methodist Men shifted to Tuesday this week because most of them will be here for today's emergency meeting of a new group: Mr. Alfred and his executive board are meeting. I put it down in the book as Boys' Board because they work mostly with the boys who have problems in school. I told Mr. Alfred he needs a better name. I think I'll tell him Wild Steer Wrestlers is a good name."

I scrubbed my hands then tied my apron in back. "I think it fits. How did you come up with that?"

"Me and Dad watched a cowboy movie that had wild steers last night after we got tired of watching wrestling."

"We can put them in the planner book as WSW for Wild Steer Wrestlers until they come up with a name."

I waited while Andrew carefully marked today's group in the planner as WSW.

"What's our menu?" I asked.

"Me and Woody planned classic glazed vanilla scones except no glaze for Mr. Alfred, vanilla frosted donuts, and strawberry frosted donuts with pink sprinkles. Woody knows what Mr. Alfred likes."

"Yes, he does. He is far more perceptive than most eleven-year-olds, isn't he? I could thin a bit of the vanilla frosting to glaze the scones, but I'll leave two plain ones for Mr. Alfred."

Andrew nodded. "I have to work now."

I glanced at the front of the shop; the shadows covered the window but disappeared after I motioned them away with my hand, but a dark figure remained on the sidewalk for a moment then shifted out of my view.

I stared at the window. "Did you see that?"

"See what?" Andrew asked.

"Nothing; for a minute there, I thought we had an early customer."

I checked the door to be sure it was locked before I hurried to fill the large coffee machine with water. After I removed the lid, I rolled my eyes. *I should have known that Andrew would have already poured in the water and measured the coffee.* I pushed the start button on the machine before I gathered my ingredients for the day's scones.

As I pulled out my last batch of scones from the oven, a flash of lightning and a sudden crack of thunder overhead startled me, and I jumped. Roxie scrambled to lean against me, and Colonel raised his head then went back to sleep.

"Colonel's not bothered, Roxie; it's just a rainstorm." I stroked her ruffled hackles to soothe her, and both of us relaxed.

Andrew wore his hearing protection earmuffs when he came out of the storeroom. "Miss Lady, did you know we have gray sugar dots? I can't remember why Woody got them, but can I sprinkle vanilla frosted donuts with gray dots and call them rainy day donuts?"

"I think that's a great idea. Do you want to write up our donuts and scones for the day and draw a rainy day cloud on the board?"

Andrew grinned. "I'd like to do that."

After Andrew finished, he and I stood back and admired our menu board like seasoned art critics.

"I like the dark, puffy clouds, and the lightning bolt adds the perfect touch. It will be a nice surprise for our customers," I said.

Andrew nodded.

When Sheriff Grady Hayes parked near the front door, I unlocked the door before I poured his coffee, and Colonel strolled to lay down next to the sheriff's stool at the counter. The sheriff dashed inside, but Andrew had already plated two donuts: a pink sprinkled and a rainy day.

"Maybe I wanted just one donut today." The sheriff's eyes twinkled as he removed his rain jacket; after he scanned the room for a place to hang it, he draped it across the counter stool closest to the window.

While the sheriff took two strides to sit at his usual place at the counter, Andrew's eyes twinkled as he reached for the sheriff's plate.

"Wait, Andrew. That was just a joke."

"Oh." When Andrew turned, he winked at me, and I laughed.

"What's so funny?" Sheriff asked.

I raised my eyebrows. "Your joke."

"I think the joke's on me," the sheriff mumbled.

He examined the donuts on his plate then read the board. "Rainy day donut? Oh, I see the cluster of dark clouds on the donut. Well done, Andrew."

Andrew's cheeks reddened as he ducked his head then hurried back to his donut station. "Thank you."

"How did you know?" I asked.

"Tell you later." He pointed to the front door. "There's His Honor, Mr. Retired Mayor."

"Right on time." I smiled.

The bell over the door jingled when David came inside then set his umbrella next to the door; when Roxie trotted to the door to greet him, he reached down and scratched her ear. "Karen, we need one of those boot trays to catch drips, some coat hooks, and an umbrella stand by the front door, so our customers will have a place to leave their dripping umbrellas and raincoats."

"Won't happen unless it goes on a list," I said.

Andrew hurried to the storeroom then returned. "I wrote tray, hooks, and umbrella stand on the inventory needed board."

David rushed toward the storeroom for his apron then paused to read the menu board. "Rainy day donut? The artwork is perfect."

Andrew carried dishes into the pink meeting room, and David picked up napkins and small plates.

"Who's our group today?" David asked as he joined Andrew.

"Wild Steer Wrestlers," Andrew said.

David nodded. "Been a while since Alfred's brought his group together; it must be something important."

Roxie supervised while David and Andrew rearranged chairs around the table in the pink room as they discussed how many men would be present at the meeting.

"How did Alfred come up with Wild Steer Wrestlers?" Sheriff whispered.

"He doesn't know about it quite yet. Andrew thought of it." I explained the sources of the name. "Now, your turn. How did you know rainy day donuts was Andrew's idea?"

"He hovered because he didn't want to miss my reaction."

I chuckled. "You're right, he did. I thought for a minute there that he was going to ask you to move over one more stool."

Sheriff turned to stare at the meeting room then turned back to his cup on the counter. "David didn't miss a step at the name of the new group. In fact, he even knew it was Alfred's group of guys. How could he have known?"

I shook my head. "I have no idea, but I'll have to ask because he'll have a great story."

"Get me the short version." Sheriff drained his cup, but I was ready with the pot.

He waved off a refill. "I have a big meeting with the City Council; they're floundering and driving me crazy. I have paperwork in my office I'd like to finish before they consume my morning." He sighed. "Box up a dozen rainy day donuts for me."

"I always did that before a meeting too," David said when he and Andrew came out of the pink room. "It helps sweeten their sour attitudes."

Sheriff chuckled. "We'll have to chat sometime; I have a feeling I'll need a lot more coaching."

Andrew boxed up the donuts then handed them to the sheriff.

Sheriff smiled. "Thanks for putting them into the plastic sack, so they won't get wet."

Not long after the sheriff left, Shirley hurried into the shop. "I need a new umbrella." She left her open umbrella on the floor near the front door. "I had to fight with it to open it, and now I'm afraid to close it. I'm probably wetter than I'd have been if I'd just run inside without it."

Shirley's signature red jacket was soaked. "Where can I put my jacket, so it will dry out?"

"Give it to me, and I'll drape it over the stool close to the oven," I said.

Shirley was four inches taller than me and outweighed me by thirty pounds. She struggled out of her jacket then handed it to me. "I have to lose a few pounds. This is my favorite jacket; I'd never find another one just like it. How's my makeup? Is it all runny?"

Her makeup was impeccable, as always.

"It's fine."

She ran her fingers through her short, curly, blonde hair with streaks of highlights. "At least my hair will dry quickly. I can't stand to look a mess."

I poured and doctored Shirley's coffee the way she liked it in a large to-go cup then set it on the counter while Andrew sacked up two donuts and a scone, and David hurried back into the pink room.

Andrew placed the sack next to the coffee then rushed to the pink room and closed the door.

"I know why David and Andrew always work in the pink room with the door closed. I used to wonder if I'd said something because every time I came into the shop, that's where they went, but now I know why. Woody told me that men like to focus on their work without interruption, so I quit dropping by the bank several times a day because Woody said Alfred was too polite to tell me I was distracting." Shirley giggled. "Isn't that the cutest thing you've ever heard? I can't stay all morning and visit with you, though. My accountant is bringing me some paperwork to review and sign, and I need to straighten up the office, so she won't be uncomfortable. Every time I go to her office, it looks like a showroom with everything in its place."

Shirley grabbed her donuts and coffee then hurried to the door. Before she picked up her umbrella, she said, "I've told you that you need to have a regular appointment with Francine. Everybody knows we're the same age, and your gray hair makes you look old."

"I don't—"

Shirley interrupted, "I know you're busy, and your gray hair doesn't bother you, but I don't want people to think I'm old like you. I have a certain image to project as a businesswoman, and a gray-haired peer doesn't fit my persona."

Shirley patted her hair before she picked up her umbrella. "I made an appointment for you; Francine will be ready for you today at two. Don't be late because she rearranged her schedule for you as a favor to me. She made it a point to tell me she doesn't do that for anyone else."

After Shirley left, I opened the pink room door, and Mia scooted out before Andrew hurried to his donut station to fry his last batch of donut holes.

"You need anything?" I asked as David came out of the pink room with the whisk broom and dustpan.

"No, we're all set."

"Good. How did you know Alfred planned to have a meeting this morning?"

David grinned. "I'm extremely perceptive, plus Alfred told me yesterday after church."

"You'll have to think up a good story I can tell the sheriff." I smirked.

"I accept the challenge." David saluted me before he dumped the few crumbs in the dustpan into the trash then returned to the pink room.

"I have every confidence in you." I finished loading donuts and scones into the display case while Andrew washed the bowls and utensils we'd used to make the dough and frostings.

After Alfred and the other men in the group were in the pink room, David hung up his apron and ballcap in the storeroom then returned to the meeting room.

"Off duty for now." He closed the door.

"That's not fair; I was going to eavesdrop," I muttered as I sanitized the counter and the seats.

One of the older city council members came into the shop. "Donut Lady, I need six of those pink-sprinkled donuts for our meeting this morning. It starts in fifteen minutes, and I forgot I was in charge of the pink sprinkles."

Andrew handed him the sack, and I took his money.

After the councilman left, Andrew said, "Pink sprinkles are the sheriff's favorite."

I nodded. "Yes, they are."

I headed to the storeroom for the mop to dry up the wet floor near the entrance and stopped. *Sheriff's favorite.*

I called the sheriff.

"I'll be there in two minutes," he said.

"Wait. Everything's okay here. I'm calling to warn you about an ambush. One of the councilman was here and bought six pink-sprinkled donuts."

"Oh, really? Thanks for the heads up."

He hung up, and I snickered. "You're welcome."

"Andrew, the sheriff said thanks for the heads up."

"You're welcome. Tell him that."

"I did." I walked out of the storeroom with the mop, but Andrew blocked my way.

"I'll mop, so you can check on Mr. David."

"Good idea; thank you." *Andrew knows I'm busting to know what is going on in there.*

I hurried to the pink room, quietly slipped inside, and picked up an empty platter then checked their coffee pot. Roxie grinned at me but didn't move from her spot near David. I smiled. *She and David are becoming fast friends.*

I glanced around the room and raised my eyebrows. *I didn't know Ned had joined Alfred's group.*

When I stepped out of the room with the empty platter in my hand, Andrew whispered, "Is everything okay? Were you surprised when you saw Mr. Ned? Ms. Barbara said he has rough edges. Does he?"

I nodded. "Seems like it doesn't take much to be nice, but I guess it just isn't natural for everyone."

After I gave Andrew the empty platter, he handed me one filled with donuts and donut holes.

I carefully closed the door and set the full platter in the middle of the table then stepped back and pretended I was invisible, or at least inconspicuous, as I stood near the coffee station.

I frowned as the men discussed the issue of missing inventory and brainstormed on how they could find the troubled boy who was stealing. Jeff, one of the sheriff's senior deputies, and Randy, Andrew's father, agreed to serve as the committee to investigate the options the group had discussed and bring back their findings at the next meeting. After more discussion, the group agreed to meet on the following Tuesday, and the meeting was adjourned.

I remained near the coffee station as David hurried to put himself back on duty; the rest of the men rose from their seats and left except for Ned, who waited until everyone was gone then sauntered over to talk to me.

"Alfred and I were nominated to attend a meeting at the Georgia Sheriffs' Association Boys Ranch on Friday. It's only an hour or so drive from here. It's a residential care program to help children who have been abandoned, neglected, and abused. The meeting is for their staff to learn more about programs like Alfred's and for us to understand their program. We're hoping to make it simpler for some of our youth to be selected for their residential program."

"Is that something that could be an alternative for a boy or girl who is in the same situation as Woody?" I asked.

"Exactly," Ned said, "and I think Woody is Alfred's inspiration to pursue a relationship with the Boys Ranch. One of the men recommended that we visit one of the other Sheriffs' association facilities in north Georgia that's specifically for girls before the Friday meeting, and another man, whose father is a retired Florida deputy sheriff, suggested we visit a Florida Sheriffs' Boys Ranch too for additional ideas. The Florida program is a little different than Georgia's, and he thought we may be able to use the best of both programs."

"That sounds good; it's nice that you'll be able to accompany Alfred."

"There's a little more to the story," Ned said. "I need another cup of coffee."

"Sit at the counter, and I'll pour you one." I pulled out a clean cup and filled it for Ned.

"We were talking about the logistics. Alfred was balking at sleeping in a hotel, and he wasn't interested in camping. He's not much for restaurant food, either. When it turned from a day trip on Friday to four days, Alfred claimed he can't be away from work that long."

I nodded. "He is particular."

"Peculiar," Ned said. "You mispronounced it. Anyway, Jorge offered to go. He said his main mechanic at the gas station, Josh, can manage it as well as he can. Alfred's going to fund the trip, so there's no financial burden on Jorge or me. I'd like to take my camper, but it makes more sense for us to travel together and stay at a hotel. The retired deputy's son will schedule our Florida visits for Tuesday and Wednesday morning, then on Thursday, we'll visit the Georgia program that is specifically for girls before we got to the meeting on Friday."

"Sounds like quite a road trip, but I'm sure you'll bring back a lot of ideas."

"You should go with us; you have women's prison experience nobody else around here has. You'd be very useful on our Thursday visit."

I rolled my eyes. *Ned definitely doesn't have the knack to approach a subject with finesse.*

"I don't know; I'd have to see if Barbara and David can cover the shop on Thursday and Friday. It's hard for Barbara to be around people, so I'm not sure I'd want to put her through two days. I'll have to think about it."

"We'll see what works out." Ned strolled to the door. "Are you free for dinner? I have a couple more things to talk over with you."

"I'm not sure I'm up to going out. Why don't I cook?"

"You know it's hard for me to turn down one of your homecooked meals, but it's my turn to treat you. Be ready at five thirty. I'll have reservations for six."

I raised my eyebrows as he left. *Since when does anyone need reservations at Ida's Diner?*

"My hair better not look weird, or I'll be cooking," I muttered.

"If your hair looks weird, Miss Lady, you can wear your ballcap," Andrew said. "That's what I do."

Oops. Didn't realize I'd said that aloud. "That's great advice, thank you."

When all our donuts, donut holes, and scones were gone, we began cleaning the shop.

"Are you going on the fact-finding trip with our resident curmudgeon, as Barbara calls him?" David asked.

"I'd like to because I do think I have a unique viewpoint, but I'm not sure I can spend two days with that man," I said.

Andrew nodded. "Mr. Ned needs to work on his manners."

"That's exactly it, Andrew," David said. "A few manners always sweeten up a cranky attitude."

After we finished cleaning, I said, "I'll lock up, Andrew. I have some invoices to review."

"I'll stay until you leave, Miss Lady." Andrew crossed his arms.

I raised my eyebrows. "Only if you let me give you a ride home."

David nodded. "She's right, Andrew. I'll see you two in the morning. Barbara and I are meeting Shirley at her office right after lunch for a list of properties that we can drive by; I hope it's still raining this afternoon because it's the best way to see how weatherproof an old house is." David hugged Roxie and whispered to her then headed to the door.

"No fair picking sides, Mr. David," Andrew said.

"You're right, Andrew. I'll be on your side the next two times, so you'll be ahead."

"I won't be long, Andrew." I hurried to my office, and Andrew picked up Mr. Otto's old recipe book for scones and donuts.

Andrew came to the office door as I finished recording and filing the invoices. "Are apple fritters like apple scones?"

"Fritters are more like donuts because they are usually fried. Did you find an apple fritter recipe in Mr. Otto's book?'

"He has a whole section on fritters." Andrew handed me the recipe book.

I scanned the recipes. "This is really interesting; he has apple, peach, blueberry, and strawberry fritter recipes, and here's a note that says fresh fruit only."

I gave the book back to Andrew. "If they're in his recipe book, I'll bet he made them. He may have stopped making them because of the extra work."

"Ms. Darlene would know." Andrew glanced out the window. "It's stopped raining; I won't need a ride."

Andrew carried Mia in her carrier to my minivan, and Colonel climbed onto the backseat while Roxie splashed in the gutter then jumped into the minivan.

"Oh, Roxie, look at the muddy footprints all over the seat," I grumbled.

Roxie grinned as I pulled away from the curb, and I shook my head. *Guess it was worth it to her.*

When we reached the house, I called Roxie to join Colonel on the porch before she dashed to the puddle she was eyeing. I quickly opened the front door, then after they were inside, I hurried to the minivan and picked up Mia's carrier as she meowed her complaints about being left alone.

I leaned against the door after we were all inside. "I know how much you love puddles, Roxie, and I'm sorry I was cranky; something's bothering me; I'm not sure, but I think it's because the shadows are worried." I frowned. "It sounds strange when I say it, doesn't it?"

While I swept the floors, Colonel nosed the back door, then he and Roxie dashed outside.

I rolled my eyes. *I probably don't want to mop until tomorrow.*

After I put away my broom and dustpan, I stood at the back window and ate my yogurt while Roxie raced around the backyard, and Colonel relaxed on the porch in the sun.

I gathered up laundry then started the washer before I dusted the living room. I glanced at the clock and sighed. *One thirty. Guess I'd better head out.*

I opened the back door. "Ready to come in?"

Colonel lumbered inside, and Roxie trotted in behind him.

"I'm going to the beauty shop; want to go with me?"

Colonel flopped onto the kitchen floor, and Roxie trotted to her favorite rug in the living room. After she rearranged it to her nest, she circled it then curled up in the middle of it. Mia meowed from the pantry; when I opened the door, she growled at me.

"I'll go by myself then."

When I parked at the hair stylist's shop, I frowned at the shadows that lurked on the side of the building.

"Are you here to snoop or to make sure my hair looks right?"

They disappeared around the corner.

They are acting so bizarre. I closed my eyes then slowly exhaled before I opened the minivan door. *I'm talking to myself about shadows acting strangely. I need a vacation.*

When I went inside the shop, the overwhelming, cloying, floral odor assaulted my nose and throat, and I coughed. *It's fragrance, not odor.*

I stepped back in shock and stared at the eye-exploding décor: the chairs were deep purple, the four stylists' stations were fiery red trimmed in neon green, and the floor tiles were yellow and orange.

Francine hurried to the door from the back room and snorted when she saw me. "Not your taste, Donut Lady? Mine neither, but the clients love it. I should have warned you to rub mentholated camphor cream under your nose and to wear sunglasses."

I chuckled. "Might have been the jolt I needed to break my every day, boring routine."

"I like that. Maybe I should change my tagline: cut, color, and a jolt." She snickered.

"Please don't," I grinned. "Shirley will know exactly how you got the idea."

"So, we're doing cut and color, right? Here's my chair." She covered her mouth with her hand. "Please excuse me, I just ate lunch and had a nice bowl of spaghetti with garlic bread." She sniffed her hands. "I can still smell it on my hands, and I've scrubbed them three times."

"I'm fine." I smiled. After I was seated, she floated the cover around me and peered at me in the mirror. "Now, what did we have in mind?"

"To get Shirley off my case." I smirked.

"So, no gray and a cut you can live with?" Francine lifted up my hair with her fingertips.

"Yes, something that isn't high maintenance."

"So, you're not high maintenance?" She chuckled. "Got it. I'll mix your color then be right back. Your gray is mousy around your face, but the rest of it is more silver, so I'm not going to try to cover up the silver. I'll just blend."

I nodded. *Blend is good.*

"Do you want music?" Francine called from the back.

"I'm fine." I scanned the shop then rose to look more closely at the collection of wigs in a corner.

Francine smiled when she returned. "I started carrying wigs at the request of some of my customers who were undergoing chemotherapy. These are hand-tied and soft, so they won't irritate an already sensitive scalp. I didn't realize there was such a demand

and have increased my inventory as word of mouth has spread the news that I have wigs that don't look wiggy. Does that make sense?"

"I can understand how that would be important for self-confidence."

"I can order anything a woman requests, but most of my customers don't what to bother with waiting, and I don't blame them."

"The variety of style and color you have is amazing. I'm not an expert by any means, but I can almost guess the age of the owner by the style; you're performing quite a valuable service for the community."

"Thank you, I do what I can."

Francine raised an eyebrow and pointed to the chair, then after I returned to my seat, she kept up a running monologue of gossip as she deftly applied hair color goo on my hair. I tuned her out until she said, "Come sit under the dryer for a few minutes."

She escorted me to the dryer then turned it on low before she placed a small stool in front of my seat, so I could prop up my feet. The smaller room was painted a soft beige, and the floor tiles were a warm, chocolate brown.

This is heavenly. I closed my eyes and listened to the drone of the dryer.

I was startled when Francine turned off the dryer. "Okay, time to rinse."

"I think I dozed off." I rose from the chair.

"I hope so; it's supposed to be relaxing in here for everyone." She led me to the sink.

As she rinsed and shampooed my hair, her hands and breath had an even heavier garlic odor. *I'll be nose-blind to it soon.*

She wrapped my head with a towel. "Back to my station."

When I rose from my chair, I caught a glimpse of an open, half-full bottle of red wine in the back room. *Not my business.*

While she carefully combed out the tangles, a man stormed into the shop, and I turned to stare at him as I held onto my phone under the drape.

"Where is it?" he growled as he opened his jacket and flashed the exposed butt of a pistol in a holster on his left side.

Francine side-glanced me, and I quickly averted my eyes. "It's at my desk," she said.

She turned my seat, so my back was to the man, but I could see him in the mirror.

Does she know I can see him?

He met my gaze in the mirror, and I was surprised at the flicker of apprehension in his eyes. He scowled as he turned his face away from me then hissed in a low voice, "Nobody was supposed to be here."

He leaned over the counter to examine her desk. "Hurry up. You have it, don't you?"

Francine strode to her desk and reached into the top drawer then pulled out a fat envelope. The man ripped it open and peered inside.

"It's all there," she said.

"Better be." He snarled as he counted it then stuffed it into his jacket pocket and left.

CHAPTER TWO

Francine sighed. "Sorry about that, but I'm glad you were here and not any of my other customers because they would have freaked. I didn't expect him until five o'clock, but there was no sense in challenging him."

"Are you okay? Are you in some kind of trouble?" I asked.

"It's not me; my younger sister, who lives in Conway, got herself in a little trouble. Sissy owns a small furniture shop and fancies herself to be a decorator; maybe she is, but we don't have the same taste. She designed my shop, and my customers claim they love it, but I think they are too nice to say anything negative."

Francine picked up her comb and continued untangling my hair, but she stopped to wave her arms for emphasis as she talked.

"You should see my sister's shop. Never mind, her shop makes mine look like a prim church lady's home with carefully placed doilies. Everyone thinks Sissy is a nickname for Sister, but our Italian mama named her Sicily; Sicily asked me to call her Sissy when she was five, so I did, and the rest of the family picked it up because they thought it was cute."

Her weak smile disappeared as she scowled. "She had a boyfriend who is scum. From what Sissy said, he could turn on the charm; I never met him, but I'll bet I would have seen right through him. I haven't heard much about him lately from Sissy and thought he was gone for good until I found out he took over her business bank account, invoices, marketing, and ordering."

Francine scanned the shop then lowered her voice. "I don't have any proof, but I think he was smuggling drugs."

There's no one in the shop but us. I shrugged. *I guess there are some things one must say in a whisper. I am surprised she didn't add, "Bless his heart."* I cleared my throat to keep from laughing at my inappropriate, witty reply to myself.

She continued in a normal tone. "He emptied her checking, savings, and retirement fund then bailed on her. Sissy told me more than once that she would invite me to her house to meet him, but she never did because he was working or busy; then she claimed it was just as well because he wasn't all that good at socializing."

I'm having trouble keeping up with her.

"I hired an investigator, but he was too pricey and didn't have any results after a month. The investigator told me he was close and needed more time, but that was what he'd said every week since I'd hired him. I had almost drained my savings, so I declined. Not long after that, Sissy told me a man showed up at her furniture store and insisted that her boyfriend owed him a lot of money, and she'd better pay up. She laughed at him and told him she had contacts then told me she called Mama, who told her not to worry because Mama would call in some favors, but that night around midnight, Sissy got a call saying her shop was on fire. She rushed to her shop, but it was fine."

Francine stopped and finished combing. "What do you think? Two inches off? More?"

"Two inches sounds great," I said.

Francine cut one side then waved her scissors as she continued talking, and I cringed.

"When Sissy got home, fire engines blocked the road in front of her house; a neighbor who worked the late shift at the hospital spotted flames coming out of Sissy's bedroom window and called the fire department. Sissy had homeowner's insurance, but her boyfriend changed it from her usual company, and the new one didn't have the best of coverage. Sissy was sleeping in her car until her house is cleaned and repaired. The only furniture she was able to save were her kitchen appliances and her kitchen table and chairs. She told me Mama tried to talk her into staying with them and even offered to pay the rent for an apartment, but she wanted to stay close to her house; I don't really blame her. There have been extra costs that Sissy told me weren't covered by her insurance, and Papa gave her access to his bank accounts, so she wouldn't have to max out her credit cards. I have been helping with what little I have."

"What about the man who came here? How does he fit in?"

Francine finished cutting my hair then handed me a mirror. "Your hair is going to be gorgeous, if I do say so myself."

She turned my chair, so I could check the back of my hair. "This is pretty. You do good work."

She nodded. "The first guy returned to her shop a week after her house fire; he told her that Mama's people couldn't do anything to him, and it would be her fault if Papa's house burned with the old folks still inside, then he upped the amount of her so-called weekly payment on the supposed debt. After she had sold all her personal belongings that were worth anything, including her car, she called me in the middle of the night. She was sobbing because her house was so cold, and it broke my heart. I caught up her back payments for her utilities after Papa gave me some money, so they could be turned back on; Sissy told me Mama took over paying her utilities, and she has been sleeping on a cot in her kitchen. The last time the guy showed up for money, she told him she didn't have it. He told her to find a way to pay it or find her old boyfriend, so the boyfriend could pay up, so she told him I'd give him the money if he came to my shop after five o'clock, then she called me and told me how much he wanted. I was glad I had enough left in the bank to cover it from the money Papa gave me to help her out."

That was pretty presumptuous of Sissy.

"Really? That's what he wants? He wants the boyfriend?"

Francine exhaled. "That's what she told me. How do you want me to style your hair?"

"This is perfect like it is; if Shirley saw my hair styled, she'd always expect me to fix it like you did. What did you give your investigator?"

"A friend of Sissy's recommended him; all he wanted was a photo and the scum's last known address."

"That's not much." I furrowed my brow as she led the way to her desk. "I don't understand why the goon didn't look for the boyfriend himself."

Francine frowned. "I'm starting to wonder if there's more to the story than what Sissy's told me. What are you doing tomorrow night? Come to my house for an authentic Italian dinner, and I'll invite Sissy too; the three of us can chat. Maybe between the two of us, we'll be able to piece together something I can go on to find her boyfriend. Come at five-thirty, and we'll eat at six."

"Sounds wonderful. What can I bring?"

"I can't think of a thing, but if you feel strange coming empty-handed, lend me one of your books." Francine smiled.

"That I can do."

After I was home, I relaxed on the back porch with a tall tumbler of sweet tea while Colonel napped in the sun, and Roxie romped with the butterflies. I closed my eyes and listened to the cardinal as he claimed his territory, the traffic hum from the state road, and the faint sound of classical music from the house across the alley.

When the tumbler hit the porch with a clatter and cold liquid splashed on my ankle then trickled into my sock, I jerked my head and opened my eyes. The tumbler lid had come off when it fell, and my pants and sock were soaked.

Roxie dashed to my side to clean up the sweet tea that had spilled on the porch.

"I really must be tired. I need to check the time; I hadn't planned a shower, but plans change, don't they, Roxie?"

I pulled off my socks and shoes. "Good thing I was wearing my old sneakers."

When the three of us went inside, I tossed my shoes, socks, and pants into the washer then checked the time. Good. *Five o'clock. I'll have to hurry because Ned will be early.*

After my quick wash and rinse, I dressed, and Ned knocked on my door at five fifteen. *I knew it.*

I opened the door, but he stayed on the porch. "You ready? Let's go."

"I have to feed Colonel, Roxie, and Mia first," I said.

Ned strode inside and crossed his arms as he stood by the front door. "I'll wait."

I rolled my eyes and resisted saying, "Suit yourself."

After I set Mia's food dish down, she pushed it into the pantry while I measured then poured food into the dogs' bowls.

"Let's go," Ned said.

"I'd like to give the dogs one last break."

Roxie finished eating first, then Colonel joined her at the back door. They took a quick break before they trotted back inside and flopped onto the cool kitchen floor. I locked the back door and glanced at the clock.

"Five twenty-five; I'm ready." I picked up my purse then strolled to the front door. Ned opened the door for me, and I stared at him. *Now, he's scaring me. Who is this polite gentleman?*

I locked the front door, and Ned hurried past me and opened the passenger's side door. After I sat on the passenger's seat, he closed the door. *Ned's been cloned by a monster from outer space: that's the only possible answer.*

"There's a new family-owned restaurant in Conway; I thought you'd like it," Ned said.

"Oh, I didn't know. What kind of food?"

"Colombian." He narrowed his eyes. "You don't have any food allergies or a delicate stomach, do you?"

I snickered. *Ned always goes straight to the point.* "Not at all. I'll eat almost anything."

Ned nodded. "I will too; I like a woman who isn't afraid to eat."

I side-glanced him. *Is he hinting that I'm fat?*

I watched the landscape as we traveled through the countryside. *No, Ned doesn't have a subtle bone in his body. If he thought I was overweight, he'd say so.*

"There's been a change in plans. Jorge and I had a long talk with Alfred, Randy, and Jeff. We all agreed that our big fact-finding tour would be interesting but not really relevant to the work that the men in town have been doing with our local boys. We still think the group should have a representative or two go to the Friday meeting. I told them I'd go, and I didn't volunteer you, but it's only a day trip. What do you think?"

"I'll definitely think about it," I said.

Ned nodded. "Some people might think that's a polite way to say no, but I know you mean it, and that's good enough for me."

When he stopped at a light, Ned peered at me. "Do you always brush your hair that way? It looks different."

"No, it's pretty much the same way I always brush it."

He frowned. "Still looks different."

When he parked at the restaurant, I said, "This looks nice. Is the building new?"

"It used to be an old bar."

When Ned opened his car door, I started to open mine too, but he rushed around the car and opened the door for me.

If he takes my hand to help me out, I'll spill water on him and watch him melt. No, wrong movie. Water burns an alien. That would be too mean; I don't think I could do that.

I was so deep in thought that I stumbled on the step, and Ned caught me before I fell.

"Are you feeling okay, Karen?"

I smiled. "I'm fine; I got lost in my thoughts."

"I thought something was bothering you because you were so quiet on the ride here, but I guess you never do talk much."

When we went inside the restaurant, I smiled at the old saloon-style décor. *I like these people.*

"Nice, isn't it?" Ned scanned the high ceilings then rubbed the host stand lightly with his fingertips. "Really smooth. Vic would drool over this wood."

"I love that they kept the old bar's personality alive." I glanced down. "I can almost see the saw dust that belongs on these old, wood floors."

A young woman with long, black hair pulled into a low ponytail hurried to greet us. She flashed a big smile, and her black eyes twinkled. "Mr. Burke? Table for two?"

Ned beamed. "That's right."

I returned her smile. *Her smile is contagious, and that old curmudgeon's heart just melted.*

"I'm Elena; follow me to your table, please. My mama's the chef, and when she heard who was coming, she wanted you to sit close to the kitchen, so she could visit with you, Ms. Donut Lady."

Ned held my chair for me. *I'll skip tossing any water. I want to see what he does next.*

As she handed us our menus, Elena said, "Mama will be out in a few minutes. She's actually my mother-in-law, but she's Mama to my husband, Dan, so she's Mama to me and all my family."

Elena strolled to the kitchen and pushed open the door. "Mama, Donut Lady is here."

The chef burst through the swinging door and squealed, "It's you! You're actually here!"

"Devlin!" I leapt up from my seat so quickly that I knocked my chair over in my rush.

As we hugged, she laughed. "Dang. I was hoping you'd have gotten shorter since the last time I saw you."

I laughed. "I always loved that you were shorter than me. You're in a very rare category."

"I'm short? I hadn't noticed." Devlin rolled her eyes.

We giggled and hugged again.

After she sat with us at the table, I asked, "I saw you sold the motel. There's a nice strip mall there now with lots of parking. How did you end up here?"

"A chef in a Colombian restaurant?" She giggled. "It's a long, really interesting story, but I'll give you the short, mildly interesting one. Do you remember the sheriff offered Daniel a scholarship in law enforcement? Daniel took him up on it and became a deputy sheriff then a few months ago, a state trooper. While he was a deputy sheriff, he met Elena, and they were married almost two years ago. Elena's family embraced both of us; even Bianca, her mother, calls me Mama except when we get into a heated argument, which is fairly often, then I'm Diabla."

"No," I chuckled. "Your co-mother-in-law sounds like a force."

She giggled. "You got that right. I was at loose ends after I sold the motel, so Elena and I became partners and decided to open a Colombian restaurant at Bianca's urging. Bianca taught me how to prepare authentic Colombian dishes: hence the arguments. Elena is the General Manager and takes care of the finances, marketing, hiring, training, and all the other management and administrative trivia I have done in the past and have no desire to touch ever again. I'm living my dream of being a chef and owning my own restaurant without all the drudge work that drags me down. Daniel works in this region and goes home to his wife at the end of his shift, so he and Elena are happy too." She pointed to the kitchen. "Even Bianca is happy because she has somebody she can yell at who yells back."

"Mama," Elena said, "Donut Lady might like to eat dinner tonight."

"Elena's right as usual," Devlin said.

"Are you eating with us?" I asked.

"Are you kidding?" She dropped her voice to a whisper. "Guess who is in the kitchen about to explode because she gets lonely if I'm not there to ignore her advice?"

After she rose to leave, she said, "One huge side feature of this new career of mine is that I've become fairly fluent in Spanish. Bianca and I communicate at full volume, so if you need a quiet table, let Elena know. She will understand."

Elena came to our table after Devlin left. "What would you like to drink?"

"I would love a cup of hot tea," I said.

"Coffee for me," Ned said.

I raised my eyebrows. *I forgot he was here. Do I owe him an apology?*

"I can't drink coffee after ten o'clock in the morning," I said.

He shrugged. "It relaxes me."

After our young server brought us our drinks, Elena returned. "You can read your menus and even order if you like, but Mama has already decided what she's cooking for you."

"We surrender," Ned said as we handed her our menus, and Elena giggled.

As we sipped our hot drinks, Ned asked, "Do you feel like you need a vacation?"

I exhaled. "I certainly do. Are you a mind reader? I was thinking that just this morning?"

"Really? That's great. Where would you like to go?"

"I didn't even get that far. Good question. What about you?"

"I'm definitely ready for a vacation too. What do you think about a cruise?"

I shuddered. "Not for me. I've seen pictures of their so-called suites, and they're just too…confining."

Ned nodded. "Like a cell: I can see that."

I crossed my arms. "Prison is behind me; leave it alone."

I glared at him then sighed. "Unfortunately, you're right; they're exactly like a cell."

Ned shook his head. "No, I owe you an apology; our past doesn't define us, does it?"

"Thank you." I sipped my tea. "I never thought about it before, but I was in a panic when a tornado hit my house; Colonel, Mia, and I were trapped in the pantry under all the debris. That feeling solidified my claustrophobic fears of being enclosed."

"I'm not sure I knew about you and the tornado. How would you be in a camper?" he asked.

I smiled. "A camper has windows all around, and I can see the outside or open a window to feel a breeze or hear birds. Does that make sense?"

"That's how I feel too. I think that's why I like my camper so much. In fact, I'm not crazy about hotel rooms because I don't know who slept in that bed the night before." He chuckled. "I usually prop up my feet and sleep in a chair."

"We're a mess, aren't we?"

"More hot tea, Donut Lady?" our server asked.

"No, thank you." I smiled.

She raised her eyebrows and pointed at Ned's cup, and he nodded.

"Not a cruise, got it; then what would your ideal vacation be?" Ned asked.

"I don't know. I love being outside, so maybe a cabin in the mountains near hiking trails."

"I sometimes think I'd like the beach, but your mountain cabin sounds more interesting." He drank his coffee. "Glad we got that settled."

As our server brought our food, Elena hovered, and I cocked my head and stared at Ned. *What did we just settle?*

While we ate, Ned told me about a few of his most grisly cases, but in a way that was funny, and I chuckled at his stories.

While our server cleared our plates, he said, "You're a most unusual woman, Karen, because you wouldn't believe how many people don't understand how oddly humorous murder can be sometimes."

"Well, you have to remember I'm a former…" I paused for effect. "…teacher."

Ned guffawed, and when the other customers in the restaurant stared at us, I giggled.

He shook his head. "You got me there, Donut Lady. I thought I was going to have to chastise you for being insensitive."

"Dessert?" Elena asked.

"Not for me," I said.

She smiled. "Mama said you'd say that. It will be right out."

Ned laughed, and I chuckled as Elena strode into the kitchen.

Elena giggled. "She said, no, Mama; just like you said."

"Devlin's got my number; she knows I always have a little pocket in my stomach set aside for dessert."

"Did you ever stay at her hotel?"

"I did when I first came to town, but it was different: homey, and I felt safe."

"No shadows?" he asked.

"I never thought about that before: no shadows and no nightmares." *I forgot Ned knows about the shadows because he sees them too.*

"That's interesting. I wonder if our cabin in the mountains would be too homey for the shadows." Ned ate the final bite of his dessert.

I stared at my almost-clean dessert plate then set down my fork. *Our?* I shook my head. *I'm probably reading too much into a casual conversation.*

"Is that it for you, Donut Lady?" Elena asked.

"I did my best."

"Mama wants you to come into the kitchen for a few minutes before you leave."

As Elena and I strolled to the kitchen, I whispered, "Make sure I get the bill."

She tittered. "You're too late. Mr. Burke already paid the bill while you and Mama were talking. He's a keeper, Donut Lady."

I rolled my eyes. *Ned Burke has been called a lot of things but never a keeper in my hearing.*

When I walked into the kitchen, Devlin introduced me to Bianca, who chattered in Spanish.

"Thank you," I said, and Bianca beamed then hurried to the walk-in refrigerator for vegetables for the pot she had been stirring on the burner.

"I expected to have to translate; I didn't know you spoke Spanish," Devlin whispered.

"Just enough to be dangerous," I whispered.

"I wanted to talk to you where the customers couldn't hear us. Have you heard about any problems here in town, like at the furniture store?" Devlin asked.

I raised my eyebrows. "Yes, my hairdresser is Francine, and her sister is Sissy."

Bianca snorted as she rushed to the sink with her vegetables.

"She's not a Sissy fan, and neither am I. I knew you might have heard something from Francine because Shirley has been one of Francine's customers for years. Bianca and I think Sissy has fabricated all her troubles, and she's bleeding her parents and her sister dry."

"Really?" I cocked my head.

"We heard she has a so-called boyfriend that is playing the part of a thug, and there are rumors that she and her boyfriend have been running a protection ring for quite some time in the town north of us, but they have expanded their operation to dealing drugs. Bianca has some friends there who have told her about the weekly cash payments they give to a woman, a different one every week, to keep their businesses safe, but they're pretty closed mouth because they're afraid for their families. We're pretty sure Sissy set her own house on fire, then the boyfriend called it in before it got too far along. She's getting a completely updated house and all new furniture that she's buying from herself, courtesy of the insurance company," Devlin said.

I furrowed my brow. *Completely contradicts what Francine told me.*

Devlin scowled. "If Bianca and I had something more concrete than just our hunches, we'd have said something to Daniel, but the gossipy suspicions of two old ladies don't go very far. Daniel would believe us, but he wouldn't have anything to take to his superiors."

"What a mess. I'm glad you told me because Francine wants me to help her find Sissy's supposed boyfriend. She's invited me and Sissy to her house for dinner tomorrow night."

"That's perfect," Devlin said. "Let me know what we can do at this end to help take Sissy down." She peered at me. "Did that make me sound fierce?"

"Very."

"Good." Devlin pulled out her business card then wrote on the back. "This is my cell; text anytime. If I'm busy, I'll let you know, then we can talk later."

I nodded. "You've certainly given me a different angle to the pitiful victim that Francine told me about, but I don't know who the extortionist is; I was in Francine's shop yesterday when a thug showed up, so I've at least seen him. Francine told me she hadn't met the boyfriend and didn't give any indication that she knew the man, but I'll check on that because Francine does seem to be vague and even confused on some details. I suspect she's bothered by the stress of it all."

Devlin nodded. "I'll let you know if we hear anything more. Bianca strolls the restaurant and speaks only Spanish in public, so people ignore her while they talk about secrets and other personal details. Did I tell you she's fluent in English?"

I giggled. "You left out that one, tiny detail."

Devlin smiled. "I forget sometimes myself because she insisted that I had to learn Spanish if I was going to cook Colombian food. Elena and Daniel speak only Spanish at home, but he's young and a sponge. I struggled for a while, but I've gotten much better."

"Self-preservation?" I asked.

"You got it." She smiled, then we hugged before I left the kitchen.

After we were in the car, Ned asked, "Anything interesting?"

"Girl talk."

He nodded. "Is it insensitive to say I can wait for you to tell me later?"

I glared at him then turned my head to gaze out my side window. *What makes him so smart?*

When we arrived at my house, I waited for him to open my door. *One of these times he's going to revert to the old Ned, and I'll be sitting in the car while he walks away.*

He walked me to the door and shook my hand. "Nice evening."

I went inside and Mia meowed from her favorite position on top of the refrigerator while Colonel rose from the kitchen floor.

"Ready to go out back?"

Colonel blocked Roxie then beat her to the door, and I giggled as I let them out.

I turned on the burner under my tea kettle then selected a book for Francine and discovered a book for myself that I hadn't read in a while. I brewed my tea and let Colonel and Roxie back inside before I sat on the sofa with my feet propped up.

When I was only halfway through the book, Colonel whined.

"Just one more chapter, Colonel."

I glanced at the clock. "The time got away from me; it's bedtime."

I stepped outside with Colonel and Roxie and gazed at the stars until Colonel nudged my hand, then we all went inside.

As I dressed for bed, Colonel and Roxie kept me company. "When I taught fourth grade, I had a child in my class whose Mother sent her to school with a thermos of coffee every day. The mother told me it calmed her daughter. I always thought it was unusual, but maybe it's more common than I realized."

I yawned and climbed into bed.

* * *

The smell of woodsmoke woke me, and I moaned as I opened my eyes. *It's still dark.* I glanced at my bedside clock, but it was dark too. *Electricity must be off.* I tried to rise, but my hands and feet were bound. I struggled to get loose but only managed to tighten the bindings. I screamed, and Colonel and Roxie barked from the living room. I rolled to my side then saw the flames in the hallway as the smoke alarm sounded its ear-splitting shriek. A swarm of bees fled the hallway by flying into my room then buzzed around my bed.

Roxie barked more frantically, and Mia yowled; Colonel dashed through the fiery hallway and into my bedroom, and I struggled to reach him as the bees crawled through my hair then down my arms as they dropped onto the bed from the smoke. I tried to shout, *We have to save the bees!* but a gag muffled my words.

The shadows slid out from my closet and billowed to the ceiling then rolled into the hall and dropped onto the flames. The flames roared and hissed as the blanket of shadows extinguished them, the bees disappeared, and the fire alarm abruptly stopped mid-screech.

Colonel licked my face; I opened my eyes and freed my feet from the sheet tangled around them then sat up as I stared at the empty hallway. "That has to be the strangest nightmare I've ever had."

Colonel whined, and I checked the clock. "You're right, Colonel; it's time to get up."

I leaned over to check under my bed before I put my feet on the floor in case there was a hidden fire waiting to flare up or bees waiting to buzz me. After I padded down the perfectly normal hallway to the kitchen accompanied by shadows, I opened the back door for Colonel and Roxie. I shivered from the cold air, then while I started my small pot of coffee, the shadows hovered close to me.

"Are you gloating or worried?" I asked.

Warm air circulated around me. "Thanks. I was cold."

I poured myself a cup of coffee. "Do you think my nightmare was a reaction to Sissy's fire?"

The shadows continued to hover then swirled under the kitchen table.

Is that an answer?

CHAPTER THREE

Colonel scratched at the back door; when I opened it, Colonel and Roxie dashed inside, and the cold air rushed in with them. I measured their food then put down their bowls.

When I said, "Okay," and pointed to their bowls, they dug in. Mia stretched on the sofa then sauntered into the kitchen while I dished up her breakfast. She sniffed at it then stalked the shadows. When Mia and the shadows chased each other around the kitchen and down the hallway and back, I smiled and drank down my coffee before I hurried to dress.

"Are you going?" I asked Mia when I was ready to leave, and she started up another game of tag with the shadows.

"Shall we walk?"

Colonel and Roxie bounded to the front door.

"Walk it is." I put on my warm coat, then we left.

I looked up at the stars. "That's why it's so cold this morning. There's no blanket of clouds to keep the earth warm."

A mourning dove called out, a male cardinal whistled to establish his territory, and a brown thrasher joined in. As the sky lightened, other birds added to the chorus.

"I love the morning songbirds." I smiled as we strolled through the still-sleeping neighborhoods and past the fragrances of magnolia blossoms and hyacinths.

Colonel and Roxie raced to the shop when we were close enough to see the light that lit up the sidewalk in front of the building.

Andrew waved when we came in and continued mixing his dough. "No Mia?"

"I think she had other plans for the day." I hurried to the storeroom and hung up my coat before I put on my apron and my ball cap.

I stopped to wash my hands. "We have the Methodist Men today. Anybody else?"

"Yes."

I waited.

"Radio Controlled Aircraft Board at nine then the Methodist Men at ten fifteen," Andrew added.

"Oh good, crop-duster donuts, and what else?"

"Woody got us some of them silver sprinkles, so we could have silver UFO scones."

"Perfect, maple donuts and the sheriff's pink-sprinkled donuts. I can make cranberry-orange scones and have half of them UFO and the other half orange glaze." I glanced toward the storeroom. "Do we have any of the gold sugar left?"

"We don't have a lot, but we do have some."

"I'll dust some of the scones with gold sugar, and we'll call them *All that Glitters*."

Andrew laughed. "Because all that glitters is not gold, right?"

"Exactly; we'll save them for the Methodist Men. How did you know about that?"

"Dad and I read about words a lot, and one of the words we learned was aphorism; that means saying something that everybody already knows is true. Dad and I decided our favorite was *if it ain't broke, don't fix it* because of the hardware store. Dad and I found a bunch of aphorisms and even made up a few until Mama told us to stop."

I coughed to keep from laughing. *Poor Kim. Stuck in an aphorism world.*

"I better get to work." I mixed my scone dough then put my first batch into the oven while Andrew dropped his first batch of donuts into the fryer while the second batch rose.

"Three or four batches of donuts today?" he asked.

"Better make it four. Yesterday was stormy, so we may have a crowd today."

"I'll make eyeball donuts for Josh at the gas station. It's been a while since we made any," Andrew said.

We were heads-down and working hard to bake, fry, and decorate all of our pastries when the front bell jingled. David and Barbara hurried inside, and Roxie danced to the door to greet David.

David leaned down and rubbed Roxie's face. "Hello, pretty girl."

"Barbara and I knew you had double groups today, so both of us came to help," David said as the two of them rushed to the storeroom for their aprons and ball caps. David hurried to the pink room to get it set up with Roxie on his heels, then Barbara came out of the storeroom; she pushed her shoulder-length gray hair behind her ears then put on her ball cap.

"I'm ready now. What do I do? Bake or decorate?" Barbara asked.

"Why don't you decorate the scones? Glaze all of them with thinned orange frosting then sprinkle half of them with silver sprinkles. Those are our UFO scones. We have gold sugar, so sprinkle the other half with the sugar until it runs out."

"That won't take you long, Ms. Barbara, because you work fast," Andrew said. "If you'll take care of the pink-sprinkled donuts, I'll do the crop duster donuts and the eyeballs."

Barbara began drizzling the scones. "How do you make crop dusters?"

"Originally, our idea was to dust them with powdered sugar, but if we mix in a little cocoa powder, they're dusty," I said.

"I didn't know we didn't always put cocoa powder in our dust," Andrew said. "I like the new way better."

While the three of us worked on donuts and scones, David made coffee and put plates, silverware, napkins, and cups on the utility cart then rolled it into the meeting room to set up.

"Are the gold scones for the Methodist group? Do I tell them it's for the streets of gold in heaven?" David asked.

Andrew grinned, and I said, "The gold scones are for the Methodist Men, and you are more than welcome to spin it anyway you wish. Your stories are always awesome."

When the sheriff came in, he said, "Nothing on the board yet. Shall I?"

"Please do. Crop duster donuts and UFO scones are our specials. Our town favorites are pink-sprinkled and maple donuts and cranberry-orange scones."

"The eyeball donut holes are a surprise for Josh," Andrew said.

After the sheriff wrote up the specials and the favorites, he asked, "Would it be okay if I draw an eyeball on the board?"

"Yes," Andrew said.

"That's an excellent idea," David said. "Word will get back to Josh, and he'll come here. It's hard to get him to take a break. We should tell Jorge to make a sign for Josh: *Will break for eyeballs.*"

Barbara tittered. "Except spell it b-r-a-k-e like on cars, since he's a mechanic."

"Brilliant, honey." David stared at Barbara.

She frowned. "You don't have to look so surprised."

Shirley bustled into the shop. "Why are you all standing around? I have a meeting with the executive real estate board, and I need donuts and scones. Half dozen of each."

"You haven't had any coffee yet, have you? Here you go." I handed Shirley her large to-go cup, and she took a long sip.

"It's too hot. People have been sued for serving hot coffee. Don't you read the news?"

"Sit down, Shirley." I pointed to a stool, and the sheriff rose. Andrew gave him a sack with two pink-sprinkled donuts, and David handed him a large to-go coffee.

"Lifesavers," the sheriff whispered then left.

"Now, what's really bothering you, Shirley?" Barbara strolled to the counter.

Tears welled up in Shirley's eyes. "I'm not made for this executive board stuff. They want me to kick off a new member because she's under thirty. Woody and I read the bylaws all the way through three times, and there is nothing there about a minimum age."

Barbara sat next to Shirley and spoke in a soft calm voice. "Tell them no then tell them you're twenty-nine and dare them to call you a liar."

Shirley stared at Barbara. "What if they get rid of me?"

Barbara smiled. "If that's the worst they can do, would that be bad?"

Shirley smiled and sipped her coffee. "No, it wouldn't."

Shirley picked up her sack and hummed as she strolled out of the shop.

Barbara blew on her nails then polished them on her shirt and preened. "I've still got the touch."

David, Andrew, and I applauded as she held her head high and princess-waved while she strutted to resume her drizzling.

Jorge dropped in to pick up donuts for his hard-working crew and grinned when he saw the menu board. "On second thought, I think I'll send Josh to pick up our order. Is that okay?"

"Yes," Andrew said, and Jorge paid me for his order then hurried out of the shop.

"Another satisfied customer." David wiggled his eyebrows then picked up the tray of donuts and scones that Andrew had set out for the pink room.

After the Radio Control Board began arriving and filed into the pink room, Josh rushed into the shop. "Jorge called the shop and asked me to pick up the order for the gas station. I was in the middle of a big job, but he told me donuts were more important than work. He must be at the emergency room or something because I've never heard him talk like—"

Josh stared at the menu board then chuckled. "That sneaky old man. I'll take his order, if you have it ready. How much?"

"Sorry, but the bill's already paid," I said.

Josh rolled his eyes. "Of course, it is. He got me good, didn't he?"

Andrew snickered. "Yes."

After he left, Andrew, Barbara, and I high-fived.

"What are your plans for dinner tonight? Want to come to our house?" Barbara asked.

"I'm having dinner at Francine's house to meet her sister."

"Sissy? Why do you want to meet her? If you need help decorating your house, you've got Gee, Darlene, and me."

I chuckled. "From what Francine told me, I definitely wouldn't want Sissy to touch my house."

Barbara peered at me. "You had your annual hair appointment yesterday, didn't you? I wouldn't have noticed if you hadn't mentioned Francine. Do you like it?"

"I thought I would hate it, but I didn't even notice it this morning." I pulled some hair close to my face to examine it. "Now I can't remember if I brushed it."

"I don't think you did, but our ball caps cover all sins, don't they? Your color is very natural and suits you."

As I handed a large to-go cup of coffee and a sack with a donut and a scone to a young mom with her baby in the stroller, the baby giggled at the laughter that erupted in the meeting room, and the mom and I smiled.

"Who is your group this morning?" she asked.

"The Radio Control Board then the Methodist Men's group at ten thirty."

"I heard there was an emergency meeting yesterday and should have known the Methodist men would reschedule. My husband's goal in life is to join their group, so he'll have an excuse to drink coffee and eat donuts at your shop once a week without any office stress. I need a group too."

"You know Amber's group meets once a week, usually on Thursdays."

She raised her eyebrows. "I'll have to check with Amber to see if she minds a gate crasher." She pointed to her baby who gestured and babbled as she carried on a one-way conversation with the men she heard talking behind the closed door. "I wouldn't mind accepting my mother-in-law's sweet offer to play with you-know-who for a few hours once a week, so I could go somewhere and have conversations that weren't dominated by babies."

The mom pinched off a tiny bite of donut and handed it to the baby who waved it like a trophy as they headed to the door. Roxie stayed as close to the baby as she dared then flopped dejectedly near the counter when they left, and I rolled my eyes.

"You'd have been in big trouble, Roxie, if you'd snagged that baby's donut."

"Karen, would you like to go for a long ride this afternoon?" Barbara asked. "David has a few more farms he wants to drive by, which means traveling on the backroads in the county. It's not quite as boring as it sounds because we always get lost, but maybe it is boring because all I'm allowed to talk about is farming. Have you ever heard of DWF?"

I slowly shook my head.

Barbara's eyes twinkled. "Driving while farming."

I chuckled. "Very tempting, but I'll wait for the sequel when he has it narrowed down, and we can see the farmhouses."

"That's a good idea. I'll encourage him to pick his top four or five, so we can critique the houses while he wanders around the fields and barns and pretends to grouse about the farm equipment he'll have to buy and all the work it will take to set up his art studio. He's very serious about moving to a more rural area, and of course, I don't mind at all because very few of us hermits are the drop-in, neighborly type. As much as I love coming to the Donut Hole that sounds odd, doesn't it? But your shop is different; it's business. Does that make sense?"

"I never thought about it before, but I can see the difference."

"Good. Can I be a regular like David?"

"Of course; I'd love having you here with me, but you don't have to be feel obligated to come every day if that doesn't work for you."

"I'll be fine. I talked to David about it, and he told me that Andrew will give me a time out if I get cranky." Barbara snickered as she grabbed a cloth and the wood cleaner for the reading table and Woody's bookshelf.

After the board members left, David and Barbara rushed to clean the room while Andrew refilled the platters and made fresh coffee, and I waited on the stream of customers that rushed into the shop for bags and boxes of donuts and scones.

"How did you know we were going to be this busy?" Andrew asked as he refilled the display case.

"I can't explain it, but I had a feeling we'd be swamped today."

Andrew nodded. "It's what you do."

I hurried to the office to review my records for the accountant, and Colonel and Roxie followed me. Colonel stayed, but Roxie pranced out to find someone who would take pity on her and give her a piece of their donut. While I was heads-down, I heard a voice that made me shudder; I peeked out of the office. *The thug is in my shop.*

He strode to David with a smile and held out his hand. My mouth opened in surprise when David shook his hand and clapped the thug's shoulder with his other hand.

"I haven't seen you in ages; what are you doing in Asbury, Quinn?"

"I retired from the force, but I was bored with nothing exciting to do, so I decided to come here and throw my hat into the ring when I heard you'd retired, and the mayor position was up for grabs."

"Well, you old son of a gun; you'd be great at whipping that lazy group that call themselves the City Council into stepping up to the plate. If you're still serious about it after you talk with them, let's get together, and I can give you some insight into alternatives for some of their more unrealistic plans."

When Colonel nudged me, I realized my mouth was still open and snapped it shut.

David poured two cups of coffee, then he and the thug sat at the counter, sipped their coffee, and chatted. When two of the Methodist men strolled into the shop, the thug left, and I hurried into my office and put away my paperwork before I headed to the cash register.

When the rest of the Methodist men flocked into the shop, they stopped to read the menu board then laughed as they hurried to the meeting room. Three men stopped at the door to talk to David.

"Got any eyeballs left, Mayor?" one of the men asked.

"Former mayor, ex-mayor, Donut Hole greeter, or old retired guy all fit my current station in life much better, and yes, we do." David chuckled.

"I heard you were looking for a farm," the second man said. "Should we add farmer to your list?"

"You're looking for a farm?" The third one asked. "Talk to me after the meeting, if you're serious. I know about one that's going to be on the market soon, and there's nothing more that would make the seller happier than to sell it to a local."

"I'd like to hear about it, and I know Barbara will too," David said as the four of them went into the meeting room, then David closed the door.

Barbara stared at the closed door, and I stepped closer to her. "Remember you have back up because I'll go with you to check it out," I whispered.

"Thanks," she said. "I don't know why I suddenly want to back out: fear of the unknown, maybe."

"Totally understandable." I nodded.

"I don't like change, either, Ms. Barbara," Andrew said. "It scares me a lot, and I shake. Dad told me I need to think of one good thing first before I start thinking about all the bad things."

Barbara swallowed. "The one good thing is that David will be happy."

I narrowed my eyes. "You can do better than that, Barbara."

Barbara sighed. "I'll have privacy and can spend time in my garden without nosy neighbors dropping by to chat."

I smiled. "Sign me up."

She matched my smile. "It does sound nice, doesn't it?"

"If I say sign me up, am I agreeing that it sounds nice, or do I get to come to your farm and weed the garden with you?" Andrew asked.

"You can do either one any time you like," Barbara said.

"Thanks."

As a steady stream of people rushed into the shop, Barbara refilled the display case. "We weren't nearly this busy while you were in your office, Donut Lady. You're our customer magnet today. I'll take care of the larger orders and keep the coffee pot going if you'll take care of the register and the counter orders. We're out of eyeballs, by the way. David took every last one into the meeting room, and I'm certain there aren't any left. Andrew erased the eyeball, but that probably won't matter; people will still ask."

"Did you know that man who talked to David?"

"You mean Quinn Norris? Sure, we've known him for years. He was with the Atlanta police department until he retired two or three years ago. All his relatives live around Conway. He'd be a real asset for Asbury. Why? Do you know him?"

"No, he just reminded me of somebody."

"He's a widower and a good-looking guy for a man who still has that cop look, don't you think?" Barbara smirked. "I'll introduce you the next time he comes in."

I bit my lip. "I suppose." *I'm not sure I'd call a thug good-looking though.*

After the Methodist Men's meeting was over, David and Barbara went into the meeting room with the man who knew someone who wanted to sell their farm; Roxie slipped in with them, so she could check the floor before it was swept. Andrew and I began our end of the day cleaning routine while Colonel napped.

"Are you okay, Miss Lady?" Andrew asked.

"I didn't sleep all that well last night, so I'm a little tired, but I'm fine."

"You can sit a minute and take a break," he said.

"I'm better off being busy." I smiled.

"I like to be busy too," Andrew said.

After Barbara, David, and the man came out of the meeting room, David and Roxie walked the Methodist man to the door, then David flipped the sign to closed and locked the door.

While David gathered the dirty dishes from the meeting room and gave them to Andrew, Barbara said, "We're going to look at a farm after lunch. It's halfway between here and Conway. We'll be looking at the house, so you'll go with me, won't you?"

I nodded. "That's what I said."

"Good; we'll pick up sandwiches at Gus's and eat at the park." Barbara hurried to sweep the pink room.

"I'll need to take Colonel and Roxie home first," I said.

"Colonel and Roxie are welcome to go along, if it's okay with you. You're the one that will be sitting in the back seat with two big dogs," David said.

"I think they'll enjoy having some room to run out in the country," Barbara added.

"I'll bring their water bowl from here when we're ready to go."

"I just realized your car isn't here, so we don't even have to drop off your car," Barbara said.

When the shop was clean and ready for the next day, Andrew said, "Clean up goes fast with double the people."

After Andrew left, I locked up while Colonel and Roxie jumped into David's car, and I laughed. "Those two are always ready to go, but especially Roxie. I don't think she'd ever turn down a ride in a car or truck."

Colonel hopped out before I could climb in next to him.

"I thought I had the window."

Colonel grinned.

"Looks like you're sitting in the middle, Donut Lady," David said. "Are you okay with that?"

"Guess I have to be," I grumbled.

On our way to Gus's sandwich shop, Barbara asked, "Do you want to split a ham and swiss?"

"I'd love it."

"Your Reuben sandwich for you, honey?" Barbara asked.

When David nodded, Barbara called in our order. David picked up our order, and we ate at the park while Colonel and Roxie chased squirrels.

On our way to the farm, David said, "We shouldn't expect too much. The property was a family farm but hasn't been actively farmed in years. The woman who is selling the house is a widow and sadly has developed signs of dementia. She's selling her house to live with her daughter. The roof was replaced with a metal roof about ten years ago, and the electrical and plumbing were brought up to code about the same time. She has it priced low before it goes on the market because she prefers a buyer recommended by a family member; she wants someone in the house who will love her home."

"I love her already," Barbara said. "That's really sweet."

I snickered. "I don't think she comes with the house, Barbara. Now I see why I'm going along."

When David pulled into the long driveway and headed toward the house, Barbara squealed. "It's a classic farmhouse. Look at that huge porch across the front. It's beautiful; I love it."

"Looks like it's been a long time since it was painted, and some of the gutters are sagging. It's going to need a lot of work to fix it up. Remember, it's old, honey."

"So are we, but I'm sure the house has great bones," Barbara said.

"I've always wondered what that really means because it sounds like something to say when a house is so ugly there is nothing nice to say about it."

Barbara wiggled her eyebrows. "The roof hasn't fallen in."

"The driveway isn't in bad shape," David said.

After David parked, Barbara and I headed toward the house; Colonel followed us while Roxie bounded after David. When we reached the porch, I pointed. "Some of these boards have dry rot and will need to be replaced."

"I'll start a list." Barbara pulled out a pen and pad from her purse and wrote a note about the porch floorboards.

When we went inside, the mustiness overpowered us, and both of us sneezed. I sneezed two more times.

Barbara snickered. "You're an overachiever. I've never heard anyone sneeze as loudly as you do."

I shrugged. "I get my money's worth."

Barbara blinked as we strolled into a large room on the left. "Is this the living room? The wallpaper is ugly."

"It might have been called the parlor. The wallpaper is cosmetic, but you'll want to put it on your to-do list if you decide to change it right away. Can you believe these floors? They're beautiful; I'll bet there was a room-sized rug. Did you notice the difference in the color of the wood? See the outline?"

"I love the floors; they add to the character of the room. I don't think I would cover them with a rug; do I add positives?" Barbara asked.

"Your choice."

"I'll add floors because they are perfect the way they are. Do you know how to replace wallpaper? Is it hard?"

"Unfortunately, I do know how, and how hard it is depends on the type of glue. We could check a section, then if it's too hard, you can hire a professional."

"Maybe it will grow on me," Barbara said.

"The mantle over the fireplace is beautiful. I'll bet it will clean right up with a little elbow grease." I leaned down to peer up the chimney. "I don't see anything; you'll want it inspected and cleaned."

Barbara added it to her list.

When we walked into the cook's kitchen with a prep station and gleaming, commercial appliances, Barbara said, "Wow."

Colonel flopped down on the floor and stretched out on his side.

"Colonel and I approve. If you don't buy this house, I will. This is the most well-equipped kitchen I've ever seen in my life."

"I'll cook and make Gee help me while you and Darlene host dinner parties. Do we want to see the rest of the house?" Barbara asked.

"Not really, but we probably should, then let's find David to see what he thinks about the property; another option is that we return to the kitchen to examine the appliances in more detail."

After we searched the first floor, we climbed the majestic staircase and admired the smooth, ornate banister, before we explored the second floor.

"The bedrooms are small," Barbara said, "but there are six of them and three bathrooms. Do you suppose this was planned to be a bed and breakfast? That's not for me."

"It doesn't matter what was planned; you can do whatever you like with the house, except if you cook in that kitchen, you have to invite me."

"You got it; let's go find David."

We went out the back door; Colonel followed us out then disappeared around the corner. We strolled to the barn and greenhouse near the wellhouse.

"I would love having a greenhouse. I can start my garden early with seeds," Barbara said as we peered inside.

As we left the greenhouse, Barbara stopped and stared at the house. "If I could talk Darlene into moving in with us without making Gee mad, Darlene could take care of the customers, and I could cook and manage the finances. We'd hire a weekly cleaning crew to clean all our public areas and guest rooms."

"That would definitely be the right business model for you, but are you sure you want Darlene to take care of your customers?"

"She's a natural; we could call the B&B *Were You Raised in a Barn?*"

We giggled as we strolled to the large, old barn. I smiled at the cooler air and the faint scent of old hay.

"This reminds me of a barn from years ago, but I'm not sure whose it was. One of my relatives must have had a farm with a few cows and chickens," Barbara said.

"The stalls need repair, but the barn is in great shape."

As we continued our stroll, we spotted a small cabin-style building that could have been a guest house or a studio on the other side of the driveway. We headed toward the building then stopped as a pickup truck rolled to a stop and parked.

"Were you expecting anyone?" I frowned.

"No." Barbara clutched my arm.

CHAPTER FOUR

The man climbed out of his truck and waved, and I waved back.

"Don't do that," Barbara hissed. "He might attack us."

David and Roxie came out of the building. He had placed the dog bowl filled with water on the porch, and Colonel trotted to the bowl for a drink.

The man smiled as he strode to David, and they shook hands.

"David Lehman?" the man asked. "I'm Rafe. I heard you might be looking at this old place and thought I'd stop by. I live down the road; I own a small engine repair shop north of Conway. Are you still the mayor in Asbury?"

David grinned. "Recently retired."

Rafe nodded. "You having any of that protection trouble in Asbury?"

"Hadn't heard of any. What's going on?"

"Not much; nobody's bothered me, but I've heard some of the less-established businesses are having trouble." He shrugged. "It's rumors, so I don't have any facts. You thinking about buying this house? My missus used to tell me if it ever came up for sale, she wanted to buy it for a bed and breakfast and even did some research. She hasn't mentioned bed and breakfast since then." Rafe chuckled. "It needs work, but it has good bones. Let me know if there's anything I can do for you."

After Rafe left, David said, "*Good bones.* Kind of makes you want to run for the car, doesn't it?"

Barbara narrowed her eyes. "I hope the small house has air conditioning because it certainly has a lot of windows."

"Come see inside; this is perfect for my art studio."

We stepped into a large great room with large windows on three sides and a small kitchen in one corner.

Barbara's eyes widened. "Wow."

David grinned. "Exactly. It has a bedroom and a bathroom. I'm not sure if it was a guest house or a yoga studio."

Barbara checked the refrigerator. "We could put cold water and sweet tea in here and even sandwich fixings if you've hit a creative spurt and don't want to take much more than a short break."

After we peeked into the bedroom and bathroom, Barbara said, "I love the house, and it has real possibilities. I hate to ask about the price, but can we even afford this?"

"We can afford the current price for family friends. If it goes on the market as the same price as the other comparable properties in the surrounding area, I'm not sure we could afford the small guest cabin."

When Barbara raised an eyebrow, he continued, "I researched it."

Barbara scowled. "Is that fair to the seller if we pay below market?"

"If it's what she and the family want to do, and they are willing to sell her property to us, then it's fair. What did you think about the house?"

"I love it; we'd need to hire someone to perform a house inspection, so we could prioritize repairs and have the chimney inspected and cleaned, but I didn't see anything that would stop us from moving in. If we can't have a fire in the fireplace, it can be decorative."

As the three of us strolled back to the car, Roxie raced to the barn then back before she joined us, and Colonel waited near the car in the shade of an old oak.

"Roxie loves the farm too," Barbara said.

"Have you noticed she's turned into David's girl?" I asked.

"Now that you mention it, she has. Does that bother you?" Barbara asked.

"Not at all; I love that they are bonding. I think she's a man's dog at heart."

On the way back to town, Barbara asked, "What are our next steps?"

"I'll call Amber," David said.

"I'll start planning what I should pack and what I should donate; even if we decide against buying the house, it wouldn't hurt for me to go through those boxes I haven't opened in years."

David dropped us off at my house, and Mia scolded me for not coming straight home from work. I gave her a treat, and she settled down.

While Colonel and Roxie trotted to the back door, I poured myself a glass of iced tea, then the three of us went outside.

I smiled at how excited David and Barbara were over the farm with the two houses. *They deserve to be happy.*

I finished my glass of tea and rose; when I reached the back door, I paused. "I'm going inside."

Roxie continued to chase a butterfly, and Colonel didn't move from his cool spot on the grass in the shade.

I checked my phone and had two texts: one from Francine with her address, and a second one from Barbara that said, "Call."

When I called Barbara, she said, "We're afraid If we buy the farmhouse, we'll get all tied up and neglect our Donut Hole duties. David is really stressing about abandoning you."

"The Donut Hole was an extension of David's duties as mayor. He's entitled to retire from the Donut Hole too and embark on his new career."

"Well, that won't happen. The Donut Hole is his social life. Amber asked her assistant, Leah, to research a few things before she drew up an offer. David's calling the woman's relative to talk to him to see what the family sees as next steps, but it's obvious the owner isn't living in the house anymore. If she wants to meet us, would you go along with me?"

I rolled my eyes. "Only if I could play the part of the wicked stepsister."

Barbara laughed. "I'll take that under consideration, and you're right in your own subtle way: I can do this."

I smiled as we hung up. *I should shower before I leave for Francine's house.*

After my quick shower and change to clean clothes, I opened the back door. "Anybody interested in supper?"

Roxie raced to the house and pranced to the pantry while Colonel strolled inside. Mia hissed at Roxie for going too close to the pantry door while I dished up her food into her bowl then measured food for Colonel and Roxie into their bowls. Mia pushed her bowl until it was under the kitchen table. She glared at the dogs then delicately picked at her food.

I set down the bowls of dog food and waited for Colonel and Roxie to sit then pointed at the bowls. "Okay."

Both of them dug in; after their food was gone, Colonel checked Roxie's bowl to see if she missed anything while Roxie checked Colonel's bowl.

I smiled. *I love our regular routine.*

After they took their after supper break, I said, "I'm going out to dinner, but I don't plan to be very late."

As I pulled out of my driveway, I sighed. *I'm sorry I told Francine I'd go to her house for dinner. What could I possibly learn from her sister that Francine couldn't have discovered herself?*

I parked in front of Francine's house then trudged toward the house with the book I'd selected for her in my hand. *I wonder if there's any way I could give her the book then leave?* I shook my head when I reached the porch and rang the doorbell. *I'm a terrible guest.*

"I'm so glad to see you, Karen." Francine beamed when she opened the door, and the tantalizing aromas of garlic, basil, oregano, and baked bread welcomed me, and my stomach growled.

My face warmed. "I didn't know I was hungry, but I'm suddenly ravenous; everything smells so good."

"Thank you. Sissy texted me, and she'll be here in five minutes, so we'll eat in about fifteen minutes. What would you like to drink? Red wine, hot tea, or sweet tea?"

"Sweet tea sounds perfect."

I followed Francine to the kitchen then stopped to peek in the dining room. I smiled at the red checkered tablecloth and the matching napkins that were folded on the oversized, yellow plates. "The place settings are beautiful, Francine."

I joined her in the kitchen, and she pointed to my glass of sweet tea on the bar as she popped the cork on a bottle of red wine then took a big gulp before she stirred a pot of sauce with meatballs. She sliced the warm bread then dished up generous servings of salad into large bowls.

I raised my eyebrows at the amount of salad she had piled into the bowls. *There's no way I can eat all that, much less any pasta and meatballs.*

"Can I put you to work? Take the salads and bread to the dining table for me, please, while I dish up our meatballs and fettuccine. Sissy loves to come into the house and go straight to the table. No predinner cocktails or small talk for her." Francine chuckled as she drained her glass.

As I picked up the salad bowls, Francine added, "Don't worry about the serving sizes. I don't know how to cook any other way, and everybody leaves my house with their next day's meal."

Next three days for me.

I carried the salads to the dining room then returned for the bread. I placed the bread on the table and joined Francine in the kitchen; she was grating fresh parmesan over the meatballs and sauce.

There's enough food on one plate to feed three lumberjacks.

After she sprinkled each serving with fresh parsley, Francine said, "Take your sweet tea and a plate, and I'll bring the other two plates to the table. I forgot to move the yellow plates; Sissy put them on the table for decoration, but they're large enough that we can be fancy and use them as chargers. Sissy will enjoy that."

When we were in the dining room, Francine pointed. "Your seat is there. Go ahead and sit; I'll text Sissy because she's usually screeching into my driveway by now."

While Francine was gone, I considered sending Barbara a text but decided against it. I stared at the huge mound of fettuccine, sauce, and meatballs, and my stomach roiled in protest. *Take it easy, buddy. I'm not eating all that.*

After ten minutes, I rose from the table and went into the kitchen. Francine was staring at her phone. "Sissy's not answering."

I waited. *Is she going to say we should go ahead and eat or not?*

"We'll have to do this another time. I can freeze the sauce and meatballs. Sorry, but we'll have to postpone." Francine picked up her phone and began another text. I glanced at the kitchen counter, and the wine bottle was empty.

I picked up the book I'd brought for her and closed the front door quietly as I left then climbed into my minivan and drove away from the curb.

I pulled into a convenience store parking lot and stopped. *Was that petty of me to take the book with me?* I shrugged. *Probably, but I don't care. What do I do about supper? I'm all cleaned up with no place to go.*

I stared at my phone when it buzzed a text from Francine. "Sorry I forgot to pack up your plate for you. Do you want to come back, and I'll give you some sauce and meatballs."

I'm still feeling petty, but it would be rude not to reply. I sighed then sent the text. "No need."

It's been a while since I've been to Ida's Diner.

I sent Ned a text. "My plans fell through."

My phone rang. "Where do you want to go?" Ned asked.

"Would you like to meet me at Ida's Diner? My treat, and don't be sneaky."

"Why don't I pick you up?"

"I'm not home."

"Go home, and I'll pick you up." He hung up.

I'll drive to Ida's Diner. He'll figure it out. I sighed. *That was only funny in my head. I need to shake off being petty.*

I wrote a quick note on a small pad of paper then folded it and stuck it into the watch pocket of my jeans: "Check is mine. Pinky swear."

I headed to my neighborhood then pulled into my driveway. Before I could reach the porch to assume a haughty, bored stance, Ned parked behind my van and strode to the passenger's side and grinned as he opened the door and motioned to the passenger's seat. "Your chariot, milady."

I tried to contain my mirth, but I giggled. "Thank you for the rescue, kind sir."

"I'll bet this is a doozy." He headed toward Ida's Diner.

I nodded. "It was definitely bizarre."

I told him about the food that Francine prepared and the portion sizes; when I wrapped up with the absent Sissy and Francine postponing dinner and essentially kicking me out, his face reddened, and he scowled.

"You were standing right there, and your dinner was on your plate, and she canceled the dinner when you were within six inches of your food," he growled.

"Good summary," I said. "She did text me after I left and asked if I wanted her to give me some sauce, and I declined and texted you."

"Good choice; her loss is my gain." He smiled.

I stared at him. *Ned doesn't smile very often. I never noticed his dimples before.*

After he parked near Ida's, he asked, "Besides Francine being a total nut case, what do you think is going on?"

"My head hurts from trying to figure it out."

He nodded. "You need some healthy, healing food carefully prepared by Sully on his greasy grill."

"Exactly," I said as he opened the car door and helped me out.

When we went into Ida's Diner, I dropped the slip of paper into Mary Rose's waitress apron pocket as we headed to our seats.

After we sat in a booth, Mary Rose brought two large glasses of sweet tea to us. "You smell pretty, Donut Lady, what's the occasion?"

"Big night out at Ida's Diner," I said.

Mary Rose giggled and wiggled her pinky finger. "Exactly my thought. What's your pleasure?"

"I'd like a green chile cheeseburger with the works."

"Got it. Mr. Ned?"

"I'll have the same with fries."

"Kitchen sink with a roasted dee cow and a Donut Lady roasted dee cow," Mary Rose called out.

"Got it," Sully replied from the kitchen.

After Mary Rose left, Ned asked, "Roasted dee cow?"

"Roasted is green chiles; Sully roasts his own. Dee cow is a burger; it used to be a dead cow, but some people are delicate and don't want to eat dead food. I'd personally be more squeamish if my food tried to crawl off my plate."

"Takes all kinds, I suppose, but I'm with you on that," Ned said.

"Speaking of all kinds, I was having lunch here a year or so ago when a guy who was trying to be a big shot ordered a roasted decal because he thought he'd show off like he was part of the in-crowd."

"Fancy in-crowd at Ida's Diner? I'm not sure that will catch on. What did Sully do?"

"Sully made what he ordered, but Mary Rose refused to serve it and insisted that Sully burn a burger instead. Sully told her she had no sense of humor or adventure, but if you look at the cash register, there's a roasted decal on it."

Ned chuckled. "Did Sully burn the burger?"

"Burned it to a crisp and set off the fire alarm in the kitchen, and the guy raved about how great his roasted decal was."

Mary Rose refilled our glasses. "Ask Miss Donut Lady who put the roasted decal on the register over my personal protest."

Ned stared at me then guffawed when I looked away.

When Mary Rose served our plates, Ned said, "I get it. Donut Lady size is a smaller portion. You don't feel like you're wasting food, so you can order whatever you like. Sully's a genius."

"Don't say that out loud in here," Mary Rose growled as she placed a customer's order on a table that was three booths away from us.

"Busted," he whispered.

We dug into our burgers with melted swiss cheese and mustard oozing out the edges of the toasted bun, and lettuce, tomato, onion, and dill pickle chips balanced precariously on top of the roasted green chile that sat on the burger Sully had grilled to perfection. When I took a bite, the juices from the burger trickled down my hands and wrists to my arms. Mary Rose dropped off a roll of paper towels as she sailed past us. After I wiped my hands and arms then my face, my paper towel was damp with grease and mustard.

"This burger can only be eaten with friends," Ned said, and I nodded.

We took a break from attacking our burgers and munched on fries.

"I have a question: why did you call me instead of Barbara?" Ned asked.

"Barbara is in overload right now." I told him about the farmhouse, the potential for a bed and breakfast, and David's art studio.

"That is overload. Do you think she'll follow through with the bed and breakfast?"

"I'm not sure, but I don't think so. All the cooking she would be doing would be breakfast, and her best chef skills are dinner meals. I think after she investigates the cost of doing business and considers strangers roaming around her house at all hours, she'll decide against it; she may come up with something else instead or just enjoy her house."

We dug back into our burgers; Ned finished his before I finished mine, but I kept going and ate every bite. I finished my meal with half of one more fry then pushed back my plate and began cleaning my hands and face with paper towels.

I glared at Mary Rose when she dropped off spoons and warm peach cobbler with vanilla ice cream that oozed into the crevices of the cobbler.

"I'm impervious," Mary Rose sang as she breezed back to the kitchen, and Sully laughed.

Ned cocked his head and frowned. "Francine isn't a friend of yours; why did she invite you to dinner?"

"You're a good investigator; did you know that?" I asked, and Ned nodded.

I told him about my hair appointment, the thug, the threats, Francine's sister and her boyfriend, what Devlin and Bianca thought about Sissy, and what Devlin told me about a possible protection racket. "Francine wanted me to talk to Sissy for more information about her boyfriend, so I could help Francine find him."

"Coffee, Mr. Ned?" Mary Rose called out from the register, and he nodded. She grabbed a pot and a cup then placed the cup on our table and filled it before she made her rounds of refilling cups.

Ned took a sip. "This is perfect with the soupy ice cream and cobbler. What else?"

"What else what?"

"What else are you stalling about telling me?"

"That's not even a good sentence." I wrinkled my nose.

He raised his eyebrows and peered at me over his cup as I sneered then took another bite of cobbler but dripped ice cream on my shirt.

I exhaled as I wiped at my shirt with a paper towel. "I just ruined my entire aloofness."

"Is that a real word?" Ned's mouth quivered. "You're still stalling."

"It's odd, but the thug came into my shop today and said he was going to apply for David's job as mayor. David knew him; the thug's name is Quinn Norris."

"Quinn Norris? He's not a thug. He'd be a real asset to Asbury if he can adjust to the people and the small town culture. He's spent most of his career close to Atlanta."

"Then why was he in Francine's shop threatening her?"

"I'd ask if you're sure, and you already told me you got a good look at him, but I'll ask anyway. You're sure it was Quinn, not his twin brother, Richard?"

I gaped at him. "Nobody mentioned that Quinn had a twin. How much does his twin look like him?"

"They're identical, but it's easy for Quinn's friends to see the difference. Richard has an angry look about him; you can see it in his eyes."

"The thug had angry eyes, and I thought Quinn just had his respectable face on. That puts a whole different spin on everything.

Could Richard be Sissy's boyfriend? Does he have a history of fraud or extortion?" I asked.

"I'd heard Quinn considered himself to be a ladies' man, but not many women fell for it; Richard, however, had a way about him that women liked: you know, the bad boy image. Fraud, extortion, and robbery were his specialties, but if Devlin and Bianca are right, and I'd bet money on it, Richard and Sissy would be a good match of crooks. I thought he was still in prison, but he could be out." Ned picked up his phone and sent a quick text.

"Excuse me. I'll be right back," I said.

I picked up my purse and headed to the women's rest room. When I passed Mary Rose, she dropped the check into the open pocket on my purse. After I was in the restroom, I washed my hands, arms, and face before I pulled out money from my wallet for the bill and a generous tip for Mary Rose. I headed back to my booth, and when Mary Rose bumped into me, I dropped the money and the check into her apron pocket.

A man had stopped at our table, and he and Ned were in a deep conversation when I neared the table. When I slipped into the booth across from Ned, the man looked at me, and I saw the difference in Quinn's friendly eyes and the thug's angry eyes.

"Karen, this is Quinn, an old friend of mine. Quinn, Karen owns the Donut Hole."

"You're the famous Donut Lady? It's a pleasure to meet you." Quinn's eyes twinkled as he smiled and held out his hand. When we shook, his hand was appropriately firm and confident. *I like this guy.*

"Sorry I didn't get here a little sooner. Maybe we can have dinner tomorrow night, Ned? Of course, that's only if Donut Lady comes too."

"I'm pretty busy; okay if I get back to you?" Ned said.

Busy doing what?

"That's great; see you later then." Quinn strode to the counter and sat on a stool near the kitchen, so he could keep an eye on the diner. *Yep, a cop.*

Mary Rose stopped by our booth with the coffee pot. "No more for me; I'll just take the check," Ned said.

Mary Rose smiled. "It's already taken care of." She lowered her voice and whispered, "One of Donut Lady's admirers."

I narrowed my eyes at her, and she fluttered her eyelashes and wiggled her pinkie before she hurried to the next booth with her coffee pot.

"Ready?" Ned growled.

What's he so cranky about?

"Quinn's a nice guy," I said on our way to my house.

"I suppose." Ned grunted. "He told me Richard was released from prison six months ago. Quinn heard Richard has been staying with a woman in Conway. I got the impression there's no love lost between those two."

My phone rang. *Barbara.* "Barbara's calling me."

"Go ahead and answer."

"This has been a roller coaster day. One of the nieces decided the house was perfect for her, her husband, and their five children, so it's not available after all, and we're relieved."

"Really?"

"We learned I want a nice kitchen, David wants an art studio, we'd like a little land for privacy, and we don't want a mansion or a new business that would be a fulltime job. We already have perfect jobs at the Donut Hole."

"I think you're smart. I was dazzled by the kitchen too."

"We'll see you tomorrow. I thought you'd like to know."

"I appreciate it."

After we hung up, I said, "One of the seller's family members has five children and wants the house. Barbara and David are relieved."

"That's good news," Ned said.

"It really is."

Ned walked me to the door, and when we shook hands, he put his other hand over mine. "Thanks for calling me. My evening would have been boring compared to dinner with you at Ida's Diner."

He waited until I was inside then pulled away from the house. I opened the back door for Colonel and Roxie as my phone rang. *Francine?*

I answered it before it rang over to voice mail.

"I thought I'd missed you and was debating about leaving a message. I finally heard from Sissy, and she got caught up with an emergency at work. She'll come tomorrow, and you can meet her. Six o'clock."

"I have a new project that will take all my spare time. Thanks for the invitation tonight, though; it's too bad it didn't work out."

"Oh, well, good luck with your new project. Just let me know when you're available, and I'll see what I can do."

After we hung up, I shook my head. *I'll need to find a new hairstylist.*

I brewed myself a cup of hot tea then relaxed on the sofa with a book until bedtime.

* * *

While my coffee perked the next morning, I let Colonel and Roxie outside then hurried to dress. After I let them back in, I poured a cup of coffee to cool then fed Colonel, Roxie, and Mia.

I sipped my coffee until Colonel and Roxie finished eating then refilled my cup and grabbed a jacket before the three of us went out back. I rocked while I held my cup with my hands to keep them warm. *I'm supposed to ask Barbara and David about covering the shop for me while I'm gone on Friday.* I rubbed my forehead with my fingertips. *I'm not sure that's a good idea.*

When I headed to the door, Mia dashed for her carrier and slipped inside, and I zipped it up. "Glad you decided to go with us today; Andrew has been missing you."

When we went into the shop, Andrew said, "Miss Lady, my mama would like for you to stop by the hardware store sometime."

His eyes lit up, and he grinned as I unzipped Mia's carrier. "Hi, Mia. I missed you."

Mia raced to Andrew and rubbed against his legs and purred. Andrew chuckled, and I raised my eyebrows. *I didn't know Mia knew how to purr.*

"We have the Historical Society today. It's been a while since they had a meeting, so I thought they'd like their plantation donuts and shoo-fly scones," Andrew said.

"That's great, but we don't have any sweet plantains for our plantation donuts, but going along with the idea of a plantation, I could make mint julip scones, and you could make shoo-fly donuts."

"Are shoo-fly donuts regular frosted donuts with raisins on top?" Andrew asked.

"Exactly," I said.

Andrew grinned. "That will be fun. Shoo-fly and pink-sprinkled donuts. How do you make mint julip scones?"

"I'll make lemony vanilla scones with a green, mint-flavored drizzle. We might have some non-alcoholic bourbon extract. We have wild mint growing in the back; David could snip stems with leaves to decorate the platter. If we have lemons, I'll add lemon zest to the batter."

"We still have lemon zest that you froze when I zested all the lemons by mistake," Andrew said. "I'll check for the non-alcoholic extract."

"If we don't have any, it's not a problem because I'll tell David to hint that it has real bourbon in it."

Andrew giggled. "Mr. David would have fun saying that."

When Barbara came into the shop, Roxie trotted to the door and whined. When Barbara opened the door, Roxie joined David outside while he talked to a man.

When David came inside. he sat in a reading chair and rubbed Roxie's face while he talked to her.

When he rose, he said, "Hope you don't mind, Donut Lady, but I invoked your no politics rule. I'll tell you what it is, just in case someone asks you. According to me, you don't allow people who are running for an office to drop in to visit our groups in the pink room or stand in the building or in front of the building to greet people and introduce themselves as a worthy candidate for office. You're a real stickler about that."

"Yes, I am, and it was brilliant of me to make it a rule before it became a problem," I said.

Barbara rolled her eyes. "Thank you again for going with us yesterday, Karen. Now when I moan about the perfect kitchen in the wrong house, you'll know exactly what I'm talking about."

"I feel like the kitchen was an old friend who left town; I'll miss it too, but if we get too nostalgic, we can count the number of bathrooms to be cleaned."

Barbara snorted. "I hadn't thought about that; there were what? seven bathrooms, counting the one in the cabin? I could clean a different bathroom every day of the week for the rest of my life. That definitely puts everything into perspective, doesn't it?"

"Perspective always helps. Ned has a meeting on Friday at the Georgia Sheriffs' Association Boys Ranch, a residential care program for boys and girls who have been abandoned, neglected, or abused. The meeting is for their staff to learn more about programs like the one Alfred started here and for our men to understand their program, so Asbury can help youth here to be selected for their residential program. He wants me to go along to the meeting."

"That sounds like a great opportunity. We can hold down the fort here, can't we, Andrew?" David said.

"Yes, and my mama would like to help."

"Really? I didn't know that. I'll talk to her after work today," I said.

"Do we have two groups on Friday, Andrew?" Barbara asked.

Andrew opened the planner and turned to Friday. "No, ma'am, just the Motorcycle people."

"That makes it easy, doesn't it? All I need is for Andrew to show me the scone recipe for the day," Barbara said.

"We've got the shop covered, Miss Lady. You can have the day off with pay." Andrew beamed.

"Thank you," I smiled. "I appreciate it." I grabbed my phone and sent a text to Ned: "Shop is covered on Friday. I have the day off with pay."

Ned replied: "Andrew is a good man."

CHAPTER FIVE

"What's our group today, Andrew?" David asked as Barbara went to the storeroom for her apron and cap then washed her hands.

"The Historical Society. Miss Lady will make mint julip scones, and I'll make shoo-fly donuts and pink-sprinkled too, of course. Miss Lady wants you to hint the mint julip scones have bourbon in them," Andrew said.

David chuckled as he strode to the large coffee machine and added the coffee before he turned it on. "That's absolutely perfect for the Historical Society. They'll love being naughty. Thanks for filling the pot with water, Andrew."

"You're welcome. Miss Lady said there might be some wild mint behind the shop, and maybe you could cut some for decoration on the platters."

"I'll do it." David headed outside. "I love my job."

"What's my assignment for today?" Barbara asked.

"How would you like to tackle the vanilla scones?" I asked.

"Really?" Barbara's eyes were wide, and she grinned. "I'd love to. Do you have a recipe?"

"Yes, ma'am. It's right here, Ms. Barbara, and you don't have to zest any lemons because Miss Lady froze some." Andrew pointed to a page in the recipe book then put it near the station where I made scones.

"I'll make the drizzle, and the frosting for the shoo-fly donuts," I said.

"Is maple like molasses?" Andrew asked. "I could make maple donuts."

"That's an excellent suggestion. I'll make maple frosting, and you can add the shoo-flies."

"I'll start with a batch of pink-sprinkled, so we'll have the sheriff's donuts when he comes in," Andrew said.

David came inside with a bunch of mint in his hand. "Y'all are busy. What do I put on the board?"

"Our specials today are shoo-fly donuts and mint julep scones, and our town favorites are pink-sprinkled donuts and lemony-vanilla scones," Andrew said.

"I'll list them on our board then get to work on my room," David said.

"Give me your mint, and I'll wash it for you while you write on the board, honey," Barbara said

The sheriff came into the shop soon after Andrew finished adding raisins to the first batch of shoo-fly donuts. Barbara took over drizzling the mint julep scones from me while her second batch of scones cooled.

Sheriff stared at the board while I set his coffee on the counter in front of his seat. "I need one of each special and my pink-sprinkled donut. I remember when you made the shoo-fly scones, but I'm not sure I've ever had a shoo-fly donut or a mint julep scone."

Andrew served Sheriff his order then waited while the sheriff inspected his donut. "Is this molasses?" the sheriff asked.

"It's Donut Hole molasses." Andrew grinned.

The sheriff chuckled. "I should have guessed because that's exactly what I thought it was."

Andrew continued to grin as he returned to his station and started another batch of donuts.

Sheriff polished off his pastries. "I need a dozen shoo-fly donuts for the office."

Andrew boxed up the donuts while I took the sheriff's money, then the sheriff whistled as he left the shop.

"The sheriff is happy," Andrew said, and I nodded.

Shirley wore sunglasses when she bustled into the shop, and Andrew sacked up her order while I made her to-go coffee.

I peered at her face that was puffy around her eyes, at least as far as I could tell with her oversized sunglasses.

"I need to talk to you in private, Karen. Can we go to the meeting room?" Shirley asked.

"David's setting up for our group. Why don't we go into my office?"

She nodded and headed to the office, and I grabbed her sack and coffee as I followed her.

After we were in my office she sat in the visitor's chair that was next to the shelves. "Is that my coffee? I really need coffee."

I handed her the cup and the sack then closed the door and turned my office chair around to face her before I sat.

"It's actually a good thing, and I should have done this months ago." She sipped her coffee, and I longed for a cup too.

Barbara tapped on the door then opened it and stuck in her hand with a to-go cup. "Excuse me. This is for you." She closed the door.

I sipped my coffee and sighed in relief. *Barbara is a mind-reader.*

"Last night after Woody went to bed, I asked Alfred what was wrong. When he told me nothing, I asked myself what would Karen say? I told him that was nice and what was really wrong because he just hasn't been himself lately. I couldn't put my finger on it, but Woody told me over the weekend that Mr. Alfred was unhappy. Alfred told me it was something he needed to handle himself. Can you imagine what Alfred would have said to one of his boys who told him that? I asked him that very question then asked him if it would be better if we kind of put the engagement and wedding plans on hold. Karen, he was quiet for a very long time, and I was about to bust, but I kept my mouth shut."

She stopped to drink her coffee then pulled out a shoo-fly donut and picked off all the raisins before she took a big bite while I stared at her.

Did I hear her right? She kept her mouth shut?

Tears slipped down her cheeks. "He apologized and told me he can't adjust to the idea of sharing a home with someone else. He said the idea of stepping into a shower that someone else had used terrified him. Karen, I know him, and he's right. I told him he isn't wired to live with other people, not even people he loves, and I know he loves me. He got tears in his eyes, and he patted my arm. It was so sweet that he trusted me enough to tell me; I was a wreck and thought I was going to bawl."

Shirley drank down more coffee and finished off her shoo-fly-less donut. "He said he wanted to give me the freedom to quit my job and sell the brokerage if I wanted to, so I could spend more time with Woody. Can you believe he set up a trust fund for me? I have an allowance that is three times what I could make working fulltime, and he had set up a trust fund for Woody a while ago, so he could go to the school of his choice after high school. I moved my engagement ring to my right hand and told him it was a symbol of our friendship, and he patted my arm again." She smiled and glanced at me.

I smiled. "That's an Alfred hug."

She nodded. "I knew you'd understand. We're not making any announcements or anything because we'll remain very close friends. We will talk to Woody tonight, but Woody won't be surprised at all."

"No, he won't; Woody is very perceptive."

"I'm not going to jump to sell the brokerage quite yet because I enjoy working. I need time to digest all this."

I nodded. "Very wise."

She sniffed back a tear then tipped up her coffee cup. "May I have another cup for the road?" She rose from her seat. "I can't chat all day; I've got work to do."

Shirley opened the office door, but before we left the office, she said, "Thanks for being my friend."

She patted my arm and snickered as she hurried to the counter while I fixed another to-go cup for her.

After Shirley left, Barbara whispered, "You're an awesome friend, Karen. I'm glad you're one of mine too."

Not long after Shirley left, the Historical Society members entered the shop, and David was waiting for them at the door. Mia hissed and raced from our reading area to join Andrew near the fryer.

"David, I love that you're here with us today," the president said. "We heard you were retiring as mayor, and some of us were afraid the information was not complete because no one at the gas station could assure us that you hadn't retired from the Donut Hole. Will you pursue your art career? We'd love for you to be our speaker today."

Barbara elbowed me, as David beamed and accompanied the president to her seat at the head of the table. Roxie followed them like a lady-in-waiting.

The rest of the women remained near the front door until Andrew and David escorted them to their seats, and the two Historical Society men nodded to Barbara and me and tipped their imaginary hats as they made their way to the meeting room.

After everyone was in the room, Barbara whispered, "Did you want to curtsey or was it just me?"

"Wasn't just you. Our usual routine?" I asked, and she nodded.

I staffed the register and filled small orders of donuts, scones, and coffee, and Barbara filled the large orders and made coffee in the small pot when it was low and filled the empty carafes from the meeting room that Andrew brought to her. When the meeting was over, David and Andrew escorted the women to the cars lined up in the road in front of the shop as the Historical Society members' relatives waited to take them home.

Mia pranced to the reading area with her tail high in the air and hopped up on the chair farthest from the front door to groom while she narrowed her eyes in suspicion at each Historical Society member.

"Senior car loop," I whispered, and Barbara snorted. When one of the women raised her eyebrows, I handed Barbara a tissue, and Barbara glared at me.

After all the members had left, David tackled the pink room with sanitizer, broom, and mop, and Andrew dove into washing pots and pans and loading the dishwasher. Mia dashed across the floor to supervise Andrew. I waited on our last minute customers while Barbara cleaned the display case and collected dishes for Andrew.

David came out of the meeting room with his cell phone in his hand. "I have another hot lead on a farm from a friend of a friend. We can see it this afternoon if you like; it's vacant and actually already listed, so I'm going to call Shirley to see if she can meet us there. What do you think?"

"Karen?" Barbara asked.

"I'm game as long as neither of you resigns from the Donut Hole."

Andrew nodded. "No resigning."

"Good, I'll give Shirley a quick call." David stepped into the meeting room.

"Share a sandwich from Gus's?" Barbara asked.

"Sounds good to me."

"Shirley's completely different when it's business, isn't she?" David said as he came out of the meeting room. "She told me she'd meet us there at twelve thirty, and she's pulling some comps and the property tax records."

Barbara raised her eyebrows. "I had my doubts when you said you were going to call Shirley, but it will be nice to have a professional on our side."

After all our customers were gone, and we'd cleaned the appliances and sanitized the counters, I said, "I'll take my brood home."

"We'll pick you up," David said.

Andrew checked to be sure the ovens, fryer, and burners were off, turned off the lights, and locked the door.

"Would you like a ride, Andrew?" I asked.

"No, Miss Lady; it's a nice day for walking."

After I was home, I released Mia from her carrier and opened the back door for Colonel and Roxie. While Roxie rid the backyard of real and imaginary squirrels and let the neighbor dogs know she was home, Colonel sunned on the porch. I carried my laundry to the washer and started the machine. My phone buzzed a text from Barbara: "2 min."

I called Colonel and Roxie inside and gave them and Mia treats then headed to the front door to wait on the porch as David pulled up at the curb.

Barbara waved; I locked the door then hurried to the car.

"How does half a pastrami sandwich sound? It was today's special, and I felt adventurous."

"I can't remember the last time I had a pastrami sandwich, but if it's from Gus's, it will be good," I said.

"I got one too," David said. "I couldn't bear to be left out."

"Do I pass around the sandwiches now? Are we eating on the road?" Barbara asked.

"There's a roadside park that's five minutes outside of town and not too far from the farm. We don't have the dogs, so I won't worry about the cars on the road," David said.

While we ate, David said, "I looked at the listing online. It's a single story, four bedroom house; the kitchen has been updated, and there are three bathrooms. I couldn't tell if there was an appropriate spot for an art studio, but there's a large shed that was once used to make pottery."

"I love this sandwich." Barbara said. "How large is the property? What crops have they grown?"

"According to the listing, it's a tree farm and a fairly large property. Most people maintain their tree farm as a wildlife habitat and take maintaining the proper environment for their wildlife seriously."

"This is not good. I'm in love with it sight unseen," Barbara said.

David smiled. "I know what you're saying. We'd make pretty good tree huggers, don't you think?"

After we finished eating, Barbara handed out hand sanitizer and more napkins for us to clean our hands, then we continued to the farm. We passed a group of small pine trees after David pulled into the gravel driveway.

"If my tree research is right, those trees are about three years old," David said. "I think they are loblolly pines; we'll have to beef up our tree knowledge if we buy a tree farm."

Shirley stood at the end of the driveway and waved, and a man climbed out of a pickup truck as David parked. My phone buzzed a text, but I ignored it and put it on silent before I dropped it into my purse.

Shirley rushed to greet us. "David, I invited an associate along who knows tree farming better than I do. He'll be happy to tour the property with you, then he'll provide me with a written assessment before the end of the week. If you're interested in the property, we'll get a preliminary inspection. I know a man who does a good job and isn't too expensive."

David followed Shirley to the man's truck, then after she introduced them, she hurried to join Barbara and me.

Shirley handed Barbara a packet. "I've included the listing, a few comps, and the tax records. Their agent had a copy of the survey, so I included that too. Paperwork looks good, so let's check out the house."

Shirley led the way, and we hurried to keep up with her. I stared at her feet. *She's wearing heels and striding across this uneven ground like it was a carpeted floor.*

We entered the house through a wide entry way.

"Beautiful wooden floors," Barbara said.

"The kitchen is on the right. Shall we start there?" Shirley asked.

When we walked into the large, eat-in kitchen with the tiled floor, Barbara smiled. "I love how bright it is in here. What a cheerful place to cook."

"This is a commercial-sized gas stove," Shirley said. "Are you okay with gas? The water heater is on-demand gas, and there's a gas fireplace in the living room."

"A gas stove is perfect. This is really nice."

When Barbara walked through the kitchen to the saloon doors then opened the door to the garage, she smiled. "David will love this. There's room for his car and mine, and if he decides to trade in his car for a large pickup truck, both of us will still be able to park in the garage. I love the saloon doors; I'll need a holster on a belt while I cook. I could put my wooden spoons in it."

I giggled. "That's quite a vision, Barbara."

"Why? I'd be in the kitchen slinging hash and swigging down sweet tea."

I snort-laughed, and Barbara grinned.

Shirley shook her head. "I never understood Karen's jokes when we were kids, Barbara; she must have rubbed off on you."

She strode toward the front door. "I'll meet you on the front porch after you've looked through the house; there's no rush."

When we joined Shirley and David on the porch, Shirley said, "After you have had a chance to review all the documents, we can talk. You can always review the listing online too. The seller appears to be motivated to sell. The house was on the market last year, but they pulled it after six months; it most likely didn't sell because of the price. They've put it back on the market at a lower price, but we'll talk about comparable homes that have sold recently. Do you have anything you'd like for me to research before we get back together? If you want to pursue the house, I'd recommend that we come back at least one more time because it's hard to remember everything from one quick tour."

"David, we found your art studio; come inside, and we'll show you," Barbara said.

When we went into the house, Barbara led him to the dining room. I stood in the doorway while David beamed.

"The natural lighting is perfect in here. It would be easy to add track lighting for cloudy days. You're right, honey, this is my studio."

When we went out to the porch, Shirley and her cohort were in deep conversation in the driveway, then the man climbed into his truck and left while Shirley returned to the house to lock the front door.

"We'll let you know what we think, Shirley," David said.

"Take all the time you need." Shirley hurried to her car and waved as she headed to the driveway.

"Did you like the house?" David asked then smiled as Barbara chattered all the way to town until we reached my house.

"Thanks again for going with us," Barbara said.

"I enjoyed it."

As I climbed out of the car, Barbara picked up where she'd left off as she went into detail about the house and all its features. David nodded while her animated gestures continued as he pulled away from the curb.

After I went into the house, I tossed the laundry into the dryer then went out back with Colonel and Roxie and rocked until I remembered I'd silenced my phone after I received a text at the tree farm. I went inside to pick up my phone then returned to my back porch. *The weather is perfect; I love the fresh air.*

When I checked my phone, my eyes widened. I had three texts and a voice mail from Francine. Two of the texts said, "Call me!" and one said, "Left you a voice mail. Call me!"

Her voice mail said, "Call me right away."

I immediately called Francine.

"Thank you so much for calling me; I didn't know who else to turn to. Nobody else knows the story...the entire thing...it's just horrible." She began sobbing, but I couldn't understand what she was saying.

"Please slow down and take a breath. I can't understand you. Where are you?"

Francine inhaled then exhaled. "I'm at Mama's. The police came here earlier and told Mama and Papa that Sissy was murdered last night."

She began sobbing again. "To make it worse, Sissy and I had a big argument yesterday at her furniture store about her boyfriend because she gave him the money I'd given her to pay her electric bill for her store. I don't know if there were any customers there, but she called Mama and told her we had a fight over money, and she needed money to pay the electrical bill for the store. Mama was furious with me when I explained that Sissy gave the money for her electric bill to her boyfriend and needed more. I'll talk to Papa and tell him what happened. He'll talk to Mama after she calms down."

"Are you sure..." I bit my lip. *Sounds more like Mama was furious with Sissy.*

Francine gasped for breath as she wept and tried to speak. "Those mean words were the last ones we spoke to each other before she...and I can't take them back. She's always counted on me to cover for her, and I let her down. Oh, Sissy, I'm so sorry," she wailed.

"What do you need me to do?"

Francine sniffed. "Could you put a note on my shop door? Mama's neighbor called my customers and canceled their appointments, but sometimes people just pop in."

"I'll do that right after we hang up."

Francine sobbed. "Thanks."

After we hung up, I printed a note that said, "Family emergency. Closed for an indefinite time. Thank you for your support." I stared at it then included the date at the bottom before I dropped it into a plastic sleeve.

I opened the back door. "Anyone interested in a short car drive?"

I stood back as Colonel and Roxie barreled to the front door.

I grabbed my purse, keys, phone, some duct tape, and the sign then opened the passenger's back door with the remote. Roxie jumped into her private row, and Colonel hopped in then sat on his usual seat. *I should probably see Kim then go to the grocery store while we're out. I forgot to thaw anything for supper.*

After I taped the sign to the glass on the door, I headed to the hardware store. When Colonel, Roxie, and I went inside, Kim smiled and came out from behind the counter.

"Did Andrew tell you to come see me?" she asked.

"He did, but he didn't say why."

"Andrew told me you never take any time off because the shop is so busy. I am bored to tears here because there is not enough work for two people, and of the two of us, Randy is more knowledgeable, and everyone knows it. People wait for him to finish with a customer, so they can get his advice: even on the simple things. I'd love it if you would take me on as an apprentice. If I could work alongside you, I'll bet I can pick up most of what you do, so you can go on vacation for a day or a week, and I won't go bonkers from boredom."

I blinked. "Are you sure?"

Kim nodded. "I've been trying to get up the nerve to talk to you for months. When Andrew told me you needed a vacation, that was my cue."

"I do like the idea, and I'm willing to give it a try. If either one of us feels it's not a good fit after all, we can pull the plug, right?"

"Right." Kim grinned. "Do we shake hands and run outside and spit in the dirt?"

I chuckled. "I do think the handshake covers it, as much as I love the idea of shocking any passersby."

We shook hands.

"When are you starting?" I asked.

"I'll be there tomorrow morning but not quite as early as Andrew." Kim smiled.

"I gave up trying to beat him to work ages ago. I'll have your apron and ballcap ready."

CHAPTER SIX

After Colonel and Roxie were in their places in the minivan, I headed to the grocery store. When I pulled into the parking lot, my phone rang, and I pulled into the nearest spot to check my phone in case it was Francine.

Gee. I smiled as I answered.

"What are you doing for supper?" Gee asked.

"I'm in the grocery parking lot and have big plans to roam the aisles until something jumps into my cart."

"Just what we thought; come here for supper. We haven't seen you in ages, and we have news."

"Dinner and a teaser? You got me."

"Good; bring all your animals; Mandy's lonesome, and Sandy needs Mia to put him in his place."

After we hung up, I said, "We have a dinner date at Gee's. I forgot to ask what time; we should go early, so we don't miss out."

When we went inside the house, Colonel and Roxie flopped down on the kitchen floor, and I emptied the dryer then folded and hung up my clothes.

"I know Gee will feed you again, but I don't want you begging the second we get there because tomorrow we'd all have to go for a long walk to take off our extra weight." I measured their food then fed Colonel and Roxie. Mia glared until I opened her favorite canned tuna for a treat and fed her too.

After everyone ate, I took Colonel and Roxie outside for one more break, then Mia paraded around the room before she zipped into her carrier.

"You always go into your carrier with style, Mia."

When we were close to Gee's house, Colonel whined behind me. "We're almost there, and can you turn down the volume?"

The closer we got, the louder he got, then Roxie joined in, and Mia meowed.

After we arrived, I opened the door and grabbed the carrier. Gee and Mandy came outside, and the three dogs zoomed around her yard, down the block, and back. As they tore into the house, Mia yowled.

"We're excited to be here," I shouted over Mia. "If it's okay with you, I won't run to the end of the block and back."

Gee chuckled as we went inside, and the dogs raced past us on their rounds to clear the house. I unzipped Mia's carrier, and she prowled the room as she stalked Sandy.

"Are you certain you called the right number when you invited us to dinner?" I asked.

Gee grinned. "It's not boring when you show up, I'll give you that."

Darlene called from the kitchen, "Donut Lady, come say hello to a feeble, old woman."

I snorted. "Feeble, my foot."

"I heard that," Darlene cackled.

"What's the teaser?" I asked on our way to the kitchen, "or are you planning on making me suffer?"

"They say suffering is good for the soul." Gee smirked.

"They is nuts."

"You got that right, girlfriend," Darlene said as Gee and I strolled into the kitchen.

I inhaled the aroma of roasted chicken and herbs. "Mmm. Smells good in here."

"We're going old school: roasted chicken, mashed unpeeled red potatoes, gravy, and English peas," Gee said.

"Comfort food night; that's exactly what I need." I peered at the large pot of potatoes simmering on the stove. "It looks like you're cooking for an army."

Gee snort-laughed. "Armies need comfort food too."

"Leave a special pocket in your stomach, so you'll have room for dessert," Darlene said. "Gee made a sour cherry pie."

Colonel trotted to the front door, and Gee hurried to catch up with him.

"What's the occasion? I can't remember the last time Gee made her sour cherry pie."

Darlene smirked. "My slightly subtle special request; I told her it was your favorite."

"You were right; I really do like the tartness of her sour cherry pie; it's a nice change."

Darlene nodded. "You get more than enough nice and sweet at the Donut Hole. I don't see how you survive from one day to the next."

"Come on in," Gee said. "We've gathered in the kitchen."

Quinn Norris strode into the kitchen and straight to me as he smiled. "This is a nice surprise. I was hoping we'd get a chance to become better acquainted, and here you are."

I put on my plastic, polite smile. *Why do I not believe this was a surprise to you? Nice or otherwise.*

Darlene stood behind Quinn; when she made a gagging motion with her finger, I nodded, and Gee glared at her.

Roxie yipped as she bounded to the front door and whined. Colonel trotted along behind her.

"That has to be David," I said. "Roxie adores him."

Darlene smiled then turned to peek at the pie in the oven.

Gee hurried to open the door. "Come on in."

"There's my girl: good girl, Roxie," David said.

Barbara hurried into the kitchen and raised her eyebrows. "Look at all that food. Are we hosting a town meeting?"

"If we are, we'll have a quorum," I said. "What's our agenda?"

Barbara rolled her eyes. "What do you need us to do, Darlene? Set the table? Write out place cards? Establish shifts to sit at the table?"

Darlene chuckled. "Don't put me in the last shift. I know how folks around here chow down."

"Y'all stop it." Gee glared at us. "There's only going to be nine of us, maybe ten, and my dining table seats twelve."

"Are we serving buffet style or family style?" I asked.

"I had planned family style, but Darlene said buffet allows for more diversity in our conversation than we'd have if our sole topic was pass the food," Gee said.

"I agree with Darlene," Barbara said. "If you'll show us how you want everything set up, we'll do the work."

Gee, Barbara, and I went to the dining room, and Quinn strolled in behind us. "Looks like you all have everything under control, but there must be something I could do. How can I help?"

"Join David and the dogs in the living room to keep them company." Gee smiled as Quinn saluted then strode to the living room.

"I hated to turn down such a sweet offer, but I'm being bossy tonight, and y'all are used to it. It would be unnatural for me to try to tone it down."

She motioned toward the sideboard and two tables. "Put the plates, silverware, and napkins on one table, glasses, cups, and drinks on the second table, and the food on the sideboard."

Barbara nodded. "That will cut down on the congestion."

After Barbara and I set up the tables, Barbara left for the living room, and I went into the kitchen.

"Okay, Gee, 'fess up. What's going on here? Are you trying to catch up on all your social obligations for the year?"

Darlene snorted, and Gee narrowed her eyes. "Just a little friendly get-together of a few close friends. You two need to behave."

I raised my eyebrows. "Why?"

Gee sighed. "I thought it would be nice to have certain people get together for a casual evening, but then Ms. Busybody stuck her nose in and invited a couple extra people on her own."

Darlene guffawed. "Mi casa, su casa. Isn't that what you always say, Gee?"

"Did you just save me from a Gee matchmaking dinner?" I asked.

Darlene winked. "You're quick."

Gee snorted then side-glanced Darlene. "It might still work out."

When Gee strode out of the kitchen to answer the door, I gave Darlene a thumbs up, and she nodded.

"Everybody's here now." Gee told the newest arrivals. "Y'all mingle, and we'll get the buffet set up."

"Where's Miss Lady?" Woody asked.

"She's in the kitchen," Gee said.

Gee came into the kitchen and grinned as I hurried to the front door.

I met Woody, Shirley, and Ned who were halfway to the kitchen and hugged Woody.

"I didn't know you were coming. Your Aunt Gee loves surprises, doesn't she?"

Ned scowled. "She certainly does."

"I have to say hello to Colonel; save me a seat next to you, Miss Lady," Woody said.

"Save me the seat on the other side of you." Ned followed Woody.

"I have something to tell you." Shirley glanced around then whispered, "Francine was arrested for murder late this afternoon. I'm sure it's a mistake, but it will be all over town in the morning, and I wanted to give you a heads-up."

"You're right; it must be a mistake, but thanks for letting me know," I said.

She nodded then hurried to join Woody.

Barbara came to the kitchen, then she and I placed food on the buffet with Gee's directions.

"I had doubts that we'd be able to get everything on the buffet, but it's all there," I said.

"Yes, ma'am, this is not my first buffet rodeo." Gee wiggled her eyebrows, and Barbara and I giggled.

We joined the group in the living room, and Gee whistled with two fingers to get everyone's attention. "Woody, would you please say our blessing?"

Woody nodded then closed his eyes. "Thank you for our food, friends, and good cooks. Amen."

"Amen," we all echoed.

"Ladies first," David announced.

Woody elbowed me, then he and I hurried to the kitchen.

"Ms. Darlene, if you'd like to choose your seat, Miss Lady and I will fix your plate," Woody said.

"I couldn't turn down an offer like that, Woody; I accept."

Woody escorted her to the table, and Darlene sat at the end that was closest to the kitchen. While I dished up her plate, Woody poured her the glass of sweet tea she requested.

"If you're the last lady in line, Mr. Ned and I will be right behind you." Woody offered his arm and escorted me to the line.

"Save my place in line; I need to pull out the rolls from the oven," Gee said as I stood behind her.

"Will do."

Woody stood behind me then motioned to Ned to join him.

"Mr. Alfred told me about the Georgia Sheriffs' Association Boys Ranch. He said it was for boys and girls in bad situations like I was who don't have a Miss Lady to help them. Have they done that very long?" Woody asked.

"The Boys Ranch has been around for a long time," Ned said. "They started off helping just boys, but the program has expanded to a girls' residential camp too."

While Woody and Ned discussed the Boys Ranch, the line moved quickly, then the three of us filled our plates. I set down my plate across from Shirley, and Woody and Ned set down theirs next to mine. Barbara sat next to Shirley in the chair across from Ned.

"If you'll sit, I'll pour you a glass of sweet tea," Ned said.

"Mama Shirley, would you like sweet tea?" Woody asked before Shirley left the dining table for her drink.

"I'd love it, thank you." Shirley sat in her chair, and I smiled.

"What about you, Barbara?" Ned asked. "Sweet tea?"

"Yes, please. I forgot to get it before I sat down; my mouth is watering, Gee," Barbara said.

Darlene picked up her fork, and the rest of us did the same.

David chose the seat on the other side of Shirley, and Quinn sat next to Barbara. The chair across from him was empty.

While we ate, Colonel barked, and Gee hurried to the door. "Come right in; it's nice to see you."

Alfred walked into the room; Shirley's face brightened when she saw him.

Alfred smiled at Shirley. "I apologize for being late. I was a little tied up in some business."

"Join us; there's plenty of food left. Fix yourself a plate," Gee said.

Alfred swallowed hard then picked up a plate and silverware and strategically placed small portions on his plate, so that nothing touched.

David rose and picked up his plate and glass of sweet tea then moved to the empty seat across from Quinn. "Sit next to Shirley, Alfred."

"Thank you, David. I'd like that." Alfred smiled at Shirley again, and I thought my heart was going to melt.

Darlene cleared her throat, and I quit staring at Alfred.

"I heard there was a big estate sale in Macon this weekend, Gee. Are you going?" Barbara asked.

Gee and Barbara discussed the estate sale, and Gee told her about the items she planned to buy.

"Help yourself to seconds, if you like," Darlene said.

"Would you care for something else, Darlene?" I asked.

"I wouldn't mind a small helping of potatoes and gravy to carry me over until morning," she said.

"I can do that," David said. "I'm the closest, which now that I think about it, was a brilliant move on my part."

After David gave Darlene the fresh plate, he asked, "Anyone else while I'm up?"

When no one spoke up, David sat and resumed eating.

While everyone finished eating, David and Ned whispered to each other.

"If you all would go into the living room, we'll clear the table then serve dessert," Gee said.

"Ned and I will clear the table," David said.

"That's great. Darlene, Barbara, and I will set up an assembly line in the kitchen to wash dishes," Gee said.

"I think we've been fired." I smiled as Shirley and I strolled to the living room.

Quinn came into the living room. "I finally get a minute to chat with you, Donut Lady. I'm curious: how did you became interested in donuts?"

"All thanks to my real estate agent," I said. "Right, Shirley?"

"I thought you should have bought the mobile dog washing business, but now I can't imagine what I was thinking. The Donut Hole is perfect for you," Shirley said.

Woody and Ned joined us. "We'd like to hear the story too, Miss Lady."

Woody and I sat on the sofa together, and he leaned against me; a tear of nostalgia welled up in my eye as I remembered the early days when I read to him and how much I would have loved it if he had leaned on me. I sniffed then brushed away the pesky tear.

"I wanted to move to my hometown and buy a business," I said.

"Where did you move from?" Quinn asked.

"Ohio."

"Was this after you retired as a teacher?" Ned asked.

Saved by the coyote hunter.

"Exactly. I wanted to have a small business that I could run by myself, and Woody's Mama Shirley helped me find one."

Woody laughed. "That didn't work out like you planned, did it?"

I smiled. "Not at all because I have lots of help now, but it didn't start out that way. I bought the Donut Hole from Mr. Rothenberger, Ms. Darlene's father. He wanted Colonel and Mia to stay with the shop because that was the only home either one of them had for a long time, and so they did."

"Why didn't Ms. Darlene run the shop?" Woody asked.

"She wasn't strong enough to stand all morning and make donuts and scones, and it wasn't the right business for her."

Barbara stood in the doorway. "I hope this is a good time to interrupt to tell you all that dessert is ready. Pick up your slice of pie; we have two ice cream stations set up for you who want vanilla ice cream on your sour cherry pie."

"Perfect timing. It was a short story," I said.

"Short, but sweet," Woody snickered as he offered his hand to help me to my feet.

The two of us walked together into the dining room; Shirley and Alfred were sitting at the table while Shirley ate her cherry pie with ice cream, and Alfred ate his plain cherry pie with his knife and fork.

"Come get your ice cream for your pie, Woody," Gee said. "Double scoop?"

"Yes, ma'am." Woody hurried to pick up his pie and carry it to Gee for his ice cream.

"We'll have to scoot after we eat our dessert because you have school tomorrow," Shirley added.

I picked up a dessert plate with a slice of pie and skipped the ice cream then sat with Shirley, Alfred, and Woody.

Alfred set his fork and knife on his plate. "I understand you are accompanying Ned to the Boys Ranch meeting on Friday. I really appreciate that you're taking the time to go because you have a special insight from your years of teaching and your knowledge of our program here."

I smiled. "You'll be happy to know that Andrew told me I could take the day off with pay."

Alfred chuckled. "Now, that's a good boss. He really has come a long way, hasn't he? I'm astounded by how much he's grown in maturity."

"I agree," Barbara said. "He took the confidence Karen had in him and made it his own."

"Like Miss Lady did for me," Woody added before he spooned up another big bite of ice cream and pie.

After Woody, Shirley, and Alfred left, David asked, "What are your plans for tomorrow afternoon, Karen? I asked Shirley to set up our second visit to the house, and she told me tonight we're scheduled for one o'clock; Ned offered to go too. I'd forgotten he had retired from the Department of Natural Resources until he asked me about the flood zone, and we talked more about the property and wildlife management."

I raised my eyebrows. "You do know you're asking me if I want to visit our latest favorite kitchen in the world, right? I'll think about it."

Darlene smirked. "If Donut Lady declines, she can watch the Thrift Store, and Gee and I will go."

David laughed when I glared at Darlene then giggled.

"I was trying to appear casual and not too eager." I covered my mouth as I yawned. "Time for me to go home. I don't want to fall asleep behind the wheel. Thanks for the wonderful dinner, you two, and for getting us all together on short notice."

Gee hugged me. "We've discovered that when we try to plan ahead, everything falls apart. We decided to see what would happen if we didn't plan, so we cooked all day then gave everyone thirty minutes' notice to show up."

"If it hadn't worked, we would have had all our meals ready for two weeks, or we could have frozen everything for later and eaten the pie by ourselves tonight," Darlene said.

I chuckled. "I vote pie."

When I reached the front door, I picked up Mia's carrier. "We're ready to leave, Mia."

Sandy strolled alongside her from the living room then meowed when she went into the carrier.

"I'm hoping to become a permanent fixture around town," Quinn said as I zipped up Mia's carrier.

I smiled. "It was nice to chat with you."

When I went out to the car, I used the fob to open the van back door. Roxie yipped at David then dashed to her seat.

"See you tomorrow, Roxie." David waved.

Colonel hurried to his seat, and I put Mia on the floor then closed the door. Ned waited for me at the driver's door and opened it for me. "I'll follow you to be sure you make it home okay."

I pulled away from Gee's house with Ned behind me. When I pulled into my driveway, Ned parked in front of my house. He hurried to open my driver's door and waited for me to go inside with Colonel, Roxie, and Mia. After we were inside, he beeped his horn twice then drove away.

While Colonel, Roxie, and I were in the backyard, my phone rang. I rushed inside and frowned at my phone. *Someone from Conway is calling me?*

I answered, and a woman with a thick accent said, "Is this Miss Donut Lady? I'm Francine and Sissy's mama. Francine told me that you know what has been happening with our family. Papa and I think you might be able to help us. We would like to talk to you. Can you come see us tomorrow? We know a nice restaurant where we can visit. Bring a friend."

"I don't know how I can help. I'm not a lawyer or private investigator or anything like that."

"We hired a good lawyer for Francine and found an honest investigator to look into things for us. Our own lawyer told me that we needed to talk to someone with a level head. Our investigator thinks like the retired police detective that he is, and our lawyer said she could advise us from a legal standpoint. I've heard stories, and you have a reputation for sniffing out the truth. Papa and I have...well, we need to talk."

"What time were you thinking?" I asked.

"Is six thirty or seven o'clock good? We thought we could meet at the Conway Seafood House. The food is good, and I'll make reservations for four."

"Six thirty should be fine."

"Good. We'll see you then. My name is Giana; Papa's name is Papa. Everyone calls him that, even the butcher and me."

I smiled. "I'm Karen."

After we hung up, I stared at the phone. *Am I taking Ned for granted? Maybe I should ask someone else to go with me.*

I sent Barbara a text. "I need to talk. Call me when convenient for you."

My phone immediately rang. "Tell me right now. Are you pregnant or do you need bail?" Barbara asked.

"Neither."

"Good. We're on our way; we'll be at your house in two minutes."

"I didn't mean—"

She hung up, and I stared at my phone. *Was there a better way to word my text, so it didn't sound like an emergency?*

David skidded to a stop in front of my house, and I opened the door, so Barbara wouldn't break it down.

They rushed into the house, and David beelined to the backyard. "Roxie and Colonel need me."

Barbara sat on the sofa while I closed the front door then sat on my soft chair. Barbara raised her eyebrows.

"Francine's mother called me and asked me to have dinner with her and her husband tomorrow night at a nice restaurant in Conway, so we could talk. I told her I wasn't a lawyer or a private investigator, and she said they needed to talk to someone who was levelheaded and knew about Francine and Sissy. She suggested that I bring someone with me and is making reservations for four."

"Are you telling me that Ned isn't available?"

"I don't know if he is or not. He was my first thought, but now I'm wondering if I'm starting to take him for granted. Will he think I have some strange attraction for him and be repulsed, or worse, does he have feelings for me that I'm not sure I can reciprocate, and I'll be leading him on?"

"You have to call Francine's mother back right away because you are not levelheaded at all. You're totally whacko." Barbara rose. "Is that all?"

I glared at her, and she laughed much harder than was necessary then sat back down and wiped her eyes. "Tell me I'm wrong."

"I should have talked to David. He wouldn't tell me I'm whacko."

"Oh, really?" Barbara marched to the back door and reached to open the door then turned and raised an eyebrow.

"So, you're telling me that I'm overthinking this?"

"Call Ned and ask him. Don't text him; your texts are not correctly conveying your message."

"Whacko," I mumbled, and Barbara snickered.

I called Ned. "I just got a call from Francine's parents. They want to meet me at a restaurant in Conway tomorrow evening."

"What time do we leave?" he asked.

"Her mother's making reservations for six thirty."

"I'll pick you up at five fifteen."

"Thanks."

After we hung up, Barbara smirked.

I bit my lip. "I'm sorry for—"

Barbara interrupted. "You trusted me to adjust your whacko, and David's having a great time with the dogs. There is absolutely nothing to apologize for. I'm going to drag David inside then home, so you can get your rest. See you in the morning."

After Barbara and David left, I smiled then locked up the house; as I headed to my bedroom, my phone rang and startled Colonel, Roxie, and me, and I jumped. *Something's wrong.*

I hurried to answer it, and the dogs scrambled to go with me.

Shirley?

"Is Woody okay?" I asked.

"He's fine," she whispered. "I'm in the bathroom, but I had to talk to you for a minute. I almost fainted when Alfred walked into Gee's house, actually put food from a buffet onto his plate, and ate it. Were you as shocked as I was?"

"Yes." *Why am I whispering?*

She sniffed. "He's making an effort; he's actually crossing into areas that terrify him. I'm so proud of him, and I told him so. I'll see you tomorrow."

She hung up.

I smiled. *That was a phone call I certainly never expected to get.*

"It's been a wild day; let's go to bed." I turned off the lights, then Colonel and Roxie followed me to the bedroom.

I yawned as I climbed into bed. "I'd like a good night's sleep, please."

The shadows slid to the hallway, and I closed my eyes and sighed. "Another strange day."

CHAPTER SEVEN

When I woke the next morning, I opened my eyes and checked the clock. *Four thirty.* I sniffed the air. *No smoke.* I leaned over and checked under my bed. *No fire.*

"Colonel?" I called out, and Colonel lumbered down the hall then whined at the doorway as the shadows danced behind him.

Good; I'm not dreaming.

I hurried in my bare feet to the back door and let Colonel and Roxie outside then started my coffee. "My feet are freezing, Mia."

I rushed back to my bedroom and dressed then invited Colonel and Roxie inside for their breakfast. Mia came out from under the dining table and stared at me until I set down her bowl near the pantry. I put on my sweatshirt to take my coffee to the back porch, and Colonel and Roxie finished eating and joined me as I went outside. While Roxie patrolled along the fence, Colonel watched her, and I inhaled the fresh, crisp air and gazed at the clear sky while I listened to the songs of the male cardinals and brown thrashers as they established their territory.

When we went back into the house, Mia stood next to her carrier. "Andrew will be happy to see you, Mia."

She meowed, and I narrowed my eyes as I zipped her carrier. "Did you just tell me you knew that?"

Colonel and Roxie waited at the front door.

"I'm ready too; we've got another busy day ahead of us."

After we were in the shop, Mia raced to join Andrew.

"Good morning, Miss Lady. Mama will be here later. Thursday is always an easy day."

"You're right; we've got Amber's group, so our donuts today are maple and pink-sprinkled with extra donut holes. I still think it's funny that quite a few of them claim they don't eat donuts, but they'll eat donut holes. Any suggestions for the scones?"

"Maple glazed scones are our usual, but if you want something different, what about vanilla with chocolate chips?"

"I'll glaze with maple today, then tomorrow's scones could be vanilla with chocolate glaze because it's essentially the same recipe."

Kim came into the shop. "Am I too late?"

"Not at all," I said. "We just finished deciding what our plan is for today. Come with me, and I'll give you your apron and ball cap, then we can get started on the scones. Our scones today are vanilla with maple glaze. Amber's book club meets this morning, and maple donuts are Amber's favorite, so Thursday is maple day."

As Kim tied her apron, she asked, "So, you make the scones, and Andrew makes the donuts? What are the other duties?"

"David takes care of the pink meeting room and the groups. Andrew keeps David supplied with donuts and scones and keeps the coffee fresh. Barbara glazes the scones and boxes up the large orders, and I wait on the counter and short-order customers. We all pitch in where we're needed, so the responsibility lines are a little blurred."

"Sounds efficient." She smiled.

"I'd call it chaotic efficiency." I handed her a ball cap, then we washed our hands and read the recipe together before I coached her on making the first batch of scones.

After the first batch was in the oven, Kim exhaled. "I felt really slow and awkward."

"You did fine. Ready to tackle your second batch without me hovering?"

Kim swallowed hard. "Okay, if you'll keep an eye on me."

"Your timer's set, you have your recipe, and Andrew will hover."

She chuckled. "You're right."

I went into the office and finished up the paperwork that I kept setting aside. Colonel and Roxie joined me until the bell over the front door jingled, then Roxie scrambled to greet David.

Barbara wore her apron when she came into the office for her ball cap. "Smart move to stay out of the way. The first batch of scones is ready for me. I'll check with Kim for my glaze instructions."

After I stuck my paperwork into its file for the accountant, David came into the office for his apron and ball cap then followed me out.

"Maple today for my daughter, the lawyer?" he asked. "What are we going to call them?"

Andrew peered at David. "I don't know. Maple?"

"What about litigation donuts?" David asked.

"That's a great word; what does it mean?" Andrew asked.

"It means going to court," David said.

While the second batch of scones was in the oven, the sheriff came into the shop.

"Y'all fired the Donut Lady? She probably deserved it." He chuckled.

I grinned as I hurried to coach Kim. "Andrew takes care of the sheriff's donuts and scone, I pour the sheriff's coffee, refill his cup, and take his money."

She nodded. "I can do that."

I reached to pour myself a cup, and Barbara cleared her throat while Andrew shook his head. "Miss Lady."

"I always have a cup with him, but I guess I'm not supposed to touch the coffee pot today, according to certain people."

Kim snickered as she poured two cups, and I sat next to the sheriff.

"How's it going?" Sheriff asked.

"Was that a polite question, or are you asking about how well I'm dealing with being the coach of a team that won't allowed me to run onto the field and grab the ball?"

Sheriff guffawed, and David laughed as he came out of the pink room.

"I need to hear the answer to that one too," David said.

"I think she just answered my question." Sheriff took a large bite of his pink-sprinkled donut.

"How do you manage the books and ordering?" Kim asked as she pulled out the second batch of scones from the oven.

"The accountant takes care of the books. I organize the invoices for her, but that's all caught up for this month. Woody and Andrew discuss our upcoming menus for the week on Saturdays. Woody checks our inventory before he and Shirley place my orders with the wholesalers, then they shop at the local farmers market and grocery store for the items that we don't order wholesale."

"How did I get left out of this loop?" Kim smiled. "You have put the entire town to work here."

Barbara snickered as David handed the sheriff the chalk. "Do you want to do the honors?"

"What goes on the menu board, Andrew?"

"The specials are litigation maple donuts and scones. Town favorites are pink-sprinkled donuts and vanilla scones."

"Perfect for a Thursday." Sheriff wrote on the menu board. "Mr. David's idea?"

Andrew nodded.

Amber and the rest of the group came into the shop, and the women laughed when they read the menu board.

"Hey, this is my day off. This was your idea, wasn't it, Dad?" Amber attempted a scowl as she put her hands on her hips.

David raised his eyebrows then grinned. "Sue me."

"Dad, you're terrible." Amber laughed along with her group as they went into the pink room, and David and Roxie followed them.

Kim giggled. "That was hilarious."

"It's like this all the time and never gets old," Barbara said. "I still think about some of the day's events while I'm cooking in the evening and laugh."

"I think I'll go for a walk." I peered outside at the bright, sunny day. "I've done everything here that I can, and I'm too restless to sit and read. Colonel and I will go around the block."

"Take your phone, Miss Lady," Andrew said.

"Good idea."

I hung up my apron and ball cap then put on my sweatshirt. After I dropped my phone into my pocket, I asked, "Ready, Colonel?"

While Colonel and I walked around the block, I was surprised at how many of the small shops were vacant. "I'd heard that people were moving their businesses out to the new strip mall, but I wonder if some of the others folded because the shoppers stopped coming here. I'll have to ask David about that."

When we reached the Donut Hole, a car pulled up in front.

"Didn't expect to find you outside." Quinn closed his car door.

I smiled. "I take Colonel out for a walk from time to time. I have a self-sufficient crew."

"That's what I hear." He strode my way.

"Are you here for coffee?" Colonel and I headed to the door.

"Coffee and a donut," he said.

I opened the door. "You came to the right place."

When he followed us inside, Kim said, "Welcome to the Donut Hole, Mr. Norris. What would you like today?"

He peered at the menu. "Coffee and... what's a litigation donut?"

"A prank we played on one of our local lawyers who has a fondness for maple donuts," Kim said.

Quinn chuckled. "How did he take it?"

"Like a champ," Barbara said. "How are you doing, Quinn?"

Quinn sat at the counter while I continued to the storeroom then closed the door behind me. After I hung up my sweatshirt and took a big breath, I strolled back to the counter.

Quinn scanned the shop. "This is a nice shop you have here, Karen. You must be doing well to afford all the staff you have."

Barbara laughed. "We're volunteers here, and it's the best job in the world for us. David and I have a place to go together every morning; he can socialize, and I can bake and decorate."

"I never heard of volunteers working at a business, unpaid volunteers?" he asked.

"Best kind," Barbara said. "We can't be fired."

"It's therapy, not work," Kim said.

Quinn nodded.

You don't really understand, do you?

"What volunteer work are you interested in, Quinn?" I asked.

He smiled. "I haven't quite found my niche yet."

"There are definitely lots of opportunities in Asbury," Kim said, and Barbara nodded.

He drained his coffee then polished off his donut. "Sounds like a great place." He placed a tip near his plate then rose. "I'm glad I stopped by, but we'll have to have lunch sometime, Karen."

After he left, Kim asked, "Was my prank comment inappropriate?"

"Not at all," Barbara said. "Amber deserves a little privacy on her day off."

"I heard he was planning to interview for the mayor's job," Kim said. "Does he know that's an unpaid position?"

"Mr. Quinn won't like Asbury," Andrew said.

"Why not, Andrew?" I asked.

"He doesn't know how to make friends."

"Acquaintances but not friends." Barbara nodded.

David opened the pink room door, and the women in the book club hurried to the front door.

The young mom stopped before she left. "Thanks for telling me about Amber's book club, Donut Lady, and my mother-in-law said to thank you for her. This was totally energizing for me."

Amber hugged her dad. "I am so glad you walked away from the stress."

She strode to Barbara, "Mom, Dad told me about the tree farm you're considering."

"Are you free for dinner tonight, honey? We'd love to bore you with all the details," Barbara said.

Amber laughed. "Perfect, but tonight doesn't work. What about tomorrow night? Is five thirty too early?"

"Not at all," Barbara said.

"Good, I'm bringing a friend."

I narrowed my eyes. "Not Quinn Norris, right?"

"No, Donut Lady, not Quinn Norris. You'll approve of my friend." Amber laughed as she breezed out of the shop.

"Do you know who she's talking about, David?" Barbara asked.

"No, I thought you did, but she knew you'd invite her to dinner, so we could talk about the house; we have a slick lawyer in the family." David narrowed his eyes as he peered at the door. "Better lock up the family jewels."

Barbara rolled her eyes.

"Are we all going to die of curiosity?" I asked.

"That's a joke, Andrew," David said.

Andrew nodded. "Miss Lady makes odd jokes sometimes, but I won't die of curiosity because I know who Ms. Amber is bringing with her to dinner."

Kim moaned. "And you won't tell us either, will you?"

"No, Ms. Kim." Andrew grinned. "We're at work, Mama. You have to be Ms. Kim."

David hurried to the pink room, and Andrew followed him with the utility cart, so he could collect the dirty dishes.

I stood at the front door and greeted customers while Kim and Barbara took care of the orders.

When Dustin, the sales manager from the car dealership, came in, he chuckled and shook my hand. "I'll vote for you, Donut Lady."

I glowered. "Dustin, behave. I am not running for Mayor; I'm going to be out of town tomorrow, and I'm giving the team a chance to work without me."

"Oh, right." He winked. "We don't want the competition to know you're testing the waters."

I rolled my eyes. "Am I going to have to put up with this all day?"

Dustin wiggled his eyebrows. "Pretty much."

"I smell the sheriff behind this."

"I ain't no squealer." Dustin laughed as he strode to place his order.

"It's going to be a long morning," I mumbled.

Jorge came into the shop and hugged me. "We're all going to vote for you, Donut Lady. You can count on us."

He chuckled as he strode to the counter. "I need a dozen donuts and all the donut holes you have."

"Donut holes are free for Jorge," I said.

"You can't bribe a voter," Jorge said, "but today is the first anniversary of our newest gas pumps, so I accept the gift."

"Those gas pumps are five years old," I grumbled.

Jorge's eyes twinkled as he pointed to the menu board.

"I get it." I sighed as I sat at the reading table.

After all the donuts were gone, and the shop sparkled, I said, "This morning really dragged."

David, Barbara, and Kim glanced at each other but didn't say anything.

"What about Mia, Miss Lady? Can she stay with us tomorrow?" Andrew asked.

"I hadn't thought that far ahead, but that's a great idea. I'll bring Mia, Colonel, and Roxie here tomorrow morning before we leave."

"We'll take them home with us," Barbara said. "You can come pick them up when you are back in town, or if it's too late, we'll bring them to the shop Saturday morning."

I scowled. "What about food, bowls, and a cat box?"

"I'm always ready for any company that may stay at our home," Barbara said, and David nodded.

"Can Mia go home with us, Mama?" Andrew asked.

"If it's okay with Donut Lady."

"Miss Lady, can Mia go home with us?"

I cocked my head. "I wouldn't be home this afternoon, this evening, or all day tomorrow. If it's okay with Mia, it's okay with me."

"Mia, would you want to go home with me until Saturday?" Andrew asked.

Mia purred and rubbed against his leg then dashed to her carrier. Andrew grinned then zipped it up and picked up the carrier. "We're ready, Mama."

"We'll pick up sandwiches then meet you at your house," David said.

I locked up, then after Colonel and Roxie were in their seats, I climbed in and headed home.

When I opened the back door for Colonel and Roxie, Barbara called me. "We forgot that David asked Ned to look at the property. Ned's going to pick you up, then we'll meet at the park outside of town. You're bringing the dogs to the farm, aren't you?"

"They'd like that, especially Roxie."

After Ned picked us up, we headed to the park. "Did you have a rough morning? I heard about Sheriff's prank."

"He sure got me good on that one."

"I understand it's been a long time since he's been able to pull off a stunt on you."

I sighed. "I've been slacking. I haven't gotten him in over a week."

Ned chuckled. "You'll come up with something when he least expects it, although you'd think he'd expect it all the time."

"He'll be watching for something, but I'm going to lie low and let him stew in the suspense." I snickered.

"Liverwurst and onion sandwich okay with you?" Ned asked.

"It actually is, but I can't tell if you're kidding or not."

"Back atcha."

We laughed together.

"When I was in college, I had a good friend who was married to the nicest guy in the world, and he was the only person on campus who loved sardine and onion sandwiches as much as I did. We weren't allowed to eat in their apartment though; she'd send us outside with bread, mayonnaise, mustard, a tin of sardines, and an onion along with a cutting board and knife. In the winter, we cleared off snow from our bench then shivered and munched on our sandwiches. One really blustery day, the temperature dipped below freezing, and she took pity on us and brought us a thermos of hot coffee."

Ned guffawed. "All heart, that one."

I grinned. "I've always been an adventurous eater."

When we reached the park, Barbara and David were waiting at a picnic table.

"Y'all must have called in your order to Gus before you left the shop," I said.

"Of course," Barbara said. "I told Gus to give us the special, so we have ham salad sandwiches. He told me it was his favorite, but nobody would ever order it. I have a small order of fruit salad for us to share, Karen, just in case."

After we unwrapped our sandwiches, I took the first bite while everyone watched.

"What's the matter with you? This is good."

"Our foodie approves. Good enough for me," Ned said.

Barbara took a bite then stared at her sandwich. "It is good. Do you think Gus was teasing me?"

David rolled his eyes. "There does seem to be a bit of that going around, doesn't there?"

Barbara peered into the sack. "He threw in four cookies. Is that so I won't yell at him later?"

"Probably." David polished off his sandwich, then he strode along the park trail while Colonel and Roxie trotted along with him then turned toward the nearby woods.

"Don't go too far away," he called, and they bounded back to him. When he and the dogs returned to our picnic table, we had thrown away our trash.

"We can eat our dessert on the road." Barbara gave me the sack with two cookies.

Before we reached the truck, I said, "I noticed you've been opening doors for me lately." I gazed at Ned and cocked my head.

"Andrew talked to me." He sighed. "He told me I had to be nice and use manners like open your doors or something."

I nodded and waited for him to open the door. "Thank you."

I climbed inside the truck. *I should have seen Andrew's hand in this, but there's more to the story.*

As we followed David, I asked, "Ready for your dessert?"

Ned held out his hand and grinned. "Gimme, please."

I giggled as I handed him his cookie. "Are you getting all nice and mannerly again?"

"We're talking about a cookie, here, so yes." Ned winked and took a bite.

Shirley and Alfred were waiting for us at the house. David, Alfred, and Ned strode away to look at the tree farm, and Roxie raced ahead to find a rabbit.

Colonel dashed to the house then waited for Shirley, Barbara, and me on the front porch.

Before we went into the house, Shirley said, "Today, don't look for what you like; instead, look for imperfections, things that aren't right, and stumbling blocks. Do you understand what I'm trying to say?"

"Maybe, so if I don't look for what I like, I'll see other things, is that it?"

"That's right." Shirley exhaled in relief. "It's hard to do for most people."

"Let's start with the bathrooms: they'll be good practice for me."

As we headed down the hall to the first bathroom, Colonel disappeared.

"Do you feel like we should stretch or something? Aren't we about to step into a house hunting fight ring?" Barbara whispered as she and I stepped into the guest bathroom. Barbara closed the door after we stepped inside.

"There's only one towel bar in here," she said.

I pulled out the drawer closest to the door then opened the door, and the door hit the handle on the drawer.

Barbara closed the drain on the tub then ran two inches of water. After she turned off the faucet, she watched the water. "No leak."

She opened the drain, ran the shower until the water was hot then held her hand in the spraying water.

"Okay, flush the toilet."

When I flushed, she said, "It maintained water pressure."

I unlocked the window and opened it then closed and locked it.

"I can't think of anything else," Barbara said.

"I'll look under the sink to see if there are any signs of old leaks." I knelt down and sniffed. "No problems here. Let's check the closets in the bedrooms before we go to the master bath."

After we checked the master bath, Barbara said, "We're ready for the kitchen."

As we strolled down the hallway, I saw the thermostat, and turned down the temperature.

"Are we ready for the kitchen? Did we stretch appropriately?" I whispered.

She shrugged. "I don't know, maybe we should actually stretch; it couldn't hurt."

"Yes, it could."

We giggled as we went into the kitchen.

"There you are, Colonel. I thought you'd be in here on this cool floor," I said.

"I love the stove, let's turn on all the burners," Barbara said.

"I'll turn on the lights."

Barbara turned on the burners to the highest setting then turned on the oven and the hood fan.

We stood back and admired the fire and the bright lights then the air conditioner kicked it.

"The air conditioner blower isn't effecting the burners. That's good," I said.

Barbara turned off the stove and oven, and I turned off the lights.

"We'll have to change the thermostat back; I'm freezing, which gives me an idea for another test." I opened the refrigerator and the lower freezer compartment then left them open.

"What are you doing?" Barbara asked.

"Testing."

The refrigerator beeped an intermittent high tone, and I closed the door, but the beep continued until I closed the freezer compartment door too.

"It wasn't a deal breaker, but it's useful to have a warning if the doors are left open."

Barbara looked around. "I think we've done our best. We have a short list of findings, but we didn't find any dealbreakers."

"You'll still want a home inspection. Let's turn up the air conditioning setting to its original setting," I said.

My phone buzzed a text: "I need a couple minutes of your time. Would you text me after you return from David's new farm? Quinn."

I frowned then showed Barbara the text.

"Odd request, but you will, won't you?" Barbara asked.

"I thought it was more than odd, but I needed a second opinion. Yes, I will; if nothing else, we'll know what he has been so anxious to talk to me about."

I replied to Quinn, "Okay."

"Do you want me there too?" Barbara asked.

"I don't think he wants anyone else to hear, which is why he didn't say anything last night."

"So, text me when he shows up then again when he leaves. I'll have your back."

After we returned the thermostat to its higher setting, Shirley joined us.

"How did you do?" she asked.

"We found a few things but no deal breakers," Barbara said.

"Good news, assuming David and Ned are satisfied, our next step is an inspection," Shirley said. "I'll draw up a tentative contract for Amber to review while we talk about what you and David would like to offer for the property."

"I'm going to look at the kitchen one more time," Barbara said.

"Quick question, Karen," Shirley said after Barbara was in the kitchen. "An old friend of mine who has her own agency in Conway told me one of the agents north of her learned their broker was paying what she called 'protection money.' Have you ever heard of anything like that?"

I nodded, and Shirley continued, "You need to stop it."

I stared at Shirley while she hurried toward the door to wait on the porch.

"Just stop it," I muttered as I shook my head in disbelief.

Barbara joined me. "Are you okay?"

I rolled my eyes. "I just had a short conversation with Shirley."

Barbara nodded. "I'm sorry; let's find David."

CHAPTER EIGHT

David and Ned strolled from the trees to the house in deep discussion.

When they reached us, David said, "There is a firebreak, but it's fairly overgrown. Ned said it's critical to have someone assess it and give us an estimate for a more protective firebreak, and it would also be a good idea to clear away the trees that are too close to the house."

"Ned, are any of those items dealbreakers?" Shirley asked.

"No, but you could easily use the information for a consideration in the offered price because they are existing safety concerns; I wouldn't advise David to walk away from the property because of them, though."

"I'll make it a priority to get those estimates," Shirley said.

"Are you ready to head back, Donut Lady?" Ned asked.

"I guess so." I stared at Colonel who stood next to Ned's truck. "Is there any way we could take Colonel with us? Mia's happy with Andrew, and Roxie's fine with David, but…"

"Colonel's different," Ned added. "Of course, we'll take him; if it's a problem in the meeting, we can leave, or I'll sit with Colonel in the sun and take walks."

I smiled. "I noticed you picked the best option for yourself."

"You're more qualified to attend the meeting, and I'm highly qualified to be outside; I spent my entire career perfecting my outdoor skills. I'll tell David that Colonel's going with us, but he won't be surprised."

Ned opened the back door for Colonel, and Colonel hopped into the truck; Ned winked at me then opened my door, and I smiled as I climbed in while Ned strode to David.

After a brief conversation, the two men shook hands, then Ned returned to the truck.

On our way back to town, Ned whistled under his breath.

"What's that tune you're whistling? It's haunting but strangely comforting."

"I didn't know I was whistling."

"You were, what was it?"

"It must have been a tune my grandpa used to whistle when he took me fishing; he told me fishing made him happy." Ned glanced at me. "I haven't thought of it in years."

"I liked it, and I'm glad you're having a fishing kind of day."

Ned smiled. "That's exactly the kind of day I'm having."

I absently stared at the passing trees and farmland. *Should I have ignored Quinn's text? What could be so urgent that it couldn't wait and so private that he couldn't talk in front of other people.*

"Something's on your mind," Ned said.

I exhaled. "I got a text from Quinn saying that he needed to come by my house and talk to me for a few minutes today, and I said okay. Now, I'm not so sure it's a good idea, but it seems awkward to change my mind."

Ned nodded. "Tell him you and Colonel will be at the park and to meet you there."

I raised my eyebrows. "A public place is a perfectly reasonable request, and Colonel and I go to the park frequently. I like it, thank you."

"You're welcome." He shook his head. "This polite stuff is kind of habit-forming, isn't it?"

I chuckled. "I think it's supposed to be."

After we reached my house, Colonel and I climbed into the minivan, and I sent the text then headed toward the park. When I glanced into my rearview mirror, I didn't see Ned behind us. *He's going to lurk not hover.*

I parked near our favorite path; I strolled along behind Colonel while he cleared the area ahead of all squirrels and any other critters.

When my phone buzzed a text, I read the message from Quinn: "Sorry. Plans changed. Will have to reschedule for next week. See you Monday."

I sent Ned a text. "Meeting canceled."

He stepped out from behind a small grove of trees and strode to me. "That was unexpected."

"I know. Want to walk with us? This is Colonel's favorite trail."

"Might as well. What did he say?"

I showed him the text. After he returned my phone, he said, "Not very informative."

We strolled along the path in companionable silence.

After we reached my van, I used the fob to open the door for Colonel, and Ned opened my door. As I slid into my seat, I frowned. *He's been opening my door, but I haven't been polite. I hope Andrew doesn't find out.*

"Thank you," I said, and Ned's cheeks reddened as he nodded.

What an old softie. I embarrassed him.

After Colonel and I returned home, I sent Barbara a text. "Quinn canceled. I'm relieved."

Barbara replied, "Me too."

I showered then stood in front of my closet while I stressed over what to wear.

I sent a text to Barbara: "What do I wear tonight?"

She replied immediately. "Green dress or green shirt."

I texted, "Ha-ha. You know I don't have a green dress."

"Imagine that."

I rolled my eyes and put on my green shirt and black pants.

After I fed Colonel, we went out back, and Colonel flopped down on the porch at my feet while I rocked, drank my sweet tea, and listened to the birds sing and the neighborhood children laugh and call to each other while they played.

When I finished my tea, we went inside. "Ned and I are going to dinner and will be a little late. You can go to David's with Roxie, if you like, or stay here if you won't be lonely."

Colonel circled a spot in the kitchen then lay down and sighed.

"You're right, the house will be quiet this evening."

When I heard Ned's truck pull into the driveway, I glanced at the clock. "It's five minutes after five; that's Ned's version of on time, Colonel."

Colonel opened his eyes and grinned his big doggy grin. I picked up my black sweater and purse. When I opened the door, Ned stepped out of his truck.

"I take it you're ready. Will Colonel be okay?" he asked.

"Colonel is looking forward to a quiet evening without Roxie and Mia," I said.

On our way to Conway, Ned asked, "Have you ever been fishing?"

"No, I don't remember anyone in my family going fishing, and I was the bookish girl most of my life. I love being outside now, but that might be from my years of being incarcerated."

"That makes sense. My grandpa told me I was born with a fishing pole in my hand, and I still love to fish and hunt. We'll have to go fishing sometime if you think you could put up with the bugs and boredom. Colonel's a calm guy; he'd be a great boat dog. We'd have to be sure our cabin is near a lake."

"Do you have a boat?" I asked.

Ned smiled. "Nope, but I don't have a cabin either, and you don't have a fishing pole. Those are easily corrected details."

I smiled at his dimples and the twinkle in his eyes as he glanced at me.

"True. I'll need a fishing hat too."

"We'll need a list."

I pulled out a small notebook and pen from my purse and wrote cabin, lake, boat, fishing pole, fishing hat, and bug repellent then read my list to him. "What else?"

We argued and laughed about what we'd need for the boat and fishing, our requirements for a cabin, and the boat safety class that Ned told me I had to take.

"You have to be a boat captain, so you can save me and not cut me up with the propeller if I fall overboard," Ned said.

"You'll just have to make it a priority to stay on the boat," I said.

"Maybe I have to jump in to save a drowning boater," he said.

"I'm sure I have a snappy comeback for that," I said. "Give me a minute."

"Too late. I win." Ned pulled into the restaurant parking lot.

I narrowed my eyes. "I wasn't watching; how many times did you circle the block until you had the last word?"

"Not more than a dozen, why?" He widened his eyes with the worst innocent look I've ever seen, and I giggled.

When he opened my door for me, he said, "It's nice to hear you laugh."

"Thanks, I like your smile."

I slipped my arm through Ned's as we walked into the restaurant.

"Fancy place," he whispered, and I nodded as I glanced at the carpeted floors, white tablecloths with black napkins on the tables, and a large crystal chandelier over the host stand.

"Are you Giana and Papa's friends?" The host wore black pants, a white shirt, and a yellow bow tie.

"Yes, but how did you know?" I asked.

The host grinned. "Giana told me to watch for a successful businesswoman with her distinguished companion."

Ned elbowed me and whispered, "Distinguished," as the host led us to Giana and Papa's table.

Papa rose when we approached the table, and Giana smiled. "Welcome."

Ned held my chair then sat on my right as the host handed us our menus.

"Sweet tea?" the host asked.

"Yes, for both of us," Ned said.

The host disappeared, then a server appeared with our glasses of sweet tea.

"Everything is good," Giana said.

Ned's eyes twinkled. "Trout dinner?"

I smiled and handed my menu to the server. "Perfect."

"Yes, ma'am. Same for you, sir?"

Ned nodded as he handed his menu to the server.

After the server left, Giana pulled out a large folder from her oversized handbag then placed it on the table.

"Francine did not murder her sister, but I'm certain any mother would say that about her child. However, Sicily was not a child that would make a mother proud."

Giana tapped the folder. "Sicily has had access to four of our bank accounts. I first noticed that she was making periodic, small withdrawals, then when the withdrawals escalated in frequency and amount, I quickly closed the accounts. When Sicily complained to Papa that the accounts were closed, Papa told her we were audited and had to pay penalties to the government."

"She cried big tears and wanted to know how we could do that to her," Papa added.

Giana nodded. "Sicily told Papa she needed to show that she had collateral, so she could get a loan for her furniture store. He told her to talk to me."

"Mama is not the soft touch." Papa smiled.

Giana nodded. "She begged him for help with her furniture store, so we decided to give her one last chance. Papa gave her access to one of his smaller bank accounts and told her it was the only one we had left. She began draining it more rapidly than she did the other four then asked Papa about his retirement. Papa told her he lost all his retirement money in the last stock market crash, and she was very angry."

"Francine told me you were angry at her because she gave Sicily money for her power bill," I said.

Papa shook his head, and Giana sighed. "Francine always blamed herself when Sicily got into trouble and frequently tried to cover for her. We've told Francine she wasn't responsible for her sister, but it's a blind spot for her."

I frowned. "It was unethical but not illegal for Sicily to take the money from the bank accounts because she'd been given access."

Giana and Papa exchanged looks and smiled.

"Which is why we hired a private investigator to follow her." Giana tapped the folder again. "We have his detailed report and surveillance photos of her activities from the first time I noticed the withdrawals on the four accounts. Maybe you are thinking we are strange parents, but we've been wary since she was sixteen, and our oldest daughter, Alessandria, discovered Sicily had convinced their grandmother to give her access to Grandmama's checking and savings. Sicily robbed that poor woman of all her money and her dignity."

"When Mama confronted her, Sicily laughed," Papa said.

"That was the most evil laugh I'd ever heard in my life, and it took every bit of strength I had to walk away," Giana growled, "but from that time on, we watched Sicily, and we were ready."

"I'm so sorry," I said. "No parent should have to go through that."

Giana reached for my hand and squeezed it. "You are a good woman, thank you."

Our server brought us our meals, and Giana said, "We eat, then we can talk more."

Papa bowed his head and said, "Thank you for our food and the kindness of strangers."

"Amen," Ned said.

"Eat, eat." Giana passed the basket of bread to me.

"How's your fish?" Papa asked.

"Delicious," I said, and Ned nodded.

"How are your crab cakes, Papa?" Ned asked.

"Good, but not like Mama's."

Giana laughed. "He's a smart man; crab cakes are his favorite seafood, and I always make them for his birthday dinner."

"You have a bakery?" Papa asked. "Do you bake bread and cakes?"

"I have a donut shop; we have coffee, donuts, and scones."

"We'll visit your donut shop on Saturday," Papa said.

"I look forward to seeing you." I smiled.

"Dessert?" our server asked.

"Yes, and coffee too. Papa prefers decaf," Giana said.

"Decaf for me too, please," I said.

"Yes, ma'am."

"A local bakery makes their lemon meringue pie every afternoon especially for them," Giana said. "It's a perfect ending for a seafood dinner."

While we ate our pie, Giana said, "We traced the money she stole from us to a local bank. It wasn't hard because Sicily threw away her deposit slips and bank statements and set her trash sacks out on the curb or in the street gutter rather than shred the papers or sign up for online banking. She was always untidy and careless; I learned she had taken her grandmother's money when she was sixteen after I found the bank statements on her bedroom floor and her grandmama's checkbook under her bed. She went crying to Papa and told him I'd been snooping in her bedroom. He told her that she should thank me for cleaning her room because it was a fire hazard."

Papa chuckled. "Pericolo d'incendio."

Giana nodded. "She had to ask her sister what that meant; Francine was shocked that Sicily didn't know. I thought Sicily would have learned to be more careful with bank statements after that, but I was obviously mistaken."

"Excuse me." Ned rose from the table and headed toward the host station and the restrooms.

"I may not have much time for the documents until Sunday," I said as the server picked up our empty dessert plates.

"I appreciate how busy you must be, so please don't think I expect you to make them a priority. I'll be interested in your assessment after you've had time to review the papers and photos. Call, text, or email me anytime you have questions; my email address is on my business card that I included in the folder," Giana said.

"Stai attento," Papa said.

Giana nodded. "Be careful."

"We will. Thank you again for a wonderful dinner and for trusting me with your information."

After Ned returned, he held my chair while I picked up the folder and rose, and the host appeared at our table. "Is there anything else?"

"A little more coffee, please, and the check," Giana said.

The host widened his eyes then glanced at Ned. "Yes ma'am; coffee."

"And the check," Giana repeated.

The host disappeared, and Ned said, "He's reluctant to tell you that I have already paid the check. I can't tell you how much it means to me for the Donut Lady to have a problem she can tackle with her amazing skills."

Papa laughed. "Well played, Signor Ned. I said that right, no?"

Ned smiled. "Yes, you did."

Giana narrowed her eyes, but her quivering mouth gave away the mirth she was trying to hide. "I let my guard down; it won't happen again."

"I will walk with you to the door," Papa said.

"Papa's old world; it's polite to see guests out." Giana sipped her coffee.

When we reached the host stand, Papa hugged me and shook hands with Ned. "Mama and I may leave the country in a few days on an extended visit. We'll get new phones and leave the old ones behind because the old phones won't work right. We apologize in advance for any inconvenience."

Before we left, Ned said, "Papa, I'm not certain what Giana expects Karen to assess. Is she looking for a way to clear Francine that your lawyer didn't see?"

"Our lawyer told us the records may help or hurt Francine and didn't even want copies. Mama wanted someone not connected to the family to have the records in case something happened to us. She's not a donna nervosa, but she's afraid..." Papa pursed his lips.

"Of what?" I asked, and Papa shook his head then returned to Giana.

On our way to the truck, Ned asked, "What do you think?"

"I thought at first they wanted me to find any evidence in Francine's favor, but after Papa talked to us, I'm a donna nervosa too. Do you think there could be something that could implicate the killer?"

"Now I'm an uomo nervoso. Do you suppose I said that right?"

I shrugged. "It's beyond me."

"I guess it would be rude to give the records back to them," Ned said.

I nodded. "That wouldn't feel right. I'll see if I can discover what could make Giana nervous, then we'll have better information, so we can decide what we want to do."

"That works, especially the 'we' part." Ned smiled.

After we were on the road to Asbury, I said, "You certainly gained the admiration of Papa, and Giana too, when you paid the check, but she didn't want to admit it."

"It just seemed appropriate."

"It was impressive; I'm glad you thought of it. I wonder how many times they've gone to dinner with someone who assumed Giana would pay the check because that's what she always does."

"Now that we're going fishing, let's talk about that cabin," Ned said.

I smiled. *Not the smoothest way to change the subject.* "After looking at the two farmhouses, I can't help but wonder if cabins have gas stoves like those two houses did. I really loved those stoves."

"Sounds like the kitchen can't be too tiny. If we find a cabin we like, and it doesn't have a gas stove, that's an easy fix, at least for the local propane company."

"What about a fireplace?" I asked.

"I think it's a law that cabins must have a fireplace," Ned said.

"If it isn't, it should be. I don't want a scary steep driveway."

Ned nodded. "We don't want the cabin right next to the road either."

"I'd rather have it next to the road than at the top of a steep hill."

"No, that won't work."

We argued the rest of the way back to Asbury about how close to the road is too close.

"I've got an idea," Ned said. "What if we have veto power? If you veto a cabin, we move on; if I veto a cabin, same."

"That sounds fair. Is there a maximum number of vetoes allowed?" I asked.

"No, we can always revisit a cabin if the veto is voluntarily lifted, but otherwise, we'll keep looking."

"Good. What time do we leave in the morning?"

"The meeting starts at eight, and it takes a little over an hour to get there. If we left at five forty-five, we'd have time to have a nice breakfast before we go to the meeting. The program says there will be a continental breakfast and coffee at seven thirty, but it will be store-bought pastries, and if word got out that's what I put in front of you for breakfast, I'd be run out of Asbury."

I chuckled. "Barbara, Darlene, and Gee would head up the mob, wouldn't they?"

After Ned parked in front of my house, he walked me to the porch, then after I unlocked the door, he hugged me. "Thank you for a wonderful evening."

I was surprised, but I returned his hug. "Thanks for going with me."

As I went inside, I heard him whistling his grandpa's tune on his way to the truck, and I smiled. *I need to learn that tune too.*

"Ready to go out back, Colonel?" I asked.

I turned on the burner under the tea kettle, then we went outside. Colonel stayed by my side for a few minutes then went on his evening stroll around the yard. I slipped inside and brewed a cup of tea then took my hot tea and phone to the porch.

I sent Barbara a text. "We're back."

She replied. "Interesting. How was dinner?"

"Great food. Nice people."

My phone rang.

"What about Ned? How did he do?"

"He was charming."

Barbara choked. "I was drinking hot tea, and now I have peach tea all over my phone, but I'm sure I misunderstood what you said. Ned was what?"

"It was a nice evening, and he charmed Francine's parents. They love him. We argued and laughed all the way there and back. It was fun."

"How much wine did you drink?"

I chuckled. "No wine."

"What did you argue about?"

"Whether or not I should be a boat captain and how close to the road is too close."

"Fine, I'll tell David we need to relax with a glass of wine because you're ahead of me."

She hung up.

Ten minutes later, she texted me. "David and I are discussing how close to the road is too close. He's wrong. Enjoy your meeting!"

I giggled. "My friends are fun, Colonel. Are you ready to go inside?"

My phone buzzed a text from Devlin. "Don't know if this is important, but the pickup woman always picks up on Wednesday but didn't show this week."

That is interesting.

Colonel stared at the back fence and growled his low warning growl. The hair on my arms and the back of my neck stood up. The shadows slid under the back door and joined us on the porch; I rose from my chair and stepped away from the illumination of the neighbor's security light and into the shadows that fanned out in front of the back door.

Colonel slowly stalked from the porch to the middle of the yard then barked and raced across the yard after a raccoon that had hidden behind the neighbor's trash can. When the raccoon lumbered away, Colonel trotted back to the porch and nosed the door, and I inhaled then exhaled.

"Okay, we'll go inside, everyone." When I opened the back door, the shadows and Colonel dashed inside, but my heart was still pounding.

I set up the coffee pot for my morning coffee then made myself a fresh cup of tea and glanced at the folder. *I'm not in the mood to dive into that right now. I wonder how long a boating safety course is.*

I turned on my laptop and checked the Georgia Department of Natural Resources. *Only three hours. I can do that.*

I picked up my book and stretched out on the sofa, and Colonel stretched out on the rug next to me. I rose on one elbow for a better look under the dining table, and the shadows were stretched out too. *We're all relaxed; that's good.*

The low rumble of a storm interrupted my reading. I checked my flashlight and changed its batteries then returned to read and set my flashlight on the table next to me. When I was on the last chapter, the lights flickered then went out; I turned on my flashlight and held it with my chin, so I could finish my book. When I closed my book, the lightning flashed, then I jumped when a crack sounded overhead.

I yawned. "I'm really tired. Wake me if the storm gets worse."

Colonel and I went to my bedroom, and I quickly changed. Colonel lay across my doorway, and I climbed into bed and turned off my flashlight as the rumbles grew louder.

I was on the edge of sleep when the brunt of the storm hit, and the rain battered the windows while the wind howled.

"You win." I turned on my flashlight and padded to the living room. I exhaled as I sat on the sofa and propped up my feet before I closed my eyes.

* * *

When Colonel nudged me, I opened my eyes. *Where's my clock?*

I rolled over to see the time and fell off the sofa onto the floor. "Oof." When I tried to get up, my right calf muscle cramped, and I leaned over to massage it.

Colonel whined, and I rose to my feet by hanging onto the sofa and pushing myself up. I hobbled to the back door, and after Colonel went outside, I turned on the burner under my coffee pot.

I automatically dropped into my morning routine.

I rolled my eyes, flipped the switch next to the back door, and turned on the kitchen lights.

I smiled as I opened the door for Colonel to come back inside. "I can take a shower, Colonel. Isn't that exciting?"

Colonel grinned as I measured then filled his bowl as he patiently sat.

"Okay," I pointed to his food; Colonel gobbled down his breakfast while I sipped my coffee and gazed out the back window at the puddles in the tracks left by the garbage trucks behind the house.

I hurried to the shower and enjoyed the hot, soothing water as it beat down on my muscles that had stiffened from my overnight on the sofa.

After I was dressed and refilled my cup, Colonel and I went out back. Colonel wandered the yard while the birds sang cheery songs. "The birds say there won't be any rain today, Colonel."

After we were inside, I stuck the folder, my laptop, and a portfolio with a notepad into my backpack then put Colonel's spare water bowl, three bottles of water, and treats for Colonel into a canvas tote.

When I put on my sweatshirt, Ned parked next to my minivan in the driveway, and Colonel trotted to the front door and whined.

I quickly gathered my purse, backpack, and tote, then Colonel and I headed to Ned's truck.

Ned grinned as he took the tote and my backpack from me. "You and Colonel are definitely ready for today."

As we headed out of town, Ned said, "It's cool enough that Colonel can stay in the truck while we eat breakfast. I'll put down the windows, so he can enjoy the smells."

"Did you hear the storm last night?" I asked.

Ned nodded. "I got up to check the radar and didn't see anything to worry about, so I went back to sleep. What about you?"

"It was noisy for me, and it took me a while to relax."

"I spent the rest of the evening last night researching cabins. I found five that might be worth looking at," he said.

"Really? I checked the Georgia Department of Natural Resources for more information about the boating safety course. It's only three hours."

"You did? That's great."

"I found some late afternoon and evening courses in Conway, and several classes in Asbury toward the end of the month," I said.

"If you take a class in Conway, we could have dinner at our favorite Columbian restaurant; or if you'd rather take a class in Asbury, we could still have dinner at our favorite Columbian restaurant without the constraint of a class," Ned said.

"I'll check the times on our way to breakfast, so we can discuss them, but what will you do for three hours?"

"I could sit in the class with you and intimidate the instructor," he said.

I narrowed my eyes. "I would absolutely die of embarrassment; find something else to do."

CHAPTER NINE

Ned shrugged. "I'll go look at boats."

"You can't look at boats without me because I need to learn about them. Maybe we should look at boats before I take the class; I don't want to embarrass myself by being totally ignorant."

"You don't have to have boating experience for the class. You'll learn the laws, then we can look at boats."

"It's all lecture? I won't have to keel a haul or whatever?"

Ned glanced at me then snorted. "Sorry. No, you won't have to torture anybody. Keelhauling was a particularly harsh disciplinary practice that was actually a method of execution on the high seas during the seventeen hundreds. A sailor would be tied with ropes then thrown into the sea and dragged under the ship from one end to the other. The underside of the ship had barnacles that sliced the sailor, or if he was dragged slowly enough, he drowned."

"Good to know for the next time I'm in a heated discussion with a pirate. You can attend the class with me but don't heckle the instructor because I think I'll be able to embarrass myself quite sufficiently without your help."

Ned laughed. "You, my dear, have a pirate's sense of humor."

I grinned. "What a nice thing to say, thank you."

Ned laughed even harder. "See? Just like I said."

I pulled out my phone and checked class times and dates and jotted them down.

When we reached the diner, Ned pulled into the parking lot. "You can go inside and get us a table if you like, and I'll give Colonel some water and a break."

I glanced at the full parking lot. "That might be a good idea."

When I went inside, the server waved a coffee pot. "Sit wherever you can find a spot. How many cups?"

"Two."

A young man who sat with an elderly woman motioned to me, and I excused myself as I made my way to their table through the standing crowd. "My grandmother and I are about to leave. Mimi wants you to sit with us, so you can have our table." He smiled.

"Are you sure?" I asked.

"Please join us," Mimi said as the young man pulled out a chair for me.

I smiled as I sat down. "Thank you so much, my friend is walking our dog, so please take your time."

"Your gentleman friend looks nice," Mimi peered at Ned and Colonel as they strolled through the grass along the front of the diner on their way to the truck. "Rough edges?"

I chuckled. "He is nice and definitely has rough edges, but he's improving."

She rose from the table with her grandson's help. "Don't let him get smooth; you don't want to have to chase off the hussies."

"Mimi, Mom said you're not supposed to be sassy." The young man shook his head.

The old woman took her grandson's arm and winked at me while a young woman quickly bussed and cleaned the table; the server set down two cups and filled them with coffee before she sailed away with her coffee pot, refilling cups as she headed back to the kitchen.

Mimi spoke to Ned as he came in the door, and Ned smiled while the young man frowned.

"Do you know why the elderly woman told me not to be too smooth?" He asked as he joined me at the table.

"She told me if you became too smooth, I'd have to chase away the hussies."

Ned chuckled as he handed me one of the menus he had picked up at the door when he came in. "Did you tell her there wasn't much chance of that happening?" He peered at the menu. "What are you having? Eggs or pancakes?"

"That's a hard choice. What about you?"

"Easy choice. I'm having both."

"What would you like, ma'am?" the server asked.

"One egg over medium, grits, and a biscuit," I said.

"Honey or strawberry jam with your biscuit? Both are local."

"Strawberry jam."

She nodded. "You, sir?"

"I'll take the farmhand special; eggs over easy," Ned said.

"Got it."

I found the farmhand special on the menu: Two pancakes, two eggs, and four thick-sliced pieces of bacon. *Not bad at all compared to some of the other specials.*

I handed Ned my list of dates and times of boating classes. After he read it, he asked, "What do you think?"

"I like the idea of not trying to go to the class and have a nice dinner on the same day. I'll be stressed before the class and hyper after the class."

Ned gazed at me. "I'm not sure I've seen you stressed."

I narrowed my eyes. "Careful; that sounded smooth."

Ned snort-laughed. "Pirate Lady."

Our server side-glanced us as she placed our plates with fluffy pancakes and eggs with dark orange yolks and a small bowl of grits on the table. "Y'all must get up before daylight because you're livelier than our usual morning crowd that just dragged themselves out of bed. I'll be right back with a biscuit, your bacon, and coffee."

She brought us Ned's crisp bacon, my pillowy biscuit, and a small bowl of strawberry jam then refilled our cups. "Your eggs and jam are local-grown; we buy them from the farmers' market down the road, and we buy our bacon from a nearby farm that raises and processes their own meat. The field corn for the grits came from Georgia, and I'm pretty sure the wheat for the pancakes grew just up the road in Kansas. Enjoy."

I smiled then whispered after she left. "Only in Georgia would Kansas be 'just up the road' because everything on the table is locally grown or raised."

After I ate my egg, grits, and the top half of my biscuit, I stared at the other half that was still on the small plate.

"Is that half of your biscuit terrorizing you? I'll take it off your hands."

I pushed the plate and the bowl of jam towards him. "Be my guest."

He scooped up a big spoonful of jam and plopped it onto the biscuit. "I want you to know I'm not being smooth." He broke the biscuit in half then crammed one piece into his mouth.

I rolled my eyes. "You're right. That was not smooth."

After Ned finished eating, we argued about the check until a man two tables from us said, "Criminy, lady. Let your brother pick up the check for once."

I turned to glare at the man, but everyone around us was laughing, so I glared at Ned instead as he said, "Yeah, Sis."

When we walked to the truck, Ned said, "You're not going to tell Mom, are you?"

"You mean Darlene? Darn tootin', I am."

His shoulders shook as he walked around the truck after he helped me climb into the passenger's side.

I giggled as he slid into the driver's seat. "It was funny, wasn't it? Have you ever seen an entire restaurant get into a joke like that?"

"It was beautiful." He grinned. "I paid for the man's breakfast and told the cashier to tell him Sis bought his breakfast."

I laughed until tears ran down my face.

When we arrived at the high school where the meeting was being held, we found the registration table and signed in. After the friendly registration woman checked us off her list, she gave us name tags and a goodie bag with promotional items from the DNR, the Sheriff's Association, and the Boys Ranch.

She peered at Colonel. "Name, please?"

I glanced at Ned. "Colonel."

She tittered. "I could tell right off he was an officer." She wrote Colonel on a name tag with a permanent marker then slipped it into a sleeve with a clip on it. "Colonel can wear his ID if he likes, but it's not mandatory. He's all registered."

She dropped three dog treats into a bag then handed it to me for Colonel. "My teenage daughter told me this is called swag; she said it's what celebrities get when they go to a fancy event. Thank you for coming, Colonel."

We stepped away from the table, and I picked through my swag.

"What's he doing here?" Ned asked, and I looked at the registration table.

Quinn?

"Good question."

My eyes widened as Quinn signed in. *It's not Quinn; it's Richard.* The registration woman checked him off her list then gave him his swag. He spoke quietly, and she giggled.

When he turned and saw me, he stopped then turned toward the hall.

I intercepted him. "Richard? I'm Karen O'Brien." I held out my hand, and he stared at it then shook it.

"You recognized me," he said.

"Yes. I didn't the first time I saw you though because I didn't know you and Quinn were twins."

"I owe you an explanation. Can we sit somewhere?"

I nodded, and Ned, Colonel, and Richard followed me to a table. After I sat, Ned sat next to me and took my hand under the table.

I examined Richard's face. His face was hardened from years of prison, but his eyes softened.

"You survived it," I said, and he nodded then peered at me.

"You did too." He said in surprise then rubbed his face. "Sorry, I shouldn't have blurted that out, but I didn't know."

I nodded and waited, and Ned squeezed my hand.

"I'm here to represent the sheriff from the county north of Conway. I'm a mechanic, and a good one. I've been training boys to repair small engines. My boss is awesome; he started the program with the sheriff ten years ago then hired me after I was released. You know Sicily and Francine?"

"Francine is my once-a-year hair stylist; I never met Sicily."

"Sicily and I had a gig going before I went to prison; I'm not proud of it, but I avoided her after my release. She called me and asked if I would help her pull a prank on Francine. I didn't think that was unusual because she and Francine were always trying to one-up each other, and I helped her with a lot of stunts before I went to prison. She told me she needed me to demand an envelope from Francine and that was all I needed to do. You're lucky you didn't know Sicily. She was very persuasive to the point of being manipulative, and against my better judgement, I agreed."

Richard's face darkened. "I met a lot of people like her in prison."

He glanced at me. "You?"

I nodded. "There were good people too, though."

"Yeah." He smiled. "All the good people were crazy."

I chuckled. "Aren't we all?"

"Never thought about it, but you're right." He shook his head. "That might have been how I survived that hell hole, pardon my language. So, anyway, that's why I went to Francine's shop, but Sicily told me nobody would be there. You know why I tore open the envelope, don't you?"

"You didn't trust Sicily or Francine; you had to be sure it wasn't drugs."

"Exactly, and I realized I was being set up when Francine turned your chair, so that you would get a good look at me in the mirror. When I heard Sicily had been murdered, I wondered if Francine was somehow involved, except it didn't make any sense. After I handed the envelope with the money to Sicily, she told me she had something else she wanted me to do. I don't know how it happened, but those words woke me up…there was never enough for her. She always had just one more little thing, and for the first time in my life, I didn't waffle and told her no."

"Where were you?"

"In a café in Conway. Nice place with excellent Columbian food."

"When was that?"

"Tuesday; about six thirty or seven. Sicily screamed and created a huge scene; I'm afraid she probably scared most of the customers. As Sicily grew louder and more abusive, a chef rushed out of the kitchen with a cleaver in her hand; she waved the cleaver and shouted at Sicily in Spanish then chased her out the door. Ms. O'Brien, you should have seen it: it was a beautiful sight, and the customers applauded with me. I was so grateful that I asked the chef to marry me, and I was only partially kidding. She laughed and handed me a menu then returned to the kitchen. The host told me the chef said for me to order a nice dinner because it was on the house. Sounds like I made that up, doesn't it?" His smile was weak.

"Only to people who don't know Bianca," I smiled, and Ned nodded.

"You know the chef?" Richard exhaled. "Thanks. It means a lot to know you believe me."

"What's your boss's name?" Ned asked.

"Rafe; you know him?"

Ned nodded and picked up our swag bags as he rose.

Richard leaned across the table and whispered, "You know he's a cop, right?"

I nodded. "A good one."

"He must be, but the ones I have known the best weren't," Richard said. "Let me know if there's something I can do for you."

"Do you know about a protection scam in your area?" I asked.

He nodded. "If I were a cop, I would assume Sicily was behind it."

"Thank you."

Ned returned and offered his hand. "I'm Ned."

Richard hesitated then shook Ned's hand.

Richard strolled to the continental breakfast table, and Ned, Colonel, and I went into the hall.

"I'd like to sit in the back," Ned said.

"I'm okay with wherever you want to sit. It makes sense for us to be close to the back for Colonel."

After Ned selected our seats, he asked, "Care for some coffee?"

"I'm afraid it wouldn't be as good as the diner's. I'll skip."

He cocked his head. "How unusual is it for people to open up to you like that?"

I shrugged. "I don't know; some do, and some don't."

"I noticed you were very open with him too."

"We found a common ground."

"That's it. That's your secret, and what you do so well. You meet people where they are." Ned shook his head. "I'm saying this very badly, but I'm starting to understand the depth of what you give, and that's what people respond to."

He smiled, and his dimples showed before he left for more coffee. "You're amazing."

I felt my cheeks warm, and Colonel grinned.

I watched as men and women strolled into the meeting room, and my eyes widened. *Everyone here is law enforcement.*

When Ned returned with Richard, I smiled. *Ned gets it.*

Ned sat next to me, and Richard sat on the other side of Ned.

I squeezed Ned's hand and whispered, "Well done; this entire room is made up of cops."

Ned turned to Richard. "You were right; she saw it too."

Richard exhaled. "It's nice to sit with friends. I want to learn how to help our youth, but I would have left if you hadn't been here."

The moderator spoke briefly about why we were there then introduced the first speaker. I wrote furiously as we listened to the practical advice being offered by speaker after speaker until it was time for our break. I rose from my seat to stretch, and Ned and Richard took Colonel outside for his break. I smiled as I watched all the men and women gravitate to the other law enforcement officers that they knew, then I noticed a young woman who sat alone. I made my way to her then sat next to her.

When she realized she was not alone, she stared at me, and I said, "Hi, I'm Karen."

I held out my hand, and she shook it. "I'm Mavis, and I'm not good at mingling."

Bright red spots broke out on her cheeks, and I shrugged. "I know you're law enforcement, but I'm not."

She smiled. "I'm new. The rest of these people have known each other for years. I felt called to a career in law enforcement to help kids like my little sister who fell through the cracks. She was an honor roll student, outgoing, a cheerleader, a drug dealer, and died of an overdose at twelve. I was fifteen, bookish, awkward, and totally unaware of who my sister was behind her façade." Her face tightened with resolve. "My goal is never to be unaware again."

I nodded. "You may find that not mingling is the best way to do that."

She cocked her head. "Really?"

Before I rose, I said, "Really, and the awkward part disarms people. You're fine."

She grinned. "Did you come to check on me?"

"Are you questioning the motives of an old woman? Of course, I did, and you're doing great."

"Thank you for reminding me I don't have to mingle."

When Ned and Richard returned with Colonel, Mavis said, "Ms. Karen, that younger man you're sitting with is not law enforcement."

"I know; pretty smart of me, don't you think?"

She cocked her head. "I don't get it."

"My world is open to seeing people as they are and not a stereotype; it helps me from becoming too myopic. If you saw he wasn't law enforcement, you aren't wearing blinders. If someone like him is in your world, you're smart too."

She examined my face then smiled. "I'm smart."

When I joined Ned and Richard, Ned asked, "Do you know her?"

I raised my eyebrows. "I do now."

The next speaker stepped behind the podium, and the room quieted, then I began writing another page of notes.

When it was time for our lunch break, Richard asked, "Can I treat you to lunch? I know about a great place where we can get tacos that's off the beaten track. There's no inside seating; everyone sits or mills around while they eat. You'll be the only cop there, Ned. Can you handle that?"

Ned chuckled. "My last assignment was to hunt down coyotes, and I ended up watching Donut Lady take down a killer. I'll be safe."

Richard's eyes widened. "I believe you."

Ned turned to me. "What do you think?"

"Sounds perfect for us."

"Do you want to follow me?" Richard asked.

"Why don't you ride with us?" Ned asked. "We've got plenty of room."

"As long as I get to ride in the backseat with my new friend." Richard reached down and scratched Colonel's ears, and Colonel grinned.

As Ned headed toward the exit, all the cars and trucks who were lined up to go to lunch turned left.

"Turn right," Richard said. "The Taco Shack is only a few blocks away; I don't know if that's its official name, but it's what everyone calls it."

We drove past two blocks of abandoned buildings and rusted-out semi-trailers then turned at a residential area. The fences around the homes were in disrepair, and the yards were bare of grass, but flowers and herbs flourished in pots, and laundry flapped on clotheslines.

"Up ahead on the left."

The Taco Shack was a former nail studio, according to the decaying sign on top of the small building. The front had been boarded up to cover where a large window must have been at one time. Two windows had been cut in the board, and each one had a small, tattered canopy. Ned parked alongside other pickup trucks.

"What do you think, Donut Lady?" Richard asked; he and Colonel stood next to the truck while Ned opened my door.

"I'm ready for a taco. Is there a menu board?"

Richard frowned as we headed to the order window. "I don't know. I always tell them three tacos and tea."

"One taco and tea for me, then."

I watched as a man bit into his taco. "I changed my mind: make that one taco with guacamole and tea."

Richard chuckled. "I just changed my order too."

Ned and Richard stood in line while Colonel wandered to visit with two young girls who had finished eating and had returned to their mother at a picnic table after throwing away their trash.

"Can we pet him?" the older girl asked.

"He'd like that," I said.

The girls stroked Colonel's back then hugged him and giggled when he grinned, and the mother smiled at me.

"Would you like to sit? Not many dogs can take that kind of attention," she said. "What's his name?"

I sat on the bench the girls had vacated. "Colonel; he has a soft heart when it comes to children."

"Colonel," the smaller girl whispered.

"We like Colonel, Mommy," the older one said.

When Ned and Richard headed toward us with lunch, the mother said, "It's time for us to go home, girls. Tell Colonel good-bye."

The girls hugged Colonel again then reluctantly left with their mother.

"We need a dog, Mommy," the smaller one said.

"You might be right."

"An old, big dog like Colonel," the older one added.

"We'll talk to Daddy; he always has good ideas."

While we ate, a man approached our table. "Mr. Burke? After you eat, could I talk to you for a minute?"

Ned nodded. "Be right there."

Ned and Richard finished eating before I did.

"Go ahead," I said when Ned turned to see where the man was.

Ned glanced at Richard, and Richard nodded.

Ned just handed off the Donut Lady watch to Richard.

I rolled my eyes, and Richard chuckled. "You caught that. Now tell me, am I in charge of guarding you, or are you in charge of guarding me? Do both of us watch Ned's back?"

I giggled. "I like how you think."

I glanced over my shoulder at Ned who listened intently as the man gestured while he spoke.

"Ned's giving the man his full attention," Richard said.

"That's who Ned is." I frowned. *Nothing lost, nothing gained.* "When you came to Francine's shop, you had a pistol on your hip."

"You don't miss a thing, do you? You want to know how I could carry a pistol, right?"

I nodded.

"I helped Sicily and did almost anything she asked me to do, but I drew the line at anything illegal. She had plenty of help with that. She was the state's star witness against me, and my lawyer at the time was not really engaged. My friends in prison helped me get in touch with a brilliant lawyer, and she appealed my case and won. Sicily's testimony was riddled with holes, and my lawyer highlighted each one. When Sicily stumbled and changed her story more than once, the state's case fell apart." He shrugged. "I'm not a convicted felon, but I'm still treated like one because I was in prison."

I'll bet it was Amber.

"I understand. There are still parts of me that twelve years of prison changed. Friends don't care, but there have been others who did."

Ned's conversation with the animated man concluded when Ned and the man shook hands.

Ned returned to our picnic bench. "Ready to go?"

After we reached the almost-empty parking lot, I asked, "Where is everybody?"

"Standing in line somewhere waiting for mediocre food," Richard said, and Ned snorted as he backed into a spot near the building entrance.

"Care to go for a walk before our next sitting marathon?" Ned asked as Richard headed to the building.

We walked to the city park across the street then strolled along the path while Colonel investigated the trees and grounds.

CHAPTER TEN

"Can I be nosy and ask what you and the man were talking about at the Taco Shack?"

"He worked at a butcher shop that closed three months ago when the owner passed away and wanted to know what I thought about opening a processing business to serve local hunters. He has money put away, and his wife does bookkeeping; I gave him some names of the right people who could help him understand what it would take to get started."

"How did he know you?"

Ned chuckled. "I wrote him a citation fifteen years ago for hunting out of season."

"You remembered him?"

He nodded. "He was a nice guy; still is."

"Do you think Richard was telling the truth?" I asked.

"I should be asking you because you're the one that's perceptive. I think he was as open as he could be and is trying hard to keep his old days behind him. What do you think?"

"I think he has a better chance than most in being successful."

When we returned to the building, there were more vehicles in the parking lot.

"How are you doing? Are you going to be okay for the rest of the day, or would you like to leave early?" Ned peered at me.

"I'm enjoying the speakers. It's been a great break for me to get away from the Donut Hole too."

Ned checked the time. "Twenty minutes until we start up. Ready to go inside?"

"That's fine with me."

On the way in, Ned asked, "You don't have dinner plans for this evening, do you?"

"I was thinking about opening a can of soup, but the warm weather changed my mind."

"What do you think about having pizza with me?"

"I don't think I want to go anywhere after we get back."

"Good, because I was thinking we could stop by the grocery store and pick up a frozen pizza and a salad to share."

"That's really a good idea. I don't feel like going out, but I'll be too tired to think about cooking anything."

"I have some people to see after we eat, so you'll have your evening to yourself."

When we reached our seats, Ned elbowed me; when I looked in the direction he indicated, I watched Richard, who was relaxed as he and two other men were in a conversation near the front.

"That's a good sign," Ned said, and I nodded.

My eyes widened when Mavis strolled toward the group then hesitated before she approached them. Richard and one of the other men moved back a step to include her in their conversation circle, and she joined them.

Ned whispered, "Did you see that?"

"I talked to her earlier; she was reluctant to join a conversation because this morning it appeared that everyone was catching up with old friends, and she didn't know anybody here."

"Small groups are more approachable," Ned said. After the moderator stepped to the podium and invited everyone to find a seat, Richard sat with the two other men, and Mavis returned to her seat that was closer to the back. Her face was flushed as she glanced toward me, and I gave her two thumbs up; her smile was weak, but it was a smile, nonetheless.

"What was that for?" Ned asked.

"Socializing is difficult for her. She did the best she could," I said.

After the second speaker finished, the moderator announced that we'd break into small groups for discussion, and the questions were in our packets.

My phone buzzed a text. *Barbara.* "Francine released on bond. Will be returning to Asbury."

I showed the text to Ned.

"That's not surprising," he said.

Mavis made a beeline toward us. "I'm in your small group," she said. "That was pretty forward of me, wasn't it?" She smiled.

"I'm Ned." He and Mavis shook hands, then Mavis turned a chair around from the table in front of us and sat with us.

Ned pulled out his packet. "The first question is what are your unique experiences that will help you work with troubled youth? I've got a story."

Ned talked about taking a social worker and a small group of boys who had always lived in Atlanta on a four-day hiking and camping trip along the Appalachian Trail. "We spent a month discussing and preparing for the trip, but it was still culture shock for them, especially the social worker."

I smiled.

"You were brave to take all those tenderfoot, city folks camping. What was their worst shock?" Mavis asked.

"Charging cell phones and the bugs, but that's an even longer story for another time," Ned said.

Mavis giggled then told us about working with an experienced leader as they mentored a group of girls from low income families. "The leader asked the girls what they wanted to learn, and the group came up with a list. At the top of the list was to be independent, so we worked on hygiene and cleanliness, getting up early and showing up on time, and simple, cheap meals. Not one of them dropped out of the program or became pregnant: that was our goal."

"That's impressive," Ned said.

What about you, Ms. Karen?" Mavis asked.

I told them about the first time I saw Woody outside my shop, our bartering, and teaching him to read.

Ned shook his head. "I never knew you and Woody had such a rocky beginning. I'm surprised you didn't become his foster mother instead of Shirley."

"I was crushed when I learned I couldn't foster a child because there were absolutely no loopholes for a convicted felon, but Shirley surprised me when she announced she had taken the classes and undergone the background check to be certified, so she could foster Woody."

"I wouldn't have thought of Shirley as a likely foster mother candidate," Ned said.

"Why not?" Mavis asked.

I smiled. "Shirley's my age and has never been around children. Have you ever known a person who talked nonstop, mostly about themselves, was meticulous about their clothes, hair, and reputation, and was a terrible cook?"

"Oh, my." Mavis's eyes widened. "How is she doing?"

"She joined a parents' group, and Woody is thriving in school and with all his activities."

"I think Woody learned the fine art of self-preservation," Ned said, and Mavis and I laughed.

"Shirley and Woody did take cooking classes together, so you may be right because Shirley does all the cooking, but I suspect that Woody coaches her."

"Isn't it amazing how things work out in ways that you never expected?" Mavis said as the moderator announced time was up for the small groups.

"Thank you for joining us," I said.

"Thanks for letting me be a part of your group. I learned far more than I expected." Mavis shook hands with Ned then hugged me before she hurried back to her seat.

One last speaker took the podium, then the moderator closed the program by reminding everyone to be safe and to fill out the survey that would come by email.

As most of the crowd rushed to the exit to leave, others lingered to talk. After the crush cleared, Ned asked, "Ready?"

I nodded, then Richard came to our table. "Ms. Karen, I did think of something you may not know. Sicily was not a creative, independent thinker, in spite of what people thought with the wild colors she splashed around her shop. She always looked to her older sister for guidance."

"Alessandria?" I asked.

He chuckled. "No, Alessandria is a dry, by-the-book person; I'm certain Francine was always the brains because she carefully calculated her actions, but Sicily was impulsive and ready to jump without any thought of how her actions might harm others."

"That's not the impression I got from what everyone else says and what you said earlier."

"I know, and I apologize. I need to get past the old habit of going with the flow and repeating what I know to be only a partial truth."

"What else do you want Karen to know?" Ned asked.

Richard stared at Ned then sighed. "Once, Sicily told me she had a silent partner, and she was branching out and was getting into bigger things and was going to be making more money than I could imagine. I don't have anything concrete, but I got the impression it was drugs. She told me if I didn't join her, I was a dirty loser." Richard snorted. "I told her that sounded just fine to me. If you looked into Sicily's finances and bank account, you may find evidence of money being siphoned to a company with a sole owner, that I suspect is Francine. I don't have any proof, or I'd give it to you; it's only my gut suspicion from the years I worked with the two of them."

"Thanks, Richard. I know it was hard for you to tell me more than you planned." I hugged him. "Be safe."

He nodded then headed to the parking lot.

"What do you think?" Ned asked after we were on the road to Asbury.

"I think we're a good team."

Ned beamed. "So do I. When can we go to our cabin?"

"Don't we have to find one first?"

"We can't just pack a suitcase and go looking." Ned frowned then tapped his thumb on the steering wheel. "Maybe we should."

"Should what?"

"Don't they say it's the journey, not the destination? We should just pack up and go looking instead of just talking about it."

"What are you talking about?"

"Fishing. We need to go fishing."

"Don't we need a boat first?"

"We will eventually, but first, we need to sit on a riverbank and fish."

"Wouldn't that be scandalous? If we just take off and go fishing?"

He shrugged. "Yes."

I laughed.

"I'm a reasonable man—"

"Says who?"

"You interrupted me; that's not polite."

I laughed even harder.

"Are you done?" he asked after I wiped my eyes.

"Maybe."

"I'm a reasonable man. As soon as we solve Sicily's murder, we'll go fishing. That's our reward: a fishing honeymoon." He side-glanced me.

Honeymoon? I stared at him. "What?"

Not my snappiest reply.

"You know, if that's what we want to do. It's good to keep our options open. What do you think?"

I stared at the passing scenery. "It's not scandalous."

Ned nodded.

I don't know what I think.

I watched the countryside and thought about why I didn't know what to think. *What have I been missing? Would Mavis scold me for not paying attention to the people closest to me?*

"What kind of pizza?" Ned asked.

"What?"

I should copyright my snappy comeback.

"We're almost at the grocery store. What kind of pizza do you want?"

"I like pepperoni, but I'm okay with mushrooms, onions, tomato, whatever."

"Pineapple?" he asked.

"Of course; I'm just not crazy about green peppers."

"I'm not either. Are you staying with Colonel in the truck?"

"Yes, so you can pick whatever you like."

"Anchovies?" he asked.

"If that's what you like. I can pick mine off and give them to you."

After he parked at the edge of the lot in the shade, he mumbled, "I don't like anchovies."

"Then don't get any." I rolled my eyes then watched him as he strode across the parking lot to the grocery store.

Colonel stretched out on the back seat and fell asleep. I watched the drivers who cruised for the closest spot then quickly parked and hurried inside and the shoppers who pushed full buggies of groceries out of the store then searched for their cars. Occasionally, someone would dash into the grocery store then hurry out with a single grocery bag. *Busy place.*

A man parked several rows away from me but left several parking spots available between his car and the others then climbed out of his car. My eyes widened as he scanned the parking lot before he headed to the store. *What's Richard doing here?* The man strode through the automatic door. *That's not Richard's walk. That's Quinn.*

I watched the door until Ned came out with several sacks in his hands. As Ned continued across the parking lot, Quinn came out of the store, and when he saw Ned, he stepped behind a column. I watched the front of the store while Ned put the groceries in the back of the truck and slid into the driver's seat, but Quinn didn't appear.

As we drove away, I said, "I saw Quinn go into the grocery store, then he came out not long after you did, but he didn't continue to his car. He walked behind a column, then I didn't see him again."

"There's an ATM on that side of the building; maybe he waited in a line to withdraw some cash. Are you sure it was Quinn, not Richard?"

"I'm positive; I know Richard's walk."

Ned nodded. "It wouldn't take long for you to notice that slight outward swing Richard does with his left foot."

"Could you tell if Richard faked his walk?" I asked.

"I've tracked animals and men most of my life; Richard's walk was too smooth and consistent to be faked."

I smiled. "When in doubt, ask an old tracker. Well, it was strange to see Quinn after he told me he would be out of town all weekend." I frowned then checked my phone. "Actually he didn't say he'd be out of town; I just assumed he would be. He said his plans changed, and he had to reschedule; he said he'd see me on Monday."

"Natural assumption." Ned rubbed his chin. "He didn't tell you he needed to reschedule until you told him you'd meet him at the park."

I cocked my head as Ned pulled into my driveway next to my minivan and parked. "Do you suppose he didn't want anyone to see him with me?"

"I don't know, but I'm glad you had second thoughts and asked me for a suggestion. I guess Papa and Giana's paranoia is catching."

I snickered. "Between my shadows and my feelings that something's not right, tension is an old friend of mine."

As we headed into the house, Ned said, "I picked up the fixings for a salad because the ready-mades didn't look that great. If you'll make a salad, I'll preheat the oven for the pizza."

"What kind of pizza did you get?"

"Pepperoni, mushrooms, black olives, and onions. I don't think it has sweet green peppers."

"If it does, we'll pick them off."

While Ned turned on the oven, and I scrubbed the vegetables, my phone rang. *Barbara.*

"What are you doing?" she asked.

"Making a salad, and Ned just turned on the oven. He's in charge of the pizza."

"Perfect, as soon as you eat, come here for dessert, and bring Colonel." Barbara hung up.

"We're invited to the Lehmans' for dessert, and she deliberately hung up before I could ask any questions." I put the vegetables on a paper towel to dry.

"Weren't Amber and her friend supposed to go to their house for dinner tonight?" Ned slid the pizza into the oven and set the timer.

"You're right. Do you suppose they didn't show, and Barbara has extra dessert?" I finished dicing the cucumber and tomato into the salad then added feta cheese crumbles.

"A more likely possibility is that Barbara wants you to be as surprised as she was by the elusive guest." Ned set the crushed red peppers on the table.

I served the salad into two bowls then put our salad bowls and the bottled creamy Italian salad dressing that Ned had bought on the table. "Do you want sweet tea to drink?"

"Sounds good. Five minutes until the pizza's ready. Shall I feed Colonel then take him to the backyard for a romp?"

I nodded as I poured two glasses of sweet tea and put paper towels next to our plates.

When I glanced at Ned, he grinned as he stopped at the back door. "We're not the delicate eaters that Alfred is, are we?"

"Not at all."

After they went outside, I put the whole roll of paper towels on the table.

When the timer dinged, I pulled out the pizza from the oven and slid it onto a sturdy cutting board then cut it into slices: small for me, and large for Ned.

Ned came inside alone and headed to the sink. "Colonel's enjoying his outside time."

After Ned washed his hands, we sat at the table. He served me two of my small slices and put two large slices on his plate while I sprinkled pepper flakes on my pizza then dressed my salad with the creamy Italian.

While Ned poured dressing on his salad, I pulled away the crust on the edge of my slices.

"I never thought about eating the crust by itself like that. It's almost like having garlic knots, isn't it?" Ned asked as he pulled away the edge of his crust too.

"I can't remember who it was that told me to pull off the crust to eat my pizza bones first, but I've done it for ages."

"Pizza bones. I like it." He tapped his pizza bone with mine. "Cheers."

I giggled. "Cheers."

"Rafe called Richard and asked him to go into work tomorrow morning to help with a rush job. Richard expects it to take all morning; I told him to text me if he'd like to go to lunch with us."

"With us? Did we have lunch plans?" I glared at Ned.

"Do you?" he asked.

"That's not the point; the point is that you just bulldozed straight to assuming I didn't have any other lunch plans." I glowered over my glass as I sipped my iced tea.

Ned shrugged. "Would this be smoother: would you like to go to lunch with Richard if he's available, and I'll tag along?"

I tried not to laugh, but I choked and spewed tea on my pizza. I grabbed a paper towel and dabbed away the tea from my plate, food, and chin.

"Can I take that as a yes?"

After I could breathe, I said, "If that was your version of smooth, I'm positive a certain grandmother would be pleased."

"What about Richard and lunch?"

"I'll pick up sandwiches from Gus's shop and meet him at the park north of town, and you can tag along."

"I'll drive you. When Richard and I walked Colonel, I mentioned that I'd known Quinn for a while, and Richard's eyes darkened. No love lost there, so I dropped it."

"When I first met him, he recognized that you were a cop and warned me; after I told him you were a good one, he said the ones he knew the best weren't. Do you suppose he meant Quinn, or did he mean the ones he knew when he was in prison?"

"I would have said the guards he knew in prison except for the look I saw on his face when I mentioned Quinn."

After we finished eating, we had almost half a pizza left.

"If you'll clear the table and wrap up the pizza, I'll wash the dishes." Ned sauntered to the back door and let Colonel inside then loaded the dishwasher.

I wrapped the pizza in foil then put it and the salad dressing into the refrigerator.

"We'll take out the trash; we won't be long," Ned said, and Colonel went out with him.

When they returned, Ned asked, "Are you ready?"

"I just remembered you have plans for this evening. Should I take my minivan, so you can leave when you need to?"

Ned's cheeks turned red. "I was trying to be polite and not monopolize your time or wear out my welcome."

I hugged him. "No chance of that, and good job with that polite thing."

Ned hugged me tight, and I leaned against him, closed my eyes, and sighed. "I guess we should leave."

"I suspect we'll be there a while." Ned turned on the porchlight as we left.

On our way, Ned frowned as he glanced in his rearview mirror. "Hopefully this is our last and best surprise of the day."

"Wouldn't that be nice. Any guesses who Amber's friend is?"

"I don't have a clue. You've been here longer; what do you think?"

"I can't think of anyone who is Amber's type, but then I have no clue what Amber's type would be. Single is the best I can come up with."

Ned snorted. "Do you think Gee and Darlene will be there?"

"I didn't even think of that. If this is some kind of big reveal, maybe."

"Or maybe Amber's friend is from out of town and it's just us for now, but doesn't that mean the pressure is on us not to scare away the friend?" Ned asked.

"That's a lot of pressure; I'd be happy to scare away Quinn, but we already know it isn't Quinn because Amber said so, unless she was trying to throw me off. If it's Quinn, I'll go into full chase-him-off mode," I said as Ned parked.

I glanced at the car in the driveway. "Amber's a cheater. That's her car, and I don't see any others around."

Ned pointed. "There's one of the sheriff's cruisers at the corner."

"Can you tell if anyone is in it? I wonder if the sheriff sent someone to see who Amber's friend is."

Ned let Colonel out then opened my door, and I held onto his offered arm to step down. "It's more likely that the sheriff assigned a deputy to spy on you."

When I smiled, Ned touched my cheek and smiled. "Nice smile."

"Yours too."

He gazed at my face, and I met his gaze. "Ready to go inside?" he asked.

Colonel glared at us from the front door.

"We're hurrying," I said.

Colonel whined; when Barbara opened the front door, Roxie bounded out, and she and Colonel raced around the yard then scrambled into the house as Ned and I went inside.

Barbara beamed as she led us to the kitchen.

Amber's eyes twinkled. "I understand you've been keeping Donut Lady out of trouble, Ned."

"So far, so good." Ned smiled at me, and Barbara side-glanced me then raised her eyebrows.

"They're here," David said from the garage. "We can have dessert now."

I blinked when David and Jeff came into the kitchen.

Ned chuckled then strode to shake Jeff's hand. "Good to see you, Deputy Jeff."

I glared at Amber, and she beamed.

"I need details and dessert," I said.

David guffawed as he elbowed Jeff. "Okay, Amber. The ball's in your court, unless you want me to tell the story."

"Oh, no, Dad. I'll help Mom serve dessert first."

I continued to glare at my lawyer and moved close to Barbara. "I'll help serve dessert. You talk."

Amber smiled at Jeff. "Jeff and I have been good friends for a long time; I guess you might say best friends, but we decided to stay low key because Jeff arrested some of my clients, and we were frequently on opposite sides in the courtroom."

Jeff continued, "It was easy, at least for us, to leave our work at work and to enjoy each other's company."

Amber leaned against Jeff when he put his arm around her. "It took a while for us to learn what a rare relationship we had. For two really smart people, we were slow learners on some fronts."

"Both of us dated other people, but there was no magic." Jeff smiled at Amber; when I put my hand on my heart at the sweetness of his look, Barbara did the same.

Ned winked at me, and I smiled.

"After I got home from a date, I'd call Jeff to tell him how boring, insufferable, or obnoxious the poor guy was. I never went out with a man more than once. I didn't realize I was comparing them to Jeff, but they certainly didn't measure up. I was resigned to a life of being an old maid."

"With a best friend." Jeff kissed Amber on the cheek, and she blushed.

"Dessert," David said.

"Right." Barbara finished slicing the homemade strawberry cream layer cake while David pulled out the maple nut ice cream from the freezer.

When I stared at the cake then the ice cream, Barbara giggled. "I know, pretty strange combination, right? It was Amber's request."

"The maple ice cream was not a surprise," I said.

"Mom's strawberry cream layer cake is Jeff's favorite," Amber said.

"Now I understand why Amber requested it so many times then took half the cake home with her," Barbara said.

"The cake is beautiful. When you first said strawberry cream, I expected the cake to be pink, but it's vanilla cake with fresh strawberries in the whipped cream filling."

Barbara nodded. "The frosting is a soft buttercream that I dreamed up because I wanted the strawberry halves to sink into the frosting."

"We're eloping tomorrow," Amber said.

"Best friends' version," Jeff added.

"Mom and Dad will be our witnesses, and both of us have all next week off; that was the trickiest thing we've ever pulled off," Amber said.

"We're going to the beach," Jeff said.

"My eyes are leaking," I said. "I'm really happy for both of you."

Barbara wiped her eyes with her apron. "Mine are leaking too."

While David and Ned shook hands with Jeff, I hugged Amber, then Ned hugged Amber, and I hugged Jeff.

After we finished our dessert, Jeff asked, "How was the meeting, Ned?"

"Let's go into the living room for a full report. Is that okay with you, honey?" David asked.

"Go." Barbara shooed him away.

Ned raised his eyebrows at me.

"Go on; I'll help Barbara with the kitchen," I said.

"What time is the wedding?" I asked.

"We're supposed to be at the courthouse at seven forty-five, then the wedding is at eight thirty, so we'll be a little late for work. I'm sure we'll be there by ten at the latest. Is that okay? I am so happy for those two." Barbara's eyes filled again.

"Not a problem at all. It will give Andrew a little solo time without David, so he can see if that's really what he wants to do."

"Have Ned's rough edges softened a little? He seems a little different," Barbara said.

"Maybe, or maybe we're adjusting to each other."

"I've been worried because you know, Jack." Barbara wrinkled her nose. "I'm sorry; maybe there was a more elegant way to bring up the subject of Jack."

I giggled. "I doubt it, but there's a big difference between Ned and Jack. Jack and I never really connected; there was never any emotional intimacy. He never let me get too close; his focus was on being my protector, not my friend. I'm saying this badly, but I understand Amber and Jeff. A good friend is rare."

Barbara nodded. "I wanted to like Jack, but there obviously was so much more going on with him than he wanted to admit even to himself. There are times when David irritates me to pieces, but he is still my best friend."

CHAPTER ELEVEN

"Ned and I are definitely good friends, and I enjoy his company. He's making an effort to drop his sour attitude, and I'm making an effort to let him past the wall I've always had around myself."

"There is definitely a chemistry between the two of you; I can feel it."

After the kitchen was clean, Barbara said, "That was fast. Do we join the discussion?"

"I'd rather go out back with Colonel and Roxie, but I did take copious notes at the meeting, so I suppose we should."

Barbara peeked out the window. "Roxie just plopped down on the porch next to Colonel. I think she missed him."

I chuckled. "She keeps him on his toes. I know he's missed her."

We strolled into the living room together.

"We were talking about the requirements for acceptance into the Boys Ranch. Do you have your notes, hon?" Ned asked, and Barbara elbowed me.

"They're in my backpack or my tote, but I think I left them in the truck," I said.

"I'll check." Ned dashed out the door.

Barbara raised her eyebrows. "Hon?"

"Hush." I glared at her while she fluttered her eyelashes, and Amber snickered.

Ned returned and handed me my backpack, and I pulled out the notes.

After I found the requirements, I quickly reviewed them.

"What do you think, David? Don't we have two candidates that would be a good match?" Jeff asked.

"Did they say anything about how many applicants can come from one agency?"

"I don't remember hearing anything like that, but they did give us a contact if we have any questions." I flipped through my notes. "I didn't write down anything about recommending more than one candidate."

"Maybe we should start a list of questions," Ned said.

I raised my eyebrows as I peered at Ned. "We?"

"Busted again." Ned chuckled, and I snickered.

"This is good stuff," David said. "We scheduled our next meeting for a week from this coming Monday."

"I seem to recall that was your suggestion, Jeff," Ned said. "Now I see why Donut Lady is suspicious of everything and everyone."

Amber laughed as she rose and took Jeff's arm. "This suspicious character and I need to pack."

"We packed up the leftover cake for you; it's in the refrigerator," Barbara said.

"Thanks, Mom," Amber said as Jeff hurried to the refrigerator.

After hugs and more congratulations, Amber and Jeff left.

"You'd think a mother would know, but I didn't have a clue." Barbara narrowed her eyes. "You did, didn't you, David?"

"No, I did wonder a time or two, but I chalked it up to being an overly protective father because Amber and Jeff have always been close friends," David said.

"That's true," Barbara said.

"I didn't even know they were friends," I said. "Thank you so much for inviting us to dessert; it was the perfect ending to a very productive day."

As we headed to the front door, Roxie followed Colonel.

"Roxie enjoyed the visit, but I think she's ready to go home with Colonel," David said.

"Are you okay?" I asked.

"I'm fine; she'll always be my girlfriend, just don't tell my wife."

Barbara giggled. "Mum's the word."

On our way home, Ned glanced in his rearview mirror several times.

"Is something wrong?" I asked.

"Just checking. I thought I saw someone following us when we went to Barbara's house, but maybe your 'suspicious of everything' is contagious."

As Ned pulled close to the house, Colonel growled, then Roxie joined him.

"Stay in the truck." Ned parked in front of the house next door to mine then removed his concealed pistol from its holster inside his waistband.

Before he climbed out, I handed him my house key, and he quietly closed his door behind him. Colonel moved past Roxie, so he could watch Ned. My eyes widened. *The shadows are with Ned.*

Ned knocked on the front door, and Colonel and Roxie bared their teeth as they barked.

"Let them out," Ned shouted as he unlocked the door; the shadows slid around the house toward the backyard.

I jumped out of the truck to open the back door, and both dogs hurdled over the seat and leapt out of my door. Roxie raced to the side of the house, and Colonel raced into the house as Ned threw open the front door. My eyes widened as Roxie vaulted over the fence into the backyard. I stayed close to the truck and called nine-one-one.

"Ernie's on the way, Donut Lady. Are you at home?"

Why do I feel like my calls always trigger an alert to the on-duty deputy and the sheriff?

"Yes, I think Ned, Colonel, and Roxie scared an intruder out of my house."

"One sec." Tess said. "Okay, Sheriff may beat Ernie there. Did you see the intruder?"

"No."

The sheriff's cruiser roared down the street, then the sheriff parked in front of my house while Ned waited on the front porch. "My pistol is on the porch, Sheriff."

"You can pick it up," Sheriff said. The two men went into the house as Ernie parked in the driveway behind my van then strode to me.

While I told him about the dogs growling and Ned knocking on the door, he took notes. When I told him about Roxie jumping the fence and Colonel running into the house, he asked, "Did you see anyone?"

"No."

He wrote more notes, and I closed the truck door before we walked together to the house.

"The house has been ransacked," Ned met us before we reached the front porch. "Come inside to see what might be missing."

I frowned at the books and cushions scattered on the floor, and the overturned sofa and chairs. When I went into the kitchen, all the cupboard doors were open, but I beelined to an empty open drawer in the kitchen. "My recipe notebook is missing."

"What was in it?" Sheriff asked.

I tilted my head. "Recipes."

Ernie hurried out the back door, and Ned stared at me.

"Why don't you sit down, hon?" Ned pulled out a kitchen chair for me.

Sheriff raised his eyebrows then smirked as he glanced at me.

I knew he'd catch that.

After I sat, Ned poured me a small glass of iced tea.

"I've been printing some of my favorite recipes and putting them into a three-ring binder because I'd rather flip through the pages for ideas than turn on my computer and read recipes on my screen." I sipped my tea. "Thanks."

"What else is missing?" the sheriff asked.

"I'll have to check. My computer and printer are still here. I don't keep any Donut Hole business records here, but I have a fireproof box in my bathroom with all my personal records."

"Your bathroom? Not your bedroom?" The sheriff asked as he followed me to the bathroom.

I frowned as I went down the hallway. *No shadows.*

I shrugged. "Everybody keeps stuff in their bedrooms."

After I opened the linen closet in the bathroom, I pulled out the toilet plunger, plumber's snake, toilet cleaner, drain cleaner, and used rags before I removed the board that was a false back then pointed. "My firesafe doesn't look like it's been disturbed."

After I put everything back, the sheriff shook his head. "Where do you come up with stuff like that?"

I glanced at Ned who stood in the doorway. "I pay attention when people talk."

"Let's check your bedroom," Sheriff said as Ernie joined us.

"Sheriff, the intruder smashed the back door windowpane that was nearest the lock, then it was an easy reach for the intruder to unlock the door. I couldn't find any footprints in the alley. The intruder must have climbed the fence into the neighbor's yard then left the neighborhood from there."

When we went into my bedroom, I gasped. My pillow and the sheets on my bed had been slashed, and my closet door was open. I hurried to look inside and grabbed onto the door frame to keep from fainting. Ned put his arm around me and pulled me away from the terrifying sight.

"Sheriff, all her clothes are in tatters and spattered with catsup or red paint," Ned said.

"Vicious," I muttered.

"I agree," Ned said.

"You're not staying in your house until it's been professionally cleaned, and we catch the heartless savage that did this," Sheriff growled.

"I can't go to a hotel with Colonel and Roxie." I bit my lip to keep from crying.

"We'll find something. If Emma was in town, I'd say stay with us, but she's taking care of her mother and won't be back for two or three weeks. I'll find somewhere." Sheriff stormed out of the room, and Ernie called Tess on his radio and asked her to contact the GBI regional office then stood in front of the closet and wrote furiously in his notebook.

Ned helped me to the living room. When he picked up the sofa cushions to put them on the sofa, they were sliced with a large X.

He led me to a dining chair. "You can stay with me, Karen."

"No, I can't; you're a single man."

He pulled a chair close to me then sat and gazed at my face. "Karen, it isn't the Victorian era. Even male and female students share apartments these days."

"I don't know." I furrowed my brow.

"My trailer is nice, for being ten years old, and it's parked in a quiet campground with nice, clean showers. I have a bedroom with a door you can close. My sofa unfolds into a bed that is very comfortable. I snore, but I can give you earplugs. There's plenty of room for Colonel and Roxie to stretch out, and who knows? Mia might like it too. Call Barbara to see what she thinks. She'll want you to stay with them, but they've got a wedding to attend in the morning, then they will be busy sorting and packing in preparation for moving to their new house."

"Maybe I should see if Gee and Darlene have room for me," I said.

"I just did." Sheriff came into the house. "I'd forgotten that Gee is leaving in the morning for Savannah to visit Tiffany and Roger and will be gone for two weeks. She offered to postpone her trip, but I told her I was afraid to tell you that. She has already lined up one of her cousins to stay with Darlene to help run the thrift shop and to make sure Darlene eats right."

"I wouldn't feel right barging in on Gee's cousin and Darlene."

Sheriff nodded. "I told her you had other options. So, what are your other options?"

"Ned offered me his bedroom in his trailer. He has a foldout sofa bed that he claims is comfortable, and we'd be at the campground, so I'd have the women's shower."

"There's plenty of room for Colonel and Roxie, and they won't be alone because they go with Karen to work," Ned added.

"Seems reasonable to me. When are you calling Barbara? You know she and David have plans in the morning, right?" Sheriff asked.

"Yes, but I didn't know you knew." I frowned.

"Jeff asked for the time off, and I had to juggle a few things to make it happen," Sheriff said.

I sighed. "I'll call her now."

Ned stepped out back then returned. "Your rocking chairs are untouched, and your shadows are out there."

We went to the back porch, and I rocked while I called Barbara, and Ned sat next to me while I put my phone on speakerphone. The shadows hovered. *They must have been scared.*

"What's wrong?" Barbara asked when she picked up the phone.

I sighed. "Ned's here, and I have you on speakerphone. Somebody broke into my house while we were gone and slashed all my furniture, bed linens, and clothes, then they poured catsup or red paint all over my ripped clothes."

"Oh, I have to sit down." Barbara repeated what I'd said to David. "I've got you on speakerphone now. When are you going to be here? You are staying with us, aren't you?"

"You are so sweet." Tears slid down my cheeks. "My eyes are leaking."

"So are mine, but you started it."

"You need to be fresh for the wedding in the morning, and after that, you'll have to pack for your move."

"So what are your options?"

"Ned said I could stay with him. His trailer has a bedroom with a door that closes and a sofa with a pullout bed. He's in a campground that has nice men's and women's showers, and pets are welcome."

"What do you want to do?"

"I'm okay with camping, and the campground sounds nice from what Ned told me, and according to Ned, it's not the Victorian era because people share apartments all the time."

"I'll give you the campground for tonight, but we already have a room for you here, and you won't interfere with any packing I'm doing except I don't promise I won't ask your opinion when it's keep or toss time. You can certainly come here if you like. What do you want to do?"

"One night at the campground would work, so you and I wouldn't keep David awake while we talked all night about tomorrow's wedding."

"Which you would," David added.

"Would not," Barbara said. "What about clothes? Mine are a little big for you, but I've got some jeans and shirts I can't wear anymore because it isn't five years ago. What about your underwear?"

"I'll check." Ned hurried inside.

"Why did they steal your recipe notebook?" Barbara asked.

"I don't know; the recipes aren't like trade secrets or anything. They're recipes I found on the internet that looked interesting to me."

Ned returned. "I checked the chest of drawers, and everything there is untouched," Ned said.

"Good. You'll still want to wash them because I know you, but you won't have to do laundry before tomorrow; I'll pack some things for you to have for an overnight and will add underwear and pajamas to the jeans and shirts. What about shoes?"

"They were in my closet, but I wore my comfortable work shoes to your house."

"Okay. How are the shadows doing?" Barbara asked.

"They were outside the house when we arrived and haven't gone back in. They're here with me on the back porch."

"You might have to sing them to sleep or something tonight. I'm sure they'll go with you to the trailer. Shadows are affected by violence; did you know that?"

"Maybe I did, but I didn't remember."

"There is no reason to dwell on it. They're safe now."

Ned took my hand and squeezed it. "I'll check with the sheriff then box up the things in your chest of drawers."

"By the time you're here, I'll have everything in a suitcase for you," Barbara said. "Be sure to tell the shadows they can go with you. They may be shellshocked and not thinking straight."

After we hung up, I said, "I'd feel better if you go with us to the trailer. You know Ned can see you too, so you'll be safe with us there."

I rocked and hummed until Ned returned. "That's a nice tune," he said. "The shadows don't look as agitated as they were earlier. The sheriff said you can't take anything out of the house including your laptop and printer until the GBI crime scene investigators have had a chance to catalog and photograph everything. I asked for the rockers, and the sheriff said no. I knew he would, but I had to ask, then I asked for your fireproof box, and he said okay. If the intruder had found it, they wouldn't have left it. When he says we can leave, we'll stop by the grocery store on the way to Barbara's and pick you up a hairbrush, toothbrush, toothpaste, soap, shampoo, and whatever else you'll need to take with you to the shower. I have a shower tote that's too flowery for me that you can use. Maybe we can get you a nice towel from Barbara; mine are ancient and threadbare."

I sent a text to Barbara: "Need a shower towel and a face cloth."

My phone rang. *Barbara.* "David said you won't be allowed to take anything from your house right now, so I'm packing a goody bag of toiletries and what you'll need for a nice shower. You won't need to buy anything for a while. What about a charger for your phone?"

"I didn't think about that," I said.

"You would have eventually." Barbara giggled as she hung up.

"My packrat friend is packing a goody bag for me, so we won't have to stop at the grocery store."

"I should have known. I have coffee, but no tea for you."

"I'll be fine. We're camping, right? Doesn't that mean roughing it?"

My phone buzzed a text from Barbara. "What size is Ned's bed?"

I showed the text to Ned.

"It's queen-size," he said.

I replied, "Queen."

"What was that all about?" Ned asked.

"I suspect I'll be making the bed with clean sheets. Barbara's getting me excited about my new adventure of camping in the woods."

The shadows danced, and Ned smiled. "I'm glad everyone is feeling better. I can use my sheets on the foldout bed; I don't remember if it even has sheets on it because it's been so long since I used it."

I frowned. "Maybe I should sleep on the foldout."

"No way. I can change in the trailer bathroom, but you'll be more comfortable dressing where you have a little privacy and space."

"Thank you; I really appreciate all your efforts to make me comfortable." *Ned remembered my claustrophobia.*

The sheriff joined us on the porch. "We have Ernie's notes; unless you can think of anything else, y'all can leave with the firebox. I'll have you sign for it, Ned. What's your plan, Karen?"

"I'm staying at the campground with Ned tonight, then I'll go to Barbara and David's house tomorrow."

"Karen, please be safe. I'm reassured for once because you'll be with Ned tonight. Karen, take your minivan to the sheriff's department parking lot. Benjamin will unlock the gate for you."

"How am I going to get to work from the campground?" I asked.

"The sheriff and I talked. Your private chauffeur will provide your transportation." Ned's eyes twinkled.

I glared at Ned then the sheriff. "I guess that's okay for tonight, but I'll pick it up tomorrow."

The two men shook hands, then the sheriff hugged me.

I pushed the key fob and the back door slid open; Colonel and Roxie jumped in and took their self-assigned seats, and the shadows slid in with them.

I waited for Ned while he put my firebox in the back of his truck, then I drove to the sheriff's department with Ned less than a foot behind me. I pulled in front of the gate then opened the back door for Colonel and Roxie. While I handed my van keys to Deputy Benjamin, Colonel and Roxie raced to Ned's truck.

"All of us are glad that you're okay, Donut Lady," Benjamin said in his soft, Alabama drawl.

"Thank you, Benjamin."

After Ned helped me into the passenger's seat, he opened the back door for the dogs, and they jumped inside while the shadows billowed from the minivan to the truck.

When Ned headed toward Barbara's house, he said, "I'm glad everybody is going to the trailer."

The shadows wiggled side to side, and I smiled. *Good, they're feeling better.*

David and Barbara waited on their front porch for us. I lowered my window while Barbara rushed to the truck, and David carried the large, heavy suitcase to the truck then pitched it into the truck bed.

"We'll see you after the wedding," she said.

"No surprise, but Barbara packed enough for your overnight to last you for two months," David said.

As Ned pulled away, Barbara and David waved from their front yard.

"Do you feel like the parents just sent you off to your first summer camp?" Ned smiled.

I gazed at his dimples and smiled. "Something like that."

When we reached the campground, a serious young man in the security booth at the entrance saluted Ned. I stared at the neatly trimmed bushes that were surrounded by flower beds. I had expected a dusty road with ruts, but the roads were paved, and each site number was marked on a post that was topped by a small lantern.

"This is really nice."

My eyes widened when Ned pulled in next to a large trailer.

"It's a fifth wheel," I said.

"Thought I told you; I'll unlock it for you and put the suitcase inside then stay out here for a while with Colonel and Roxie, so they can explore the neighborhood."

After I went inside, the shadows went in with me and danced. "It is dance worthy, isn't it?" I gazed at the far end of the trailer at the living area with a leather sofa, two leather recliners, and the large TV over the fireplace. "I wonder if that works."

Next to the large window near the door was a teak dining table with two chairs. I ran my fingers across the cool island and gazed at the cabinets underneath the island on my way to the stove. The cooktop had four burners, and the oven was large enough to accommodate a standard cookie sheet. I checked out the full-sized refrigerator with a freezer drawer under it. *This is large enough to store a month's worth of frozen food.*

I opened the bathroom door. "Nice shower for camping, but I can see how larger campground showers might be more comfortable for me." The shadows crowded into the bathroom, and I giggled.

I headed up the three steps to the bedroom. "This is roomy." I opened a door near the steps. "I thought this was a closet; I didn't expect a toilet and a sink along with the bedroom."

I lugged Barbara's suitcase up the stairs one step at a time and opened it. I laughed at the small tin of tea bags that was on top of the sheets. After I stripped the bed and folded Ned's sheets, I carried the bed linens and the tin down the stairs. I dropped off the tin at the kitchen and placed the sheets on the sofa then returned to the bedroom and made the bed.

Barbara had organized the clothes by packing three shirts on top of each pair of jeans. *She did pack enough for two months' worth of choices.* I selected clothes to wear the next day and put them on the bed then found the toiletries and bath items. Barbara had stuck in a pair of flip flops for me to use as shower shoes. *If Barbara missed anything, I don't need it.*

Ned, Colonel, and Roxie came inside the trailer. "David gave me a water bowl, food bowls, and some dog food. What do you think about the trailer?" Ned filled the dog bowl with water then set it down, and Colonel and Roxie trotted over for drinks.

"This is really nice. I see why staying in the trailer is far superior to staying in a hotel."

"Is there enough closet space?"

"I didn't need to hang up any of the clothes. Barbara folded the shirts like a pro."

"Shall I heat a pot of water for your tea?"

"I can do that."

"Of course, you can, but it's my turn. Coffee for me and tea for you. Try out the recliner."

I sat in the recliner, and Ned pointed to the side of the chair. "Pull up the lever for the footrest."

I raised the footrest then leaned back and sighed. "I needed to relax with my feet up."

"Where's your backpack and tote?" Ned asked.

"I must have left them in the truck."

Ned poured the hot water into a mug and dropped in a tea bag to steep then went outside and returned with my backpack and tote.

While we relaxed, I sipped my tea and listened to the barred owl. "Whoo-cooks-for-you? Whoo-whoo-cooks-for-you?"

"What do you eat for breakfast? What do you think about oatmeal? That's my specialty," Ned said.

I shrugged. "I've had only coffee for breakfast since I've moved to Asbury."

When I gazed at him, he shifted his glance to Colonel and sipped his coffee. *He's trying not to be nosy.*

CHAPTER TWELVE

I gazed at Ned. "I've never really thought about it before, but I wasn't comfortable eating alone because there was no one to watch my back."

"What about lunch?"

"Sometimes I'd pack a sandwich, but I didn't always eat it."

"It's a wonder you didn't starve," Ned said.

"I was a hearty eater when I was younger, but I don't need as many calories now; I think my metabolism has gone into retrograde."

Ned chuckled. "Sure can tell you were a teacher."

After I finished my tea, Ned said, "I'll walk you to the bathhouse, so you can check out the showers. Here's your flashlight."

He handed me a flashlight, and I smiled as I hefted it from one hand to the other. "Tactical flashlight; this is nice. Walk me through the features."

Ned rolled his eyes then showed me how to click to maximum, strobe, dim, and signaling lights. "I was going to tell you I'd get you a lighter weight flashlight tomorrow, but I think this is yours."

"I always wanted a really cool flashlight when I was a kid, and my aunt gave me a tiny pink one. I told her thank you to be polite then cried for two days. I felt terrible when I dropped it the third day, and the case shattered."

Ned laughed. "Love it. It sounds more like a David story, but I believe you."

Ned held open the door for the dogs to go out, then we followed them.

Colonel had stopped near the truck to see which direction we were going, and Roxie stood alongside him.

"Colonel's taught Roxie to stay close, hasn't he?" Ned asked.

"She's pretty good about following directions."

"So, how high was the flashlight when you dropped it and what did it land on that made it shatter?"

"I was examining a stinkbug on a window ledge at a friend's house. She lived in an apartment, and we opened windows for fresh air or to catch a breeze back in the day, you know. My flashlight slipped."

"How high?"

"Oh, she lived in a second story apartment, and the flashlight landed on the parking lot."

Ned laughed. "Why did you ask for a flashlight in the first place?"

"I stayed with my aunt in Atlanta most holidays, and she had a close friend who was a police officer; I was fascinated by the flashlight on his belt. He told me the flashlight saved his life more than once. It just seemed like the right thing to have."

When I walked into the women's restroom and shower, the terra cotta tiles on the floors and the sturdy, wooden stall doors had a luxurious feel. I opened the door to a shower and examined the private dressing area with three clothes hooks and a teakwood bench then pulled back the clean, heavy woven cloth curtain, and the shower was large and had a sleek, wall mounted shower head. *Floors, sinks, and showers are clean.*

"What do you think?" Ned sat on a nearby bench while Colonel and Roxie investigated the dog park.

"It's nice. I'll gather my shower things and take a shower tonight."

"We'll take a walk while you're in the bath house; we won't be far," Ned said.

I put the shower supplies into the tote that Ned gave me then changed into the fleecy pants, T-shirt, and flipflops that Barbara had packed, so I'd have clean clothes to wear after my shower. I headed toward the bath house with my flashlight on dim. *I love this light.*

I hung up my towel and put my tote on the bench then turned on the hot water. After my shower, I quickly dried and dressed then towel-dried my hair before I stood in front of the mirror and gently combed out the tangles.

I listened while Ned talked to a man in a voice that was too quiet for me to hear clearly; when they laughed, I smiled. *Ned's in his environment: outside.*

Colonel and Roxie bounded to me as I came out of the bath house, and the wizened man waved to me before he headed toward the end of the row. I smiled and returned his wave.

"How was the shower?" Ned asked as we headed back to the trailer.

"Very relaxing."

After we were in the trailer, I yawned. "It's past my bedtime."

Ned smiled. "Sleep well. What time do you want to leave for the Donut Hole?"

"I try to be there before five thirty," I said. "Good night."

I closed the bedroom door, but Colonel whined, so I opened it and turned off the light before I climbed into bed. I yawned again, pulled up the covers, and closed my eyes while I listened to the barred owl.

"Whoo-cooks-for-you? Whoo-whoo-cooks-for-you?"

* * *

While I battled a fat, alligator with a garden rake in a swamp, the sharp aroma of coffee tickled my nose; I dropped my rake, pointed my flashlight at the alligator's eyes, and shouted, "Coffee break," and the alligator shriveled down to a dried-up wallet. I fought my way through the tangle of slimy grass in the swamp to get to the campfire for coffee then stopped. *How could there be a campfire in a swamp?* I sighed and opened my eyes. *Strange dream, but at least it wasn't a nightmare.*

Colonel padded up the steps, then I followed him to the brightly lit kitchen, and Roxie wagged her greeting. Ned poured a cup of coffee for me and set it on the island.

I sat on a barstool and inhaled the steamy bouquet of beans. "Thanks for the coffee."

He stirred a pot on the stove. "What do you like in your oatmeal? Regular or brown sugar?"

"Either."

He nodded then put a small bowl of brown sugar in front of me. "I've fed Colonel and Roxie. I'll take them with me on my morning walk while you get ready for work."

I drank my coffee, then Ned refilled the cup and set a bowl of oatmeal in front of me. *I'm glad Ned's not chatty in the morning.*

I stirred in the brown sugar, then we ate in silence. After I finished eating, Ned put our dishes into the sink then opened the door for Colonel and Roxie, and they dashed outside.

I hurried to the bedroom and dressed then stripped the bed and folded the sheets. After I returned Barbara's sheets and my toiletries to the suitcase, I half-carried and half-slid it down the stairs. I washed and rinsed the dishes then left them to dry in the drainer while I went outside and breathed in the cool air. *I'll ask Barbara about a sweatshirt or go shopping this afternoon.*

I walked to the end of the row and gawked at the trailers and RVs. I smiled at the flowers in pots and yard decorations that marked sites of the more permanent guests. After I returned to Ned's trailer, I went inside and gathered up the dog bowls and food to return to David.

Ned came into the trailer alone. "I hope you're pretty close to leaving because Colonel and Roxie are guarding the truck. This must be about the time you usually go to work because they are ready."

I smiled. "They know the routine."

"Don't forget your flashlight." He pointed to the flashlight I'd put on the island.

"That's yours; it's a good flashlight."

"It's a gift from me to you; just don't go hanging out any windows." His eyes twinkled, then he added, "I'll grab that overnight case for you."

I giggled as I picked up my new flashlight then stuck it into my backpack. When I stepped outside, Roxie danced, and Colonel grinned. Ned hefted the suitcase into the truck bed while I opened the back door for the dogs, and Roxie scrambled to jump in before Colonel did.

Ned chuckled. "Roxie's definitely a fan of going for a ride."

"You're right; she considers an open vehicle door to be her personal open invitation to go somewhere, and she's not picky about the destination."

On the way, Ned asked, "Are you planning to pick up your van today?"

"I thought I would right after work; David can drop me off."

"I'm available if you change your mind. Do I put Barbara's suitcase in your office, or do I take it to their house later?"

"I'd forgotten how much I just overloaded David's truck with me, Barbara, two dogs, and the luggage. It might be better if you take Colonel, Roxie, and me to pick up my van, if you're available."

He nodded.

When he parked in front of the shop, he peered at the lights. "What time does Andrew come to work?"

"I have no idea; he's always here when I show up."

"Shall I come in with you?" he asked as he opened the door for the dogs then opened my door.

"We'll be fine; thank you."

"I'll see you later." Ned stood next to his truck with his arms crossed until I opened the door. When I waved, he nodded but didn't move until we went inside.

"Hi, Miss Lady. You're five minutes late, according to Mia." Andrew grinned.

Mia growled then flicked her tail, sauntered to the reading table, and meowed.

"She's probably right. Sorry, Mia; we have no excuse."

Mia turned her back on us and preened.

"She missed you, Miss Lady, and Colonel and Roxie too. She'll probably go home with you after work."

"Whatever she wants is fine with me." I washed my hands then hurried to the storeroom for my apron and ball cap.

"It's fine with me too. Woody will be here soon, and we're going to make a honey bun beehive. Our group today is our local beekeepers; Woody has been working on a science project about bees and is going to present his findings to the group. Woody told me that Mr. Alfred wouldn't allow Ms. Shirley to come because she'd make everybody nervous."

I swallowed hard. *Bees?*

I shook off my hesitation. "Mr. Alfred is very smart."

"Yes."

"What's my assignment? The honey buns?"

"Yes, Miss Lady. I have Mr. Otto's recipe. Woody decided it would be better to bake them, so we'll let you do that. I made the first batch of dough earlier, and it's ready for you. The second batch is almost ready, and I think two batches is all we'll need for the beehive. There's the recipe and Woody's plan with the drawing and directions." Andrew pointed to the open recipe book and a sheet of paper near my workstation.

I studied the plan. "Got it. What about donuts and scones?"

"Sour cherry scones, Mr. Otto's recipe is cherry scones with lemon juice and lemon zest. Mama can make those. You can make sour orange scones with orange zest. Woody will make busy bee donut holes; I'll make classic donuts, and fry donut holes first, so he can decorate them, then I'll make pink-sprinkled donuts while you drizzle the classic donuts with honey."

"The orange zest will give them a tinge of bitter; that's perfect." I placed the first batch of honey bun dough on my floured work surface and flattened it to the size specified by Mr. Otto's recipe.

When Kim came into the shop, the first batch of honey buns was cooling, and I had the second batch in the oven.

"What's my assignment, and where do I work?" she asked.

"Sour cherry scones, Ms. Kim," Andrew said. "Here's the recipe."

"You have the scone station," I added. "We are hosting the local beekeepers, and Woody will present his findings from his science project on bees to them."

"Woody said it's a sweet day with a slightly tart sting," Andrew said. "Tart scones, sweet donuts, honeybee donut holes, and Miss Lady made honeybuns to build Woody's beehive."

"Did you and Woody pick out a platter for the beehive?" I asked.

"It's on the table in the pink room. We thought it could be a table decoration."

"I'll build the hive in there, so we don't have to move it, but Woody's specifications are easy to follow. What time is the group's meeting?"

"Nine o'clock."

"Mr. David and Ms. Barbara won't be here until ten. They have an appointment this morning," I said.

"Barbara called us last night, so we heard their news. We decided not to say anything until it was public knowledge," Kim said.

"I'm going to take care of the group." Andrew beamed.

Andrew helped me carry the honeybuns into the meeting room, then I began building. After I finished, I stepped to the door. "Come see the beehive."

"That is great," Kim said. "Woody was the architect?"

"Sure was. He even planned on extra honeybuns, so they wouldn't have to dismantle the beehive right away."

Kim glanced at the drawing and the instructions. "The detail and thought he must have put into it are amazing." Kim glanced around the room. "What about flowers? Do we have any artificial flowers we could put on the sideboard?"

Andrew grinned. "Woody is taking care of that."

"This is just amazing, but I have to get back to work; I don't want to be the only one who is behind," Kim said.

Andrew followed her then called out, "Sheriff's here, Miss Lady."

I hurried to pour the sheriff's coffee while Andrew plated a sour cherry scone and a pink-sprinkled donut then set the plate on the counter.

The bell jingled as the sheriff came in and glanced in the meeting room. "What's that? A beehive?"

"Come see," I said. "Woody is presenting his science paper on bees to the local beekeepers association this morning, so today is National Bee Day. Woody is the architect of the beehive, and it's made of honey buns."

The sheriff brought his coffee and his plate with him to the pink room. "Well, I'll be. It looks real. If I listen, will I hear bees?"

"You might. As soon as Woody gets here, he and Andrew are decorating our honeybee donut holes."

"I'll have to come back and see that. What time is the meeting?"

"Nine o'clock."

The sheriff set down his plate and picked up his scone. "What kind of scone is this? It doesn't look like strawberry." He took a bite. "It's a little tart."

"Our scones today are tart to offset the sweet honey donut and honey buns," I said.

"Are you going to eat the beehive?" Sheriff asked.

"After the beekeepers see their hive, they get first dibs on the honey buns, then the rest will be available after their meeting."

"I want the beehive after the beekeepers' meeting, so wrap it up for me, and I'll send someone to pick it up." He frowned. "Maybe I should pick it up, or it might not make it to my office. So, were you able to get any rest last night?"

"The campground is very relaxing, and I was exhausted. When can I pick up my van?"

"Anytime. Your keys are in the dispatcher's office, and Tess or any of the deputies can unlock the gate for you. I didn't want your van sitting unprotected at your house, and you were too shaken up to drive, and I don't blame you. GBI will begin photographing and examining your house this morning by nine." Sheriff glared at me. "Did you know you've become a GBI priority because nothing is simple when you're involved? That's a direct quote, and I wish it wasn't true, but it is."

We strolled together to the counter, and I refilled his cup then sat next to him. Kim poured a cup of coffee and set it in front of me. When I raised my eyebrows, she smiled. "I've been trained by the best. When you sit next to the sheriff, you get a cup of coffee."

Andrew beamed.

He's proud of his mother. I smiled. "I agree: trained by the best. Thank you for the coffee, Kim."

Sheriff gazed at the blank board. "Will Woody write the menu on the board?"

I glanced at Andrew, and he shook his head.

"No, that's up to you."

Sheriff grinned. "What's the menu?"

"Honey sweet and tart for the sting. Sweet donuts: honey drizzled classic and pink-sprinkled. Tart scones: sour cherry and orange. Buzzy bee donut holes."

"Love it." After he wrote on the board, he asked, "How does that look?"

"I like it," I said.

Sheriff tossed down his coffee then left, and I mixed and baked my sour orange scones. When Woody came into the shop, he carried in a vase with a bouquet of bright yellow flowers, and Shirley followed him. I automatically fixed her large to-go coffee, and Andrew sacked up two donuts and a cherry scone.

"I can't stay because Alfred needs me to help him with a project. He said we need to spend more time together, so he can get used to being around people. We're going to an estate auction near Conway. It's been ages since I've gone to a real auction; I'm looking forward to it, but I told him we could leave whenever he liked. We might stand in the back and not sit close to anyone. I told him that might help, and he thanked me for understanding. I'm not sure anyone has ever told me that before."

"Woody's going to lunch with us, Shirley," Kim said, "so don't feel like you have to rush back."

"That's nice, Kim, thank you." Shirley grabbed her sack and coffee and rushed out.

"My mama's a whirlwind," Woody said as he and Andrew began decorating the bees.

"The bouquet is beautiful." I drizzled honey scones. "What's the plan?"

"We'll put the flowers on the table with bees around them and on the hive."

"David told me I'm in charge of taking pictures," Kim said. "My scones are ready. Where can I help?"

"If you'll take over the coffee, and take care of any customers who come in, I'll finish up my scones."

Kim nodded and hurried to start another fresh pot of coffee then filled our display case. After Andrew and Woody finished the last touch on the last honeybee, they went into the pink room with bees to place them on the hive then on a narrow tray between the hive and the vase.

I completed the final touch on my tart orange scones as our first customer came in the door. "I heard there was some kind of sting operation going on in here," Ernie said. "Suppose I could have a few bees for the sheriff's beehive?"

"Half dozen? A dozen?" Kim asked.

"Give me a half dozen. Tess has a bonnet from a sugar cane fair she attended a couple of years ago."

Kim laughed. "Bees on the hive, and bees in the bonnet?"

"Yes, ma'am, except we're going to drill holes into the hive then place the bees inside the hive."

Woody rushed out of the pink room. "Is it hard? Can you show us how to do that, Deputy Ernie?"

Ernie grinned. "I'll be right back." Ernie returned with an electric drill then closed the meeting room door.

I stared at the door. "I can't take it." Kim snickered when I strolled to the meeting room and went inside.

"Look, Miss Lady!" The excitement on Woody's face and his shining eyes made me smile. "First I drill a hole as a starter, then Andrew cuts a wider circle and puts the bee in the hive. Some of our bees are peeking out, but Deputy Ernie said that's what bees should probably do."

"Sometimes I cover the bee with the circle I cut out," Andrew added as he pointed to a hole that was covered with honeybun, "but that's tricky."

"You all are really talented."

I hurried out of the room and closed the door behind me then gave a full report to Kim.

"I can't wait to see the final product," Kim said.

Two more customers came into the shop, then our usual, steady morning stream began as Deputy Ernie left with his drill.

"I need to take pictures." Kim hurried to the meeting room and snapped photos. "Okay, back to you, gentlemen."

"I have an order for two dozen donuts," I said, and Kim hurried to talk to the customer and box up their order while Woody and Andrew stood by the meeting room door and showed off their work to their admirers who had stopped at the door to gape at the beehive before they ordered.

While I waited on a counter customer, Kim whispered, "We're almost out of bees. What do I do?"

"Tell Andrew."

After Kim whispered to Andrew and Woody, Andrew hurried to his station to mix up cake donuts that didn't need the rising time while Woody returned from the storeroom with the cake donut hole molds to bake donut holes.

"I saw that in the storeroom but didn't know what it was," Kim said.

"Mr. Otto had it." Woody grinned. "I wasn't sure what it was when I first saw it, so I asked Ms. Darlene. We've never tried it before."

"Go for it, Woody!" One of the customers called out as he stood in line. "Can't run out of bees."

After Andrew pulled out the first batch of donut holes from the oven, Woody mixed more decorating frosting while they cooled. Andrew and Woody decorated the first batch of bees while the second batch baked, then we all high-fived when all the bees were decorated before eight-thirty.

Kim's eyes twinkled as a young woman with a large red bow in her curly blond hair came into the shop. "Hello, Ruby Jean. It's nice to see you."

Andrew's face reddened, and Woody took the platter from Andrew's hands and set it on the counter then pushed Andrew toward Ruby Jean.

Andrew's voice broke as he spoke. "Hi, Ruby Jean."

"My boss sent me to get bees for the day care." Ruby Jean peered at Andrew's face. "That's okay, isn't it?"

Andrew nodded, and she continued, "Good; I told my boss we had a rule that I wouldn't bother you at work, but she said it was okay if I was a customer."

"Yes. How many bees?"

"Could you do custom bees for us? The donut holes are too big for the children, and we don't want to cut the bees because the children would cry."

"Yes, that would be scary." Andrew appeared to be glued to his spot.

"We can decorate half a dozen donuts with bee stripes then Miss Lady could cut the donuts into smaller pieces. Would that work?" Woody asked.

"Yes." Andrew handed the frosting bowl to Woody then mixed more frosting.

"How many bees per donut, Miss Lady?" Woody asked.

"Eight seems sensible to me; what do you think, Ruby Jean?"

"Eight is good."

Woody decorated donuts with stripes, and I carefully sliced each donut into eight bees while Kim waited on our customers at the counter.

Andrew arranged the bees in a box. "Ms. Kim, take pictures, please."

Kim snapped photos of the bees, then Andrew closed the box and bowed as he handed the box to Ruby Jean with both hands, and she returned his bow as she accepted them.

I smiled at the formal exchange. After Kim gave Ruby Jean her change, Ruby Jean waved as she left, and Andrew's face reddened again as he slightly raised his hand then quickly lowered it.

"We work fast, don't we Miss Lady?" Woody asked as the first beekeeper arrived.

"It's a good thing we all jumped in, so all the children could have their own bees."

Woody welcomed the beekeepers and answered questions about the beehive while Andrew poured coffee. All the beekeepers had arrived by five minutes after ten; their association president nodded at Andrew, and Andrew closed the door.

Kim smiled. "I am so proud of those two."

I raised my eyebrows at our work area. "Can you take care of customers for a bit? We don't normally make that much of a mess, but this was a baby bees emergency, wasn't it?"

I gathered the dirty bowls, utensils, and pans then loaded the dishwasher, turned it on, and quickly wiped down our stations as David and Barbara hurried into the shop.

"What did we miss?" David asked as he rushed to the storeroom for his apron and ball cap. Kim and I laughed.

"What's funny?" Barbara asked.

"Peek into the meeting room when David goes in. You'll see a masterpiece."

David opened the door. "Well, would you look at that. That's amazing."

"It is, isn't it?" the president said. "You showed up just in time, we were about to taste the beehive."

Barbara peered around David. "Wow. It is a masterpiece."

"I have pictures for you," Kim said.

Barbara hugged her. "Thank you."

David said, "I'll take care of keeping the platters full for you, Andrew."

He stepped out of the room and closed the door as Woody and Andrew began serving the extra honey buns we'd made.

CHAPTER THIRTEEN

After the customer at the counter left, Barbara said, "Amber told me she doesn't want a reception or party because as soon as they get back, they'll have to dive back into work."

"That's no fun," Kim said. "Maybe she'll change her mind. Want to see the bees and beehive pictures?"

Kim pulled up the pictures, and Barbara scrolled through. "How long did it take you to build that beehive, Karen?"

"Just a few minutes; looks like it took hours, doesn't it?"

"Certainly does."

More customers came into the shop, and Kim staffed the cash register while Barbara boxed up the larger orders.

When we heard the applause and cheers from the pink room, Barbara, Kim, and I smiled. David opened the door and handed me an empty platter. "We're getting ready to dig into the beehive. Could Kim come in and film it for us?"

I nodded and handed him a full platter then said, "Kim, would you take an evidence video of the destruction of the hive, so we can turn it over to the authorities?"

Kim giggled as she hurried to the pink room. Barbara and I were too busy with customers to peek.

"I'm glad Kim's in there," Barbara said.

After more applause, David opened the door, and the beekeepers filed out of the room.

Quinn came into the shop. "Is that a beehive?" His face paled. "I'm allergic to bees, wasps, and hornets, especially hornets. All my friends know I can't be around bees."

I stared at him. "It's built with honeybuns in honor of the beekeepers' association that met this morning."

"It's creepy to me." Quinn shuddered. "I thought maybe you might be open to changing your policy about a newcomer introducing himself to some of the groups, but now's not a good time for me. I'll see you on Monday."

I stared at Quinn who rushed out the door.

"What's wrong with him?" Kim asked.

"He's allergic to bees, and evidently is terrified of being stung." I frowned. "That's the second time in two days that he's told me he'll see me on Monday. I'm confused."

"Sounds more like he's confused. Andrew and I heard about your house. Andrew wanted to know if you have a place to stay because he wants to move into the garage and give you his room if you don't."

Tears suddenly welled up in my eyes then slipped down my cheeks. "That is so sweet. I stayed with Ned at the campground last night, and I'll be staying with Barbara and David until I can move back into my house."

As our next customer came into the shop, Kim said, "I heard that campground was really nice. Why don't you just stay with Ned?"

"It was nice, but according to Ned, I'm still living in the Victorian era."

Kim laughed, and I hurried to the pink room to box up what was left of the hive for the sheriff. *I'll have to talk to Kim; maybe I am a little outdated.*

I set the sheriff's box of beehive and bees on the counter and marked it for him, so no one would think it was for sale.

Ernie sauntered inside. "The sheriff sent me to pick up something, but he wouldn't tell me what it was, and I'm not supposed to peek."

Kim handed him the sheriff's box.

He raised his eyebrows. "That's one huge box of donuts. What kind are they?"

Kim rolled her eyes, and Ernie shrugged. "Had to try." He whistled as he rushed out the door.

Woody and Andrew came out of the pink room.

"How did the presentation go?" I asked.

"Woody was awesome, and the president of the beekeepers said so too. Some of the beekeepers asked questions, and Woody knew the answers. He's very smart," Andrew said.

"I'm glad everything went so well," I said.

"Mama Shirley and Mr. Alfred have a special meeting this afternoon. I'm going to invite myself." Woody beamed as he swaggered back to the pink room to help Andrew.

"What do you think about me staying with Ned? Am I being nervous and old-fashioned?"

"You asked, so I'll tell you what I think. As far as Ned's concerned," Kim said, "if you want to stay with him then stay and enjoy getting to know him better; if you want the time and space to know him better then take it, and you don't owe other people any excuses or explanations either way because it's none of their business."

"I haven't thought of it like that. I'm not sure what I want to do because I got all wrapped up over what other people might think."

"Pish posh," Kim said, and I stared at her.

Kim snickered. "I was trying to talk old-fashioned, but I might have gone too far."

I chuckled. "I think you nailed it. I need to understand what I want to do."

"Right."

"Pish posh," I muttered.

Jorge, owner of the gas station, rushed into the shop. "What do you have left? I'll buy everything."

"We have scones, donuts, and bees," Kim said.

"Good. Box up everything. The rumor is going around that some celebrity is going to drive through Asbury, and we've got a slew of news photographers and talking heads milling around at the gas station, and nobody can get to the pumps. I talked to a photographer, and he told me nobody knows who the celebrity is, but the television station in Tallahassee got a tip, then someone in their office leaked the word, and we've got a mess." Jorge shook his head. "I'm going to lure them to our spare parking lot with coffee and pastries. One of the photographers told me not to give the pastries away, so we're going to charge them three times what I pay for them. I have a portable card reader to take credit and debit cards, and two of my retired regulars have volunteered to manage the sales. Josh and I decided we'd give the proceeds to the animal shelter in addition to the community service we'll be providing."

I peered at him. "Community service? You lost me."

"If I don't convince the photographers and gawkers to move away from the pumps before someone runs over every single one of them, I'll have an entire parking lot of upstanding people who would willingly commit perjury and swear they saw nothing."

"You're right," David said as he helped Woody and Andrew pack all the pastries we had, then Andrew carried out the boxes to Jorge's truck while Jorge paid Kim.

After Jorge left, I flipped the sign on the door to closed, and Barbara and David cleaned the pink room while Andrew unloaded then reloaded the dishwasher.

Kim sanitized the display case, I wiped down the counter, and Woody swept the shop floor then the pink room floor.

"I've never seen anyone so terrified by donuts just because the donuts looked like something else. Does that happen often?" Kim asked.

"Never; Quinn must be terribly allergic to bees and wasps."

"What are we talking about?" David asked.

I told him about Quinn's reaction to the honeybun beehive and the donut hole bees. "It was beyond bizarre, but giving him the benefit of the doubt..." I shook my head. "No, it was definitely strange. I can usually find the good in almost anyone, but Quinn rubs me the wrong way, and I still see him as a uniquely self-centered, one-dimensional individual."

David chuckled. "Yes, but why don't you tell us how you really feel?"

"He does have nice hair." Kim wrinkled her nose. "Was that too superficial?"

David snorted, and I giggled.

I texted Ned. "We're ready when you are."

"We're leaving, Roxie." David bent down to rub her face. "You're welcome to come with us."

Roxie sat and grinned, and David said, "We've enjoyed your company."

After David and Barbara left, I said, "I'll lock up, Andrew. Ned will be here in a few minutes."

"We'll wait," Andrew said, and Woody nodded.

"Andrew wants to see you safely in Ned's truck," Kim added.

Mia rubbed against Andrew's leg then stood in front of me and meowed.

"Mia wants to go with you, Miss Lady," Andrew said.

I set Mia's carrier near the door and unzipped it. "We'll leave in a few minutes."

When Ned parked in front of the Donut Hole, Mia slipped into her carrier, and I zipped it up, then Andrew carried her out to Ned's truck.

"Nice to see you, Mia," Ned said.

When we were on our way, Ned said, "The town's in an uproar because a celebrity is supposed to be driving through town. I can't imagine where this supposedly famous person might be going or how all those news people got word of it, but it's a mess at the gas station and most of the intersections. Richard will meet us at the park. Good thing Gus's sandwich shop is on this side of town, and we don't have to go near the gas station to get to the park."

Ned parked in front of Gus's. "What do you want?"

"Whatever the special is."

Ned grinned. "Good idea; I'll order three specials."

While we waited for Richard at the park north of town, the dogs romped and explored, and Mia snoozed in her carrier that I had set in the shade near my feet.

Ned asked, "How was your morning?"

I told him about the beekeepers and the beehive that Woody designed. "Kim sent me the pictures she took of the hive and the bees." I pulled up the pictures on my phone.

Ned chuckled as we went through the pictures together. "Woody is really talented, isn't he?" When he came to the pictures of the donut pieces for the day care, Ned asked, "He did this on the spur of the moment?"

"Sure did. Isn't that amazing?"

"Did you see the talent in him when he stood outside the Donut Hole?"

"No, I saw a hungry boy that needed a friend."

When Richard joined us in the park, he said, "Sorry I was slower than I expected."

"Ready for lunch?" Ned asked. "The special was smoked ham salad."

"I've had ham salad but never smoked ham salad." I bit into my sandwich. "This is good."

Richard nodded as he ate. "Rafe offered me a promotion today. He wants me to be the lead mechanic, so he can spend less time in the shop and more time on his farm. I told him I'd like the weekend to think about it."

Richard and Ned finished their sandwiches.

"We have six cookies: two cookies each, unless you want only one." Ned raised his eyebrows as he peered at me, and his face was so wistful, I giggled.

"No luck. I always have room for cookies."

Ned exhaled. "I knew that."

"But you had to ask anyway." Richard chuckled.

Ned nodded. "Do you want to talk about Rafe's offer?"

"Yes, I think I do. I'm comfortable with the work itself; I know I'm his best mechanic, and I love training the others who are less experienced, but I don't know about the supervisory part."

"When you train someone, what do you do if your student does something wrong?" I asked.

"I stop him or her, and depending on what it is, I tell them what they need to do or give them a chance to think it through." Richard smiled. "We have two mechanics who are women, and they sure give me grief when I say, 'the guys.' I tried to play the old guy card, but they weren't buying it."

"What do you do if Rafe's not there and someone shows up late?" I asked.

Richard narrowed his eyes. "I pull them aside and tell them not to do it again without letting someone know."

"Sounds like a lead mechanic to me," Ned said. "Any repeat offenders?"

"Not so far," Richard said. "We had one quit, but that was his choice, and we need to have people we can count on."

"What do you think, Karen?" Ned asked.

"Richard, what do I think?"

Richard laughed. "You two are an amazing team. You think I've been a supervisor all along and too stubborn to see it."

"High five, hon." Ned smirked and held up his hand, and I smacked it.

Richard picked up his two cookies. "I'm going to talk to Rafe. Maybe I need to meet with my mentors on a regular basis." He grinned as he hurried to his truck then waved as he left.

"What do you think, Karen?" Ned asked.

"I think we must be a good team."

"Can I have your second cookie?"

"No." I laughed then bit into my first cookie as he pouted.

"Oh, fine; we're a team, according to Richard, so you can have it."

"If you insist." Ned took my second cookie and jammed half of it into his mouth.

As we headed to his truck, I said, "We need to talk sometime."

"Yes, we do; whenever you say." Ned opened my door.

I examined the farmers' fields as we headed toward town. "The corn looks like it grew overnight. I'd like to talk now."

"Do I pull over or do you want to pick up your vehicle?"

"Let's go to the park then pick up my van."

When we reached the park close to my house, Ned parked then released the dogs and picked up Mia's carrier.

After we sat at our picnic table, I said, "I'm not sure how long it will be before I can move back into my house, and I'm not sure I want to live there anymore."

"That's understandable." Ned picked up his phone and sent a text. "I don't expect the crime scene people to be there longer than two or three days, but I asked the sheriff for his opinion. A cleaning crew could have it cleaned and ready for furniture in two days, and Gee would find the furniture for you while you're waiting, so my educated guess is before next weekend."

"I was thinking weeks; that's not so bad."

"Are you certain you'd be willing to move into the house next week, or is that too soon?"

"I think I'll be okay; I realized I'm anxious because I feel homeless; we don't even have a comfortable place where we can have a private conversation. Barbara and David are very welcoming, but I'm a guest. Your trailer is nice, but there really isn't enough room for all of us." I gazed at his face. "Even if we shared the bedroom."

He sighed. "It will be fine for camping, but the five of us need more space to stretch out."

He returned my gaze; his face was solemn, but his eyes twinkled.

My mouth quivered to keep back a smile. *Something's up; that's his devilish look.*

"We'll find a cabin for all of us; you know I want to spend the rest of my life with you. Just promise me you'll tell me when I can ask you to marry me." He broke his gaze to watch Colonel and Roxie then side-glanced me. "Pinky swear."

I snort-laughed then held up my little finger, and he hooked his in mine.

"Pinky swear," I said.

"Pinky swear," he repeated in a solemn tone then leaned back and grinned.

Before he climbed into the truck, his phone buzzed a text. Ned read it then said, "Sheriff said by Monday."

"Let's drop off my minivan then go to Gee's thrift shop."

We picked up my vehicle, but before we reached the grocery store on the way to Barbara's, the road was blocked. I headed to the Donut Hole, and Ned followed me.

After I parked, I climbed into the truck. "That was a surprise. I just remembered Gee is out of town, but Darlene can help."

When we went into the shop, Mandy greeted Colonel and Roxie, then Ned took the three of them outside for a romp. I unzipped Mia's carrier, and she darted away to find Sandy.

"Tell me about your house. What do you need, and when do you need it?" Darlene asked.

"First, it will have to be professionally cleaned. There is either red paint or catsup all over my closet, and all my furniture is trashed except for my kitchen table and chairs. The appliances and my rockers are okay too."

"Bedroom and living room furniture." Darlene wrote on her notepad. "When?"

"Ned and the sheriff think the GBI will finish their on-site investigation by Monday, so maybe the cleaners could begin on Tuesday."

Darlene jotted down a note. "I know a good crew. I'll schedule them for Tuesday to clear out the damaged furniture and Wednesday to clean. What about any repairs to the house itself?"

"The intruder broke a window; Ned can replace that."

"That's good; You'll want a bed at least on Thursday. I assume you'll need a new mattress. What about linens?"

"Everything was ruined except my towels that were in the bathroom closet."

"Got it." Darlene continued to write. "Dishes?"

"I didn't see any broken, so I'll run all of them through the dishwasher."

"The cleaners can do that and wipe out the cabinets for you." Darlene added to her notes.

"Aren't we putting a lot of extra work on them?"

"No," she growled. "What about your laptop?"

"It's fine."

"I'm surprised, but we'll have to see whether GBI takes it. Do you think the intruder was looking for something?"

"It's hard to say; the only thing I know that was missing was my recipe book, but from the looks of my clothes and closet, it was a personal attack."

Darlene's eyes widened. "Recipe book?"

I shrugged. "I printed recipes I found on the internet and put them into a three-ring binder."

Darlene shook her head. "When are you going clothes shopping? Want to leave Colonel, Roxie, and Mia here?"

"That's a good idea, thanks."

"How's it going with Ned?"

I smiled. "He and I are becoming good friends."

Ned opened the door to come inside, and the three dogs dashed to the back of the store for water.

"What's the plan?" Ned asked.

I smiled. "Darlene will schedule the cleaning crew for Tuesday to clear out the furniture then Wednesday to clean. On Thursday, she'll schedule the furniture for delivery. Darlene invited Colonel, Roxie, and Mia to stay at the shop while I shop for clothes."

After we left the thrift shop, Ned asked, "Did you want to pick up your van before shopping?"

"I'd like that, then you won't have to sit in your truck and wait for me."

"I'll be close. Let me know when you're ready to go to Barbara's, and I'll bring the suitcase."

Ned dropped me off at the Donut Hole, and I drove to our large retailer and picked out two pairs of jeans, four shirts, underwear, and pajamas.

After I checked out, I stopped as Quinn or Richard hurried into the store. *Quinn.* He began searching the aisles systematically. *He's looking for someone. If it's me, I don't want to talk to him.*

I slipped out the closest exit then rushed to my van and called Ned. "I'm going to pick up Colonel, Mia, and Roxie before I go to Barbara's. I won't be long."

"I already picked them up, and we're all at Barbara's."

I rolled my eyes. *I should have known.* "On my way."

When I reached Barbara's house, Ned and David were on the porch. David pointed to his driveway, and I parked in his usual spot.

"The suitcase is in your bedroom," Ned said as he opened my door. He picked up my shopping bags, then we followed David into the house.

"Barbara's cooking, so Colonel and Roxie are guarding her. Barbara said Mia's been stalking shadows," David said.

"Where do you want your new clothes?" Ned asked.

"In my room for now." I hurried to the kitchen. "Barbara, I bought some new clothes, but I need to try them on before I pull the tags or wash them."

Barbara nodded. "I'm making a chicken and tortilla casserole; it's kind of like a nacho because we'll have crunchy tortilla chips to eat with it."

"Shall I make a salad?" I asked.

"We've got forty minutes after I put it into the oven, so we've got plenty of time; go try on your clothes."

Everything fit, so I removed all the tags, pulled my dirty clothes from the suitcase that Ned had brought in for me, and carried the clothes to the kitchen. "These are ready to wash. I'm not sure it's quite a full load."

Barbara slid the casserole dish into the oven then peered at the clothes. "Close enough; toss them in. I have cheese, crackers and wine. I think we need to declare tonight a night off. What do you think?"

"Sounds good," I said.

"What sounds good?" David asked as he and Ned came into the kitchen.

"Karen and I are taking the night off to enjoy a glass of wine."

David glanced at Ned. "Ned and I may not go off duty, so we'll have sweet tea with our cheese and crackers, but I'll be happy to open your bottle and serve you in the living room."

"Thank you, David." Barbara kissed his cheek and took my arm.

Barbara sat on her soft chair, and I sat on the sofa and exhaled.

"It's nice to sit." I told Barbara about Darlene's plan.

Barbara snickered. "If the crime crew isn't out of there by five o'clock on Monday, I have a feeling that Darlene and Gee's cousin will toss them out."

David carried Barbara's glass of wine and a plate of cheese and crackers, and Ned handed me my glass of wine and put a second plate of cheese and crackers on the table in front of me. Ned went back to the kitchen and returned with the two glasses of sweet tea.

When Ned sat next to me, he picked up a cheese-covered cracker as I asked, "Is something going on that you think I don't need to know about?"

He glanced at me then stuffed the cracker and cheese into his mouth.

Barbara narrowed her eyes. "David?"

David reached for a cracker, and Barbara snatched away the plate.

"No fair," David grumbled. "You had advance warning." He cleared his throat. "That's an oddly worded question. Why do you ask?"

Barbara moved the plate farther from him, and he sighed. "I bow to your well-timed, effectively executed torture. Ned and I decided we need to stay on our toes until the intruder is caught."

She smiled and held the plate for him, and he picked up five crackers with cheese.

"Emergency rations," he said before he ate a cracker with cheese.

"Did you ever hear who the celebrity was?" I asked.

"Jorge told me the news people decided it was a prank, but he sold all the donuts and has a nice donation for the animal shelter," Ned said. "So, what are your plans after dinner, Karen? Please don't say you're going anywhere."

I chuckled. "I still have those documents from Giana and Papa. I thought I'd prop up my feet and read them."

"Good plan; I'll read something too, so I'll have a cover while I watch you."

When Ned and I laughed, Barbara asked, "Why was that funny?"

"It was Ned's version of subtle." I raised my glass to Ned, and he clinked it with his iced tea.

She rolled her eyes. "I'm going to make the salad."

"I'll help," I said, but before I rose, David put up his hand.

"It's my turn to be the sous chef."

"David's version of subtle." Barbara giggled as the two of them strolled to the kitchen.

"David knows I don't drink," Ned said.

"Oh, I didn't know."

CHAPTER FOURTEEN

Ned smiled. "Now you do, but not many know the reason. My wife was an alcoholic, so I never had any alcohol in the house because she was too fragile. She was a wonderful person at heart, but…"

He looked away before he continued, "I didn't know how much she was drinking during the day while I was at work. It doesn't bother me in the least if other people enjoy their wine, and if I know what kind you like, I'm happy to have it for you as long as you're okay if I toast you with sweet tea."

"Of course, thank you; Barbara and I do enjoy our cocktail hour together for our special occasions."

"What's the special occasion tonight?" Ned asked.

"Either Amber's wedding or the house; we'll know if we have wedding cake or johnny cakes."

Ned laughed. "Johnny cakes?"

I flipped my hair. "Sometimes it's hard to make up stories on the fly."

"My condolences."

"I miss everything." David came into the living room. "Condolences for what?"

"Making up a believable lie on short notice. I failed," I said.

David shook his head. "Y'all are certainly a party in the box. Supper is on the table. You want sweet tea with your dinner, Karen?"

"Yes, please; I'll finish my wine with dessert."

While we ate, David said, "Ned, I heard they called you when someone stole a tiger cub from the zoo, and the mama escaped to look for her baby."

Ned chuckled. "The thief was easy for mama to track because the cub peed all over the man and his car."

"Smart cub," Barbara said.

"It wasn't hard to track the mama because she was not in stealth mode at all; she was in full-on mama mode and not in the mood for anything or anyone who was in her way and let them know it. The dispatch board lit up with calls about a raging tiger, but she wasn't raging, she was enraged. It took three tranquilizer darts: two to settle her down, and a small dose for the cub who attacked the man when his mama got close." Ned shook his head. "That little guy was protecting his mama. I wrote him up for a junior ranger award, and the boss signed it, had it framed, and sent the junior ranger certificate and a steak to the zoo for the cub and his mother."

"Don't tell me if that story isn't true; I love it," Barbara said.

After we ate, Ned and I cleared the table while David loaded the dishwasher.

"What's for dessert, honey?" David asked.

"Apple crumb pie with ice cream, or as you call it, crummy apple pie."

David placed his hand on his heart. "My favorite. Honey, remember when Amber was in second grade and told her teacher that her dad's favorite dessert was her mama's crummy apple pie?"

Barbara laughed until the tears rolled.

David added, "The teacher called me at the office to tell me that she called you about a problem with Amber, and you were hysterical. When she told me what the problem was, I laughed, and she hung up on me."

I laughed along with Barbara then smiled at Ned's dimples.

Barbara brushed away her tears. "The best part is word got around that I was an awful cook, and nobody ever called me again for cookies, cakes, or pies for school or a church potluck."

Barbara placed slices of warm pie in bowls then David scooped ice cream on top.

I took a bite of the hot and freezing delicacy. "Crummy apple pie is my new favorite too. This is delicious, Barbara."

Ned nodded.

After dessert, I settled down on the sofa with the folder Giana had given me and began reading. After an hour, I rubbed my forehead then strolled to the back door and went outside with Colonel, Roxie, and Ned following me.

"What have you found so far?" Ned asked.

"I see how Sicily removed the money with minimal detection. She timed the withdrawals to coincide with the dates of the regular deposits, so the balance from one day to the next was only a few hundred dollars lower. At a glance, her grandmother's bank balance appears to be relatively static on the surface. An audit of the detail records would have found it, but who would audit an elderly woman's bank account? It became even more interesting when I tracked where the money went after it left the grandmother's account. I found the records for three bank accounts that the funds flowed through, and there is a fourth. The names on the first one were Sicily and someone I assume to be her grandmother, and the second one had Sicily's and Francine's names on it, then the names on the third one were Francine, Sicily, and Q. R. Norris. It could have been Richard, Quinn, or neither, but there are six years of records here, and the frequency and the amount of money being transferred from the third to a fourth bank increased, but I haven't found any records for that fourth bank. I still have more to look through because I'm not even halfway through the papers." I covered my mouth as I yawned.

"Time to quit; otherwise you'll have to go back over everything in the morning because you'll get sloppy if you continue."

I giggled. "Sloppy? You want to pick another word?"

Ned stroked his chin. "Nope, that's the right word."

"Okay, honey. You win."

His eyes widened. "Honey?"

"Of course. Cuddles was my first thought."

Ned guffawed. "I'd like to be honey, but thanks for the offer, unless you want to cuddle, then you can call me cuddles, curmudgeon, or whatever you like."

As we headed toward the door, I hugged him, and he leaned down and kissed me.

After we broke away, we went into the house with our arms around each other.

Barbara smirked as she backed away from the window when we came in and smiled. "I emptied the dryer. Your clothes are in your room, I thought you'd like to put them away, so you'll know where they are."

"I'll see you tomorrow." Ned kissed me. "Good night, hon."

"Good night, sweetie." I smiled.

After Ned and David spoke quietly, Ned left.

"Kissing now? It's about time. Sweetie?" Barbara asked.

I shrugged. "I haven't quite figured out what I want to call Ned."

"Are you going to continue reading?"

"No, I'm exhausted."

Barbara hugged me. "I'm glad you're here. Good night, Karen."

"Good night."

"See you in the morning, David." I headed toward the hallway where the shadows danced.

"Good night. I'll take Colonel and Roxie out before I go to bed; Mia may be in your room."

I quickly put away my newly-washed clothes then changed for bed, and the shadows settled down in the corner of the room. After Mia stalked them then pounced, she curled up in the corner, and they snuggled down with her.

I turned off the light, climbed into bed, and closed my eyes.

* * *

When I woke, it was almost daybreak, and I sat up so quickly that I made myself dizzy. I glanced at the clock and gasped. *Six o'clock? I'm late.*

I threw off the covers then exhaled as I scanned the room. *I'm not home; I'm at Barbara's, and it's Sunday.*

After I dressed, I followed the beckoning aroma of coffee to the kitchen.

"How did you sleep?" Barbara poured a cup for me as I sat at the breakfast bar.

"Amazingly great; I can't believe how late I slept."

"David fed the dogs; he wants to drive by the house later today. I think we'll be stalking it until we move in. He wanted to ask Shirley to submit our offer today, but I reminded him that we have an appointment with her in the morning at eight to go over our offer. Amanda had a couple of changes, but she gave them to Shirley late Friday afternoon."

"Meeting with Shirley at eight? I thought the earliest she would schedule a meeting was nine."

Barbara chuckled as she joined me with her coffee. "David asked her to meet us at seven, then they finally settled on eight. I don't expect us to be very long."

When my phone buzzed a text, I read it and snickered.

"What?" Barbara asked.

"Ned wants to know if I'm awake." I responded, and my phone rang.

"What's your schedule for today?" he asked.

"I want to finish going through the papers."

"I thought you would; why don't I pick you up, and you can relax at the campground? The weather's going to be nice, and there's a nearby hiking trail that I'd like to explore, and I think Colonel and Roxie will enjoy it too. Mia's welcome too, if she'd like to come."

"I'll get back to you after we've had breakfast."

After we hung up, I said, "Ned invited the dogs, Mia, and me to the campground. I can read the rest of the documents in the folder, and Colonel and Roxie can go hiking with Ned. I think Mia would rather hang out here, though. Would that be okay with you?"

"That would be fine. She and the shadows keep each other entertained, don't they?" Barbara smiled. "You'll miss driving past the house five or six times, but I'm sure there will be plenty of opportunities for you until we finally close on the house. Call Ned back and tell him he's welcome to have breakfast with us, if he hurries."

I called Ned. "Barbara invited you to breakfast; we'll be sitting down soon."

After we hung up, I said, "He's on his way."

David came in from the garage then picked up the cup of coffee that Barbara poured for him. He peered at the empty coffee pot. "I need extra fortification this morning. Should I start another pot?"

"Thanks, I invited Ned to join us; I thought we'd like biscuits and gravy this morning to go with our eggs and sausage. Do you want bacon too? Never mind, I'll fry up some bacon in case Ned doesn't like sausage. When do you plan to drive past the house?" Barbara measured flour then cut in the cold butter.

"I've got a couple more things to do in the garage before breakfast, then I'll be ready to leave after we eat and take care of the dishes." David tapped his fingers until the fresh pot of coffee was ready then refilled his cup before he hurried back to the garage.

"What do you want me to do with your clothes you packed up for me?" I asked.

"If you can wear them, why don't you just keep them? They'll never fit me."

I made my bed then returned to the kitchen.

"Ready for breakfast?" Barbara asked as David came in from the garage.

David washed his hands. "As soon as Ned gets here. I still have a few more things to finish up in the garage after we eat."

Barbara pointed to the refrigerator. "I cut up some melon and strawberries earlier; they'll counteract the gravy calories."

David set out silverware then pulled out butter, jam, and the fruit from the refrigerator; Ned knocked on the front door, and I hurried to open it.

When Ned and I strolled into the kitchen, David handed Ned a cup of steaming coffee. "We're having an early brunch because my overachieving wife made more than a human can eat for breakfast."

Barbara slipped a pan of biscuits into the oven then melted butter in the skillet for gravy. "After I get the gravy going, I'll cook eggs. What do you think: fried or scrambled?"

"Fried," David said.

"If it's not extra work then fried," I said.

Barbara nodded. "I can fry up a mess of eggs as quickly as I can scramble them."

Barbara put the gravy boat on the table then pulled out the biscuits from the oven and slid them onto a serving tray. After she handed David then Ned their plates with two eggs each, she said, "Fix your biscuits however you like: butter, gravy, or both."

While the men split open their biscuits, Barbara fried two eggs, put one on my plate, and one on hers.

I buttered my biscuit and added jam to it before I poured a little gravy on my egg and served myself a spoonful of fruit and a piece of bacon.

Barbara smiled. "You have a taste of everything. I'm copying you. I'll split a sausage patty with you."

While we ate, Barbara asked, "Do you think you'll be here for lunch?"

I glanced at Ned who shrugged.

"I don't think so, and don't plan on us for supper, then you can enjoy stalking the countryside at your leisure."

Barbara crossed her arms, and David patted her shoulder. "If they starve, it's on them."

I giggled, and Barbara smiled.

David started to clear the plates, but Barbara said, "We'll take care of the dishes; it's our turn."

David shrugged, then he and Ned went into the garage.

After Barbara loaded the dishwasher, David and Ned joined us in the kitchen.

"The sheriff called me. He'll be here in a few minutes," Ned said.

"Did he say why?" I asked.

"No, but I got the impression it's not good news."

I sat on the nearest dining chair. "I hope this doesn't mean there's a change in when my house will be released to me."

"Let's sit in the living room where we can be more comfortable," Barbara said.

Ned and David waited on the porch, and I stood next to the living room window and watched for the sheriff, but the shadows rushed to the window and darkened my view.

"I think it would be better if you sit next to me." Barbara patted the sofa cushion. "The shadows are agitated about something."

"I can't imagine what it is, but you're right." I sighed and sat on the sofa.

I heard the cruiser stop in front of the house, then the three men came inside.

The sheriff's face was somber. "First, the good news. After everyone at the office had at least one honeybun and a bee, Ernie took the leftover honeybuns and bees to the GBI crew, and they promised they'd finish up the investigation by tomorrow."

"Bribery pays!" Barbara said. "Sorry, didn't mean to blurt that out."

David smiled as he patted her shoulder. "You only said what the rest of us were thinking."

Sheriff pulled a chair to sit close to me. "Karen, this shouldn't have anything to do with you, but it does. When Benjamin was making his rounds early this morning, he found Quinn Norris's body in his car near the gas station. Quinn's face and neck were swollen, and there were insect stings on his face and arms. The driver's door was partially open, and Benjamin found a jar behind the driver's seat with a large wasp nest in it."

My eyes were wide. "Quinn came to the Donut Hole yesterday and panicked at the sight of the honeybun beehive; he told me he was extremely allergic to bees, wasps, and hornets. If there had been wasps in his car, he would have waved his arms and flailed at them."

The sheriff nodded and added softly, "He would have tried to get out of his car."

I nodded. "I can't see him putting a jar with a live wasp nest in his car even if he intended it for someone else."

"Do you think anyone else knew of his allergy and fear of bees and other stinging insects?"

"He told me everyone that knew him knew about his severe reaction to bees."

"Forgive me, Sheriff, but what does that have to do with Karen?" Ned asked.

Sheriff exhaled and gazed at me. "There was a three-ring binder under Quinn's seat."

"My recipe book?" I shook my head. "It doesn't make any sense. There wasn't anything in it except recipes I found on the internet that I thought I might try some time."

"Either Quinn thought there was something in it included with the recipes, or someone is trying to implicate you." Sheriff's face was pained as he cleared his throat. "There's more. The front and back covers of the binder had been stabbed repeatedly, and the pages were slashed."

"What?" Barbara's voice rose. "The murderer used wasps to murder Quinn Norris and slashed Karen's recipes to somehow blame Karen? That is almost too bizarre to think much less say out loud."

David strode to the sofa, and I relinquished my seat, so David could sit next to Barbara. He put his arm around her. "Easy, honey, Sheriff's on Karen's side."

"I don't think you killed Quinn Norris, and we have someone in custody. When was the last time you saw Quinn?"

"When he left the shop in a panic…" I frowned.

"What?" Ned asked.

"After I bought new clothes yesterday afternoon and was headed to the exit, he rushed into the store and hurried from aisle to aisle like he was searching for someone. I was afraid he was looking for me to talk about permission to meet with the groups in the meeting room."

"I told him it was against policy." David frowned. "I hope that wasn't a mistake."

"Sounds like a perfectly valid policy to me," Sheriff said. "What did you do, Karen?"

"I hurried out as he was headed away from me and called Ned to tell him I had finished shopping."

"Are you sure it was Quinn and not Richard?"

"Yes."

"She can describe the difference between Quinn's and Richard's walks," Ned said. "If she said the man was Quinn, it was Quinn."

Sheriff nodded. "Tell me, Karen."

"Richard has a slight outward swing with his left foot."

Sheriff sighed. "I wish I could say that you are right, but I've never noticed. Who else knows this?"

I peered at him. "Other than everybody in this room? I don't know."

"When was the last time you saw Richard?" Sheriff asked.

"Ned and I had lunch with him yesterday at the park north of town."

"And you saw Quinn after that?"

"Yes."

"Can anyone here convince me that I shouldn't take Karen into protective custody?" Sheriff narrowed his eyes as he glared at Barbara, David, Ned, and me.

"She can stay with me." Ned returned the sheriff's glare. "We'll be crowded, but she'll be safe. I'll take her to work tomorrow and stay at the Donut Hole until she is ready to leave."

"The dogs and Mia could stay with us; that will make the trailer less crowded," David said.

"No," I said. "Colonel and Roxie are good backup, and Mia belongs with Colonel. I'll be safe with Ned. Cramped and irritable, but safe."

Sheriff smirked. "You sure you want an irritable Donut Lady in your trailer?"

"It's a price I'm willing to pay." Ned hugged me. I glanced at Barbara and nodded when she put her hand on her heart. *Melted my heart too.*

I narrowed my eyes. "Who do you have in custody? It's Richard, isn't it?"

"Not your business, Karen." The sheriff stormed out; I ran after him with Ned and Colonel behind me.

"Wait, Grady, it is my business because he's innocent."

The sheriff crossed his arms, and his face hardened. "No, it's none of your business."

Ned put his arm around me and led me back to the house. "I'll find out," he whispered after we were inside.

"Thank you, honey." Tears slipped down my face.

"Am I the only one here that wants to storm the sheriff's office?" Barbara growled.

"No, but you and I are the only ones crazy enough to do it." I bit my lip.

Barbara giggled. "We've got Darlene, and Gee would return to town to help. So, what's our plan?"

I smiled. "Easy. We find out who killed Quinn and set a trap."

"No," David said. "My heart can't take it."

"No," Ned said. "I don't have that many friends and can't spare David. You'll have to find another hobby like teaching alligators to dance."

"That gives me an idea…"

Barbara peered at my face. "Even I don't understand what you're talking about."

I nodded. *I don't either.* "I haven't quite worked out all the kinks yet, but our plans haven't changed for today, have they?"

Ned narrowed his eyes. "I don't see any reason to change them except the dogs and I aren't leaving you alone at the trailer. When were you planning on leaving, David? Didn't you have a couple things to do first?"

"Yes." David glanced at Ned. "In the garage."

Ned nodded. "I'll help you."

After they strode to the garage, Barbara said, "They're plotting something. We should do the same. Who do you think the killer is? Do you think it's the same person who invaded your house and attacked your clothes?"

"I think so. Don't the two crimes have the same psychological goal of causing fear and more than a casual level of knowledge of the target?"

Barbara nodded. "They seemed similar in intent to me, but why would someone slash clothes and recipes then simulate blood on the clothes and put wasps in in the car of a person who is very allergic? The actions seem sadistic to me."

I frowned. "You're probably right, and both actions seem to be revenge. I could understand how a retired police officer might be a target, but I'm having trouble coming up with anyone that would need to take revenge against me."

"You're thinking like a normal person, and killers aren't normal." Barbara emptied the dryer then carried the basket of clean clothes to her bedroom.

While she folded clothes, Ned came into the living room where I sat as I read through the records in the folder. "I'm going to the gas station to fill up. I'll be back for you in a bit."

Roxie dashed ahead of him to the door, and Colonel trotted along behind Ned.

"Not this time." Ned slipped out the door before Roxie could dart past him.

Roxie flopped down near the door, and Colonel relaxed at my feet while I spread out the papers on the sofa.

My phone rang as Barbara came into the living room.

"It's Francine," I said.

"What does she want?" Barbara sniffed.

I shrugged as I answered.

"Hi, Karen. I just heard about the damage to your belongings at your house, and I was absolutely shocked. I understand it will be weeks before you'll be able to move back in. I was worried about where you were staying, but I'm sure you have plenty of friends besides Shirley to stay with. Shirley has her hands full with Woody and his cat."

"It was nice of you to call, and I'm fine."

"Well, you're certainly welcome to stay with me, but you have those big dogs, and I'm allergic." She laughed. "Or are they being boarded at the kennel, so you can stay at the hotel?"

"The kennel is a good suggestion for me to be able to stay at the hotel; I hadn't thought of that, thank you."

"You're welcome. I saw your car was in the sheriff's lot for a while. Do you need a ride anywhere? I'd be happy to pick you up."

"Thank you; I'll let you know if I need a ride."

"Be sure to give me plenty of notice, so I can rearrange hair appointments."

"Will do. Thanks again for calling." I hung up.

"What did Francine want?"

"Fodder for gossip is my best guess. She was fishing about where I was staying, whether the dogs were boarded, and how I was getting around."

"From what I heard, she didn't get even a nibble," Barbara said.

"I guess it's just me, but her questions really rubbed me the wrong way; they were very intrusive."

Barbara smiled. "I was impressed by how subtly you told her you were fine, and it was none of her business."

"She did make me think, though. Maybe I should ask the sheriff about leaving my minivan at the department lot. She said she saw it there, and if there is someone else roaming around who might be looking for me, they could easily find my car at your house or at the campground. I'll ask Ned when he gets back from his secret mission."

"You caught that too?" Barbara giggled. "Have you noticed David is still hiding in the garage? I thought I'd make a fresh pot of coffee for our intrepid co-conspirators. Care for some coffee or tea while you read?"

"Coffee sounds great."

As I finished reading through the bank records, my phone rang. *Giana?*

"Ms. O'Brien? Thanks for picking up; I'm sure you recognized Mama's number. I'm Alessandria, Mama and Papa's oldest daughter." Alessandria's voice was raspy.

"Please excuse me, I have a bit of a cold. Mama left her phone with me and asked me to call you. Mama and Papa left town for an undisclosed location after finding a dead raccoon in their backyard early this morning. Someone had tossed poisoned food over their fence, probably late yesterday afternoon, and the target must have been their old dog, but Papa's dog is a persnickety Pekingese, according to Mama, and won't eat anything that isn't in her special food bowl. Evidently the raccoon found it in the middle of the night and ate it. Mama thinks it may have been strychnine because the raccoon didn't finish eating it, and…"

Alessandria paused and cleared her throat. "Sorry, it was a disturbing find. Mama and Papa want you to be very careful, and Mama asks you to forgive her for pulling you into this. She discovered another small file of papers that wasn't included in the folder she gave you. I've asked a friend I trust to drop off the file at your donut shop tomorrow."

Alessandria hung up.

I shuddered. *Strychnine is a very painful death.*

CHAPTER FIFTEEN

Barbara carried two cups of coffee to the living room. "What's wrong?"

I shook my head. *I won't mention the new file.* "I received a very disturbing call from Giana and Papa's oldest daughter, Alessandria. Someone tried to poison Papa's Pekingese. They're very concerned for their own safety and left town."

"That's absolutely horrible. Who would want to do such a thing?" A tear slipped down Barbara's cheek. "Giana and Papa gave you those records, didn't they? Do you think that's why Giana apologized?"

Barbara sat next to me, and we sipped our coffee in silence.

When Ned parked in front of the house, I opened the front door while Barbara went to the door to the garage and said, "Ned's here."

"Refills?" David asked when he came inside.

"Yes, please," Barbara said.

David brought two coffee mugs and the coffee pot to the living room and refilled our cups then filled the two mugs.

"What's going on?" Ned asked when he stepped onto the porch.

"We have fresh coffee; come sit," I said.

"You first," Barbara added.

"Okay, mine's quick; you were right, Karen, they've arrested Richard. Your turn."

"I knew it." I told them about Alessandria's phone call but left off the information about the new file that I hadn't told Barbara. *I'll tell Ned later.*

Ned's face darkened. "You know what strikes me about the attacks?"

"How cruel they are?" David asked.

"Besides that, none of the attacks are direct," I said, and Ned nodded.

Barbara rose from the sofa and paced. "Cruel, vindictive, and cowardly."

"Ned, how would you catch a vicious animal?" I asked.

He squinted. "One of the most conniving animals that I know is the alligator. When it's nesting season, they'll put sticks and feathers inside their mouths and keep their mouths open. Birds spot the perfect nesting material, and the alligator chomps down. The best way to catch an alligator is with bait and a good snatch hook to keep it from getting away then shoot it."

I frowned. *Alligator?* "What happens when you shine a bright light in an alligator's eyes?"

"That's one way to find alligators," Ned said. "If you shine a light across the surface of a lake, pond, or swamp, you'll see the glowing red dots of what wildlife experts call eye shine from the alligators' eyes."

Can I use this? I gazed out the window. *The better question is how.*

"Karen, what are you thinking?" Ned asked.

"I'm trying to put all the pieces together."

"Tell me later," he said.

I nodded. "After I make sense of everything."

"Are you ready to go to the campground?" he asked.

I nodded. "I think we should ask the sheriff if I can leave my car at the sheriff's department. It won't take me but a minute or two to pack my new clothes."

"I'll send the sheriff a text; once again, I wish I'd thought of it."

"I'm not sure there's room in the suitcase. I started a small box of things, and there's plenty of room for your new clothes," Barbara said.

Ned's phone buzzed a text. "Sheriff agrees. We'll take your minivan to their secure lot. Ernie is waiting at the parking lot for you."

"We're going to the trailer, Mia, are you going?" I asked.

She dashed into her carrier, and I zipped it up.

"I'm ready." David carried out the suitcase and the extra box and put them into the truck bed while Ned put Mia's carrier on the passenger's seat. Ned opened the back door, and Colonel leapt in before Roxie and grinned.

Roxie hopped in, and I giggled. "You let him win for once, didn't you?"

Roxie yipped then curled up on her half of the seat.

"We'll follow you, hon," Ned said.

I climbed into my minivan with my backpack and headed to the sheriff's department. After I parked, Ernie took my minivan keys then saluted Ned, who nodded.

Ned helped me into his truck, then we headed to the campground.

"I bought some groceries on my way back to Barbara's," Ned said. "I originally planned on just a few things, but my list expanded to the staples, according to the women who advised me as I went from one aisle to the next. We can start a list after you have a chance to see what we have, and I can shop tomorrow while you work."

I smiled. "I used to love to plan menus in advance, but it didn't make sense for one person. I'll enjoy cooking again, and it will be nice to have meals together."

"I thought we could invite Barbara and David to have supper with us tonight. I bought steaks, potatoes, salad stuff, and ice cream bars. I'll grill the steaks if you'll take care of the potatoes and salad."

Colonel and Roxie explored the trailer's small yard; I carried Mia into the trailer while Ned carried in bags of groceries.

"You don't have to live out of a suitcase," Ned said. "You can put your clothes away."

I stepped up the stairs, peeked at the bedroom, and smiled. "You didn't put your sheets back on your bed."

"Nope, I liked the sofa bed and decided that's where I'd sleep; I was kind of hoping you'd be back soon."

I smiled. "I'll put away the groceries, so I can start a list," I said.

Ned whistled as he left to bring in the rest of the bags. After he set them on the island, he went back out for the suitcase and the box. He brought in the suitcase first and sat it on the first step to the bedroom. "Do me a favor: when you want to go between the trailer and your house after it's ready, keep some clothes here, so we don't have to lug this overweight bag back and forth."

"That's a great idea; I could leave all the clothes here that Barbara gave me and buy new clothes as I need them to have at my house."

He lifted the bag to the top step then slid it into the bedroom before he left for the small box.

As he put the small box in the bedroom, I finished putting away the groceries and had a short list.

Ned peered over my shoulder. "It doesn't look like there is anything critical."

"You're right; thanks for getting the wine; it's our favorite," I said.

He nodded. "I asked David, and he said that was what you and Barbara like best. Do you want some time to read over the bank records?"

"No, I've been through what I have. I need to be outside; why don't we hike that trail you talked about?"

"Colonel and Roxie will love it. What about Mia?"

"She won't want to go on a hike, but the shadows are in my bedroom; she might like to be out of her carrier. I'll set the water bowl under the dining table for now and put her litter box in my small bathroom; she'll like that."

Ned filled the water bowl half full while I set her litter box under the sink in my small bathroom. Ned unzipped her carrier.

"We're going to be here with Ned a few days," I said. "The shadows are here too; we're going to take Colonel and Roxie for a walk if you want to explore the trailer."

We went outside, and Ned locked the trailer and his truck then waved at the neighbor across the street. "Captain, Donut Lady, Colonel, and Roxie will be staying with me until at least Thursday.

We don't expect any company unless the mayor and his wife come to supper tonight."

The man smiled. "It would be nice to see David and Barbara. I've known them for years. I already met Colonel and Roxie. Nice to meetcha, Donut Lady. My friends and I are big fans of yours. It's nice you can get a little campground relaxation because we all know how hard you work."

I felt my cheeks warm as I smiled. "Thank you."

Colonel and Roxie trotted on the trail ahead of us. "Is your neighbor a retired captain?" I asked.

"He should be, but he isn't. He's a master tugboat captain. They still call him in when they have a difficult problem."

"There's a little more to Alessandria's phone call that I didn't mention earlier because I didn't want to add to Barbara's worries, but you knew."

He nodded.

"Alessandria told me Giana found a small file that wasn't included in the records she gave me. Alessandria didn't tell me how the file was overlooked, and I didn't ask. Alessandria asked a friend of hers to deliver the file to me at the shop tomorrow. I'm hoping it has the missing information about the fourth bank account, but I'm afraid to let my hopes get too high."

"I didn't expect to hear anything like that," he said.

"I didn't either." I listened to a mockingbird as he claimed his territory.

"There's more. I've had two nightmares this week. One included fire and bees, and the second one had an alligator. The details aren't important, but I am almost afraid to go to sleep."

Ned stopped and took me into his arms. "Bees and an alligator? The bees are clear, and the poison for Papa's dog easily correlates to the alligator setting a trap for unsuspecting birds, doesn't it? You're afraid you're the next target, and you won't understand the meaning of the nightmare until it's too late; at least, that's what scares me."

I leaned against Ned, listened to his strong heartbeat, and relaxed.

"I want to do this always."

"What?" Ned asked.

I gazed at his face. "I didn't mean to say it out loud. I want to lean against your chest and listen to your heart always."

He met my gaze. "Pinky swear?"

I smiled. "Pinky swear."

He kissed me then shouted, "Hot damn!"

The dogs raced back to us, and I laughed. "Colonel and Roxie want to know what's going on."

"I want to hear you tell them."

I took his face with my hands and kissed him. "We are going to be married."

"Isn't that something? What do you think, Colonel?" Ned asked.

Colonel howled, and Roxie cocked her head as she stared at Colonel then barked as he howled.

We strolled back to the trailer with our arms around each other's waists. I watched Ned's feet then finally figured out his stride as we walked in step.

When we reached the trailer, the captain said, "I heard the howling. What's the occasion?"

"Donut Lady asked me to marry her."

I elbowed Ned in the ribs, and he said, "Ow. I mean, Donut Lady has graciously accepted my proposal of marriage."

"Congratulations, you two." The captain pumped Ned's hand then grabbed my hand and patted it.

Roxie barked, and the captain chuckled. "I stand corrected; congratulations to you all."

Colonel grinned then dashed to Ned's trailer.

"I guess we'll need to tell Mia too," Ned said.

I nodded. "Unless we can be as secretive as Amber, we've got a slew of people to tell."

"Sheriff first?" Ned asked as he opened the door for Colonel and Roxie.

"Yes, then I'll ask Barbara and David to come to supper here."

"What about Woody, Gee, and Darlene?"

I paced. "And Andrew."

"Sheriff, Barbara, and David today; Andrew in the morning, and Darlene after lunch, then you and Darlene can call or text Gee. I don't know how to catch Woody though: after school?" Ned stopped me mid-pace and hugged me. "You know everybody will ask when."

I snorted. "Was that supposed to help me relax?"

"It sounded better in my head because now I'm panicked. Want to pace together?" he side-glanced me.

I giggled and tugged on his hand to sit with me on the sofa. "Mia, Ned and I are going to be married."

Mia marched down the stairs and waved her tail while the shadows swirled behind her.

Ned grinned. "Glad you all approve, thanks."

"Let's simplify. I'll invite Barbara and David here for steaks, and you text the sheriff. After we tell Barbara and David, I'll text Gee and Darlene at the same time."

"How could you tell Woody today?" Ned asked.

"I'll text Shirley. Maybe we could pick him up if she and Alfred would like a little time together, and I'll tell Andrew in the morning."

"What about Shirley? Won't you want to tell her yourself?" Ned asked.

"That's tricky. It's not fair to ask Woody to keep a secret. I'll ask Shirley if they would like to come see your trailer. I'll ask Shirley not to mention it to anyone before Tuesday, and she'll be able to last the rest of the day, at least."

"Let's have lunch first, then if we still like our plan, we can put it into motion."

"Perfect. I'll make you a sandwich, and I'll have an apple. Can we eat outside?"

"Of course, we can; we're camping." Ned smiled.

While we ate, I said, "My house is supposed to be ready by the end of the week. I just realized we could alternate between my house and the trailer; maybe we could stay at my house during the week then come to the trailer on the weekends. I'll ask Darlene for furniture for my spare bedroom."

"I checked, and there is no waiting period after a marriage license is issued. It used to be three days, but the law was changed not long ago. If we picked up our license tomorrow, we could be married any time, even tomorrow, then stay at your house during the week after it's ready to make it more convenient for you to get to work and relax at the trailer on weekends," Ned said.

I frowned. "It take time to plan a wedding." *The more planning time that Gee, Darlene, and Barbara have, the more elaborate the wedding will be.*

I smiled. "Maybe getting married soon wouldn't be so bad after all because if we give Gee, Darlene, and Barbara too much time to plan, I'll be wearing a lacy princess dress with my best western boots, and you'll be stuck in an uncomfortable tuxedo. Who will be your best man?"

"Sheriff and Woody. Who will be your maid of honor?"

I rolled my eyes. "Gee, Darlene, Shirley, and Barbara, and David and Andrew will give me away."

"So, who will attend the wedding that isn't in the wedding party?" Ned peered at me.

I gazed at the ground in thought. *Good question.* "The killer."

"Nice. A wedding is the perfect bait for a killer."

"Thank you."

"I was being sarcastic," he growled then finished his sandwich in one bite.

I took a bite to hide my smile. *It is still a perfect idea.*

After I finished my apple, I said, "You're right; we don't want to ruin the wedding. How about an engagement celebration party? I'll get Barbara on it today."

"We are not having a killer engagement party." Ned frowned. "That came out a little strange, didn't it?"

I giggled. "Barbara will find the perfect invitations. Are we going to get our marriage license tomorrow as soon as I get off work, or maybe I can scoot out in the middle of the morning while my crack crew takes care of the shop."

"The middle of the morning would be best because I was wondering how we'd manage Colonel, Roxie, and Mia while we did the paperwork."

"What do you think about our engagement plan? Should we start texting?" I asked.

"It's a good plan. I'll text the sheriff."

"I'll text Barbara and Shirley." I sent the two texts then carried Ned's plate and our glasses inside, and Colonel and Roxie followed me. While I washed dishes, Colonel and Roxie drank their fill of water then fell asleep in front of the sofa. I received two texts and checked them after I dried my hands.

Barbara replied, "Six o'clock is great. Will bring dessert."

I smirked. *I knew that.*

Shirley replied, "Three of us will be there in an hour."

When I joined Ned outside, he said, "No dogs?"

"They're snoozing. I heard back from Barbara and Shirley. Barbara and David will be here with dessert at six."

Ned nodded. "We knew that. We'll have ice cream this week for emergencies."

"Exactly. Shirley, Woody, and Alfred will be here in about an hour."

"Too bad we don't have any cookies or anything," Ned said.

"Good idea." I hurried into the camper, turned on the oven to preheat and pulled out the ingredients for peanut butter cookies.

Ned came inside. "You're going to bake cookies? I was thinking I'd make a run to the store."

"You can, if you want to, but mine will be tastier."

Ned sat on his chair. "I'll take care of the dishes when you're finished; meanwhile, I'll watch the master baker do her magic."

When I pulled the first batch of cookies out of the oven, I glanced at Ned and smiled at my napping protector. After I pulled out my last batch, Ned said, "Are you done already?"

"Sure am. They just need to cool before we put them on a plate, and I made enough to freeze for later."

"Go unpack, and I'll wash dishes."

I opened the suitcase and removed my sheets then quickly made the bed. *I'd forgotten I'd stuck Giana's folder in there.* I put the folder in the drawer next to the bed then pulled out a pair of pants and squinted at them.

Ned furrowed his brow when I stood on the bottom step holding the pants. "What's wrong?"

"I hate this, but I'm going to have to try on all of the clothes that Barbara gave me because there's no sense in putting them away if I can't wear them."

"I'm sorry, hon, but I agree with you."

I snickered. "Thanks for sympathy and for the inadvertent joke. I needed both of them."

"Happy to oblige," Ned smiled. "How long will it take you?"

"Forever." I hurried back to the large suitcase, and as I tried on clothes, I flipped them into one of two piles: keep or return to Barbara.

When I heard the car stop in front of the trailer, I hung up the last shirt that I planned to keep and closed the suitcase with all the clothes to be returned then joined Ned on his way out after he opened the door for Colonel and Roxie.

"What do you think?" I asked as Woody climbed out of Alfred's car. His eyes were wide as he stared at the trailer.

"It's as big as a house, Miss Lady. I was worried it would be tiny like a tent."

"The campground is nicely groomed," Alfred said. "It looks like an exclusive resort."

"I've driven past it so many times," Shirley said. "I didn't know they had a security guard at the gate. It has a pool, right? When the weather gets warmer, we'll have to visit you."

"Have a seat." Ned smiled as he motioned toward the extra canvas camp chairs he had set up.

"We have iced tea, milk, and cookies," I said.

"Homemade cookies," Ned added, and Alfred smiled and nodded.

"Sweet tea for us and milk for Woody," Shirley said.

"Cookies go with milk; it's the cookie rule, right Miss Lady?"

I smiled. "If it isn't, it should be."

I relaxed while Shirley talked about the house she and Alfred were buying.

"I liked it," Woody said. 'My room is big, and there's lots of room for Chase to explore."

"Can we peek inside the trailer?" Shirley asked.

"Absolutely," Ned said. "We'll give you the grand tour."

He led Woody and Alfred into the trailer, and Shirley grabbed my arm and whispered, "You look happy. It's about time."

She climbed the steps into the trailer, and I followed her.

"What do you think?" Ned asked as Woody hopped down the steps from the bedroom.

Shirley and Alfred sat on the sofa, and Woody sat on my chair.

"Really comfortable," Alfred said.

"We have something to tell you that we'd like to keep quiet for a few days," I said.

"I asked Karen to marry me, and she accepted," Ned said.

Woody whooped, Alfred shook Ned's hand, and Shirley smirked, "I knew it. All you needed to do was to get that terrible gray in your hair covered; I don't know how long it would have taken for you to be engaged if it weren't for me."

I stared at her with my mouth open, and Ned chuckled.

Alfred whispered to Shirley, and she stared at him as he nodded.

"I'm not sure what I said, Karen, but Alfred said I need to apologize," Shirley said, and Alfred rolled his eyes.

"Thank you," I said.

"Aunt Gee is visiting Tiffany and Roger; how are you going to tell her, and what about Andrew?" Woody asked.

"I'll send a text to Aunt Gee and Ms. Darlene this evening, so they can call me if they want to talk, and I'll tell Andrew first thing in the morning. That's why I'd like for you all not to mention it to anyone before Tuesday, but I wanted to tell you before you went to school this week because sometimes it's hard to catch you."

Woody's eyes misted. "Thank you, Miss Lady. You have always been my best friend."

I brushed away a tear. "I know; you too."

"When's the wedding?" Shirley asked. "I know, it's an obvious question, but I just now thought of it."

"Thursday," Ned said at the same time I said, "We don't know yet."

Alfred laughed. "You two have obviously talked this over and have options."

Shirley stared at Alfred. "I didn't understand that."

"It's okay; we need to go, so they can continue their discussion."

"Thank you again, Miss Lady." Woody rushed to me and gave me a hug, and I hugged him tight.

"I love you, man," he mumbled.

I smiled. "I love you too."

Ned handed Woody a small plastic bag filled with cookies, and Woody grinned.

After they left, Ned smiled. "Woody's at the awkward stage of trying to be an old kid while he hangs onto being a young kid, isn't he? I had to keep it inside, but he cracked me up when he said, love you, man. You got yourself a promotion there, man."

"I was really touched because I know how hard it was for him to say the words."

Ned shook his head. "Shirley's lucky to have you for her friend. She has no filters at all, does she?"

My eyes widened. "And you do?"

"Of course. You want a cookie?" He held out the plate that had two cookies left on it.

"No, thank you."

"Good." He shoved a cookie into his mouth before he picked up the second one and carried the plate inside.

Why didn't I realize when's the wedding would be an obvious question? I stared at the trees as the crows chased away a hawk.

I missed another obvious question. I followed Ned in.

"Do we know how Sicily was murdered?" I asked.

He widened his eyes. "Why didn't we think of that?"

He grabbed his phone and sat in his recliner. "Hey. That case you're working on. Is it public knowledge how she was murdered?"

I sat in my recliner to see if I could hear the conversation, but I couldn't understand the words. Mia jumped on my lap, and I stroked her back and cooed to her as she leaned against me then leapt off to chase the shadows back into the bedroom.

"Thanks." Ned hung up. "Public information: Sicily was stabbed in the chest with a sharp instrument; there was no murder weapon on the scene, and the investigators haven't identified the murder weapon yet, but the media reported it as a knife. An interesting preliminary detail from the autopsy is that she was drugged."

"That is interesting in a morbid kind of way, but there doesn't seem to be much to go on."

"No, other than the earlier partnership she had with Richard, and I don't think the investigation will find anything more recent as far as Richard is concerned."

"I hate to say it, but he did pick up the money from Francine," I said.

Ned groaned. "I'd forgotten about that."

"Where is my fireproof box? I thought I'd pull together the papers we'll need in the morning."

"It's on the floor of your closet. I'll gather my papers too. You need a manilla envelope and a tote?" He pulled out two envelopes from a drawer and gave me one then handed me a new tote bag.

"This is beautiful; I don't think I've ever seen a canvas tote with an underwater scene of sparkling blue water with fish swimming at different depths and a man and woman in a boat fishing. That's us, isn't it?" I kissed his cheek. "Thank you."

After I had all my documents, I put them into the envelope then stuck it into my new tote along with my wallet and the other papers from my older tote and backpack, so I would have everything together.

When I joined Ned, he said, "We should probably get ready for Barbara and David."

While I washed the salad vegetables, Ned put a tablecloth on the picnic table and fed the dogs then took them for a short walk. When they returned, I had added the last of my ingredients to the salad. Ned pulled out the steaks from the refrigerator to come to room temperature, which he claimed was critical for grilling then put the silverware and napkins in a basket on the dining table and stacked plates and salad bowls next to the basket.

I put the salad in the refrigerator as David parked in front of the trailer; Ned held out his hand, and I smacked a high five.

Roxie whined when she saw David come toward the door.

CHAPTER SIXTEEN

Ned invited David and Barbara into the trailer, and Barbara carried a bottle of our favorite wine and two wine glasses; David brought in a pie pan covered with foil and a large tote then leaned down to pet Roxie after he set down the pie pan and the tote.

"We bought ice cream on our way here and have wine, chips and dip, and dessert," David said. "I'll open the wine."

Ned put the ice cream in the freezer before he filled two glasses with ice then poured the sweet tea. He set the glasses on the dining table and put a small table in front of the sofa after Barbara and I sat together.

After David poured the wine, he handed us our glasses then put the tortilla chips and dip on the small table. Ned pulled the two dining chairs closer to the table in front of the sofa.

"Tell us about the house," I said.

Barbara's eyes twinkled. "We drove from the Donut Hole to the house, so we'd know how long to allow to get to work, then we drove around the area and by the house several dozen times."

"I'm grateful that you invited us to dinner because we'd have driven past the house and circled back until we ran out of gas," David said.

"This dip is great." Ned broke a tortilla chip in half then scooped up dip with it before he popped the chip into his mouth.

"Spinach and sweet Vidalia onion dip." David scooped as much as he could with a chip. "Barbara's own recipe, and my favorite."

Ned scooped into the dip with the other half of his chip and gazed in appreciation at his chip before he put it into his mouth and went outside to check the heat on the fire by holding his hand two inches above the grate. "Fire's ready."

David handed the platter with the steaks to Ned who dropped the steaks onto the sizzling grate. David carried out the plates and basket, and held the door for Barbara, who had the two glasses of sweet tea in her hands. I followed her with our wine glasses and the bottle of wine under my arm, and the dogs followed me.

"Anything else to bring out?" David asked.

"We won't know until we sit down," I said.

"It's the picnic rule," Barbara said, "Let's sit."

Ned put a steak on the cutting board he had next to his grill, then placed a steak on David's plate then one on his.

"I thought you two would want to share a steak. I'll cut it after it's rested."

"Let's begin with salad; Barbara, serve yourself then pass the bowl to David."

After David slid the salad bowl to me, I served myself and handed it to Ned as Barbara asked, "What have y'all been up to?"

I smiled. "We'll talk over dessert. I'm going to get myself a glass of sweet tea. Care for a glass, Barbara? Any refills?"

"Can you juggle two glasses and a pitcher of tea?" Ned asked.

I chuckled then returned with two glasses with ice and the pitcher.

Ned grinned as I poured sweet tea. When Ned and David finished their salads, Ned cut the waiting steak in half then served Barbara and me our steaks.

"This is beautiful," Barbara cut a small bite. "Mmm. Really good." She inhaled. "Someone has a woodfire; love the ambiance."

Someone at the far end of the campground strummed a guitar and sang a song I didn't recognize.

Ned smiled. "We have a young man who is a songwriter. All the songs he sings are his originals."

"I'm officially in love with camping," Barbara said. "This is really relaxing, isn't it?"

I ate half my steak. "I guess I'm having a steak salad for lunch tomorrow."

"That sounds good, I have to leave room for dessert, so I'll do the same," Barbara said.

"The breeze has died down, and it's getting buggy. Do we want to have dessert in the trailer?" I asked.

"I do." Barbara smacked a mosquito on her arm. David and Ned brought in the dishes, and I washed them while Ned made coffee, and Barbara wrapped up our leftovers.

After I dished up the warm peach pie, and Barbara scooped up ice cream, we sat around the small table and ate.

"What was your day like?" Barbara asked.

"Nothing special," Ned's eyes twinkled as he continued, "Donut Lady begged me to marry her."

"I did not, you Wildlife Ruffian," I fumed as I threw my napkin at him.

My napkin floated down and covered Mia, who had been sleeping at my feet. Ned and David laughed, and Barbara snickered. Mia hissed at me as she came out from under the napkin, then she darted to the top of the stairs and glared at me.

I tried to maintain my composure but giggled. "That wasn't quite as dignified as I had planned."

"When?" Barbara asked, and I glared at Ned.

"We haven't really decided on a date," Ned said. "We're going to pick up the license tomorrow. We thought maybe Karen could take a break from the Donut Hole, and we'd go to the courthouse."

"We could be married any time after we pick up the license. We'd like for the wedding to be small," I said.

"Small like us, Gee and Darlene, Sheriff and Emma, Woody, Shirley, Alfred, Andrew, Kim, and Randy, Josh, Jorge, all the deputies, Tess, Mary Rose, Sully, Gus, Devlin and her chef, and the rest of the town?"

I laughed. "That's our dilemma. I was thinking maybe we could have an engagement party before the wedding. That will take off a little pressure."

"I think it might, then you could elope without going anywhere. Gee, Darlene, and I can pull off a party on Thursday after school, then the party can't go late. We can have hors d'oeuvres, punch, and sweet tea, and an engagement cake made of cupcakes, which keeps anyone from being tied up trying to slice and serve cake."

"When are you ready for your engagement to be public knowledge?" David asked.

"I'll text Darlene and Gee this evening, then I'd like to tell Andrew in the morning. We invited Shirley, Alfred, and Woody to the campground earlier today, and Ned texted the sheriff."

Barbara nodded. "It makes sense that you would want Woody to know right away."

David added, "You've always been his best friend, and the sheriff has always been there right by your side."

I nodded. "His mother was one of my few friends when I lived here as a child. I never fit in very well with the popular crowd."

"Well, you are the leader of the popular crowd now because that's us. Text Darlene and Gee right away, so I know I can start planning with them as soon as I get home," Barbara said.

While I composed my text, Barbara said, "Okay, Ned. 'Fess up: how did the engagement really happen?"

"Karen's version might be more accurate," Ned said.

I snorted. *You dodged that one.*

"Okay, text is sent. Barbara, I told them you'd have all the details tomorrow. I'll fill you in after you and David come to work, but I can assure you I was not the one who was begging."

Ned snorted but pursed his lips when David cleared his throat.

"I'm taking the rest of my steak, half the pie, and the ice cream home with me," Barbara said.

"I went through the clothes you gave me; there were a few things that didn't fit at all; you can take your suitcase with those clothes home with you."

"I'll be right back." Ned returned with the suitcase and set it near the door. "It almost feels empty."

David picked it up. "I think we're ready to go. Can I carry anything for you, honey?"

"I have everything in the tote, so I'm fine." Barbara hugged me then Ned. "I'm really happy for you two." She brushed away a tear then went outside with David behind her.

After they left, Ned hugged me. "Are we okay?"

I snuggled against his chest. "Yes."

"Good," he whispered. "I love you, Donut Lady."

"Good thing because I love you too, Wildlife Ruffian."

He chuckled. "That was so good; is Mia still mad at you?"

"She'll pout the rest of the day, but she'll be okay tomorrow." I yawned.

"Let's go for a walk, then you can call it a night."

As the four of us walked around the campground, we stopped when Colonel and Roxie beelined to the children who asked, "Can I pet your dogs?"

After we returned to the trailer, Ned chuckled. "That's the longest it's ever taken me to take a stroll around the campground. Colonel and Roxie certainly are popular. Did you notice they didn't approach any of the children who seemed a little cautious? They let the child approach them. How did you train them to do that?"

"Colonel must be a natural because he's always been like that; I'm impressed that he trained Roxie. I don't think she had much exposure to people until she joined us."

When we were inside, Ned hugged me then gazed at my face while he stroked my hair. "I miss your gray hair."

I smiled. "Sometimes you touch my heart by saying the strangest things, thank you."

I gathered my shower things, and Ned, Colonel, and Roxie accompanied me to the bathhouse. After we returned to the trailer, Ned and I kissed good night. When I went to my bedroom, Mia hissed at me then dashed down the stairs.

* * *

I woke the next morning to the bubbling sound of perking coffee. I quickly dressed then joined Ned, who stood at the stove with an empty frying pan in his hand.

"Good morning, hon, that green shirt looks nice on you." Ned poured two cups of coffee and handed me one. "I thought I'd try my hand at making breakfast burritos as a surprise, but it sounded easier in my head because I don't know where to start. You can take over anytime you want, and I'll run take a shower, except I hate to leave you alone."

"Thanks for the compliment." I smiled then kissed his cheek. "Colonel and Roxie can stay with me; we'll be fine, and I'd love to make breakfast burritos."

He exhaled in relief as he gathered his shower things. "I won't be long."

When he returned, Colonel and Roxie met him at the door. "I guess I'm taking them for a walk before breakfast. We'll be close."

I slid the burritos into the oven to give the tortillas a bit of a crunch then made up my bed before Ned and the dogs returned.

Mia wandered to the kitchen to supervise as Ned fed the dogs. After Colonel and Roxie finished eating, Mia meowed, and I fed her, then Ned and I sat at the table for our breakfast.

I gazed at the soft lights around the campground. "This is really a beautiful way to start a day, isn't it? What are your plans for today?"

"If you think you'll be okay at the Donut Hole without me hanging around until we leave for the courthouse, I'd like to catch the sheriff before his day gets too busy. I won't be long"

"I'll be fine. There are too many people who pop into the shop even before we're officially open for a killer to slip in unnoticed."

Ned narrowed his eyes. "What if it's someone you know?"

I sipped my coffee while I considered his question then watched as the shadows slid down the stairs from the bedroom and waited at the door. "The shadows will tell me."

Ned glanced at them and sighed. "Maybe. I'm really sorry I can see them because I'd like to tell you that's crazy, but I almost agree with you."

I smirked. "I almost appreciate it."

Ned laughed and rose to pour more coffee. "I have to remember you listen to what I say. I can't slip anything past you."

After I finished my coffee, I rose to clear the table, and Ned said, "You cooked; besides, it's my turn to do the dishes."

I selected one of Barbara's sweatshirts and picked up my backpack and the new tote. When I joined Ned, he had finished the dishes.

I scanned the trailer. "Mia, where are you? We're going to work. Are you going with us?"

She meowed, and I giggled as I peered into her carrier. "I'm glad you're going with us; I know Andrew will be happy to see you."

Ned zipped up her carrier then carried it to his truck. After Colonel and Roxie hopped into their seats, and I was situated in the passenger's seat, Ned handed me the carrier. I slid my tote under my seat then placed Mia's carrier on top of the backpack.

When we went into the Donut Hole, Andrew looked up from his mixer. "Hello, everybody."

Ned handed me my backpack and unzipped the carrier, and Mia raced to Andrew then head-butted his shin.

"Thanks, Mia," Andrew said. "I looked forward to seeing you too."

"Andrew, before I get too involved with work, Ned and I have something to tell you."

Andrew turned off his mixer and nodded. "That's good. You'll be happy."

"What?" I asked.

"I'll let you tell me," he said.

I glanced at Ned, who shrugged. "Ned asked me to marry him, and I said yes."

Andrew nodded. "Good."

"You already knew?" I asked. "How?"

"I thought everybody knew. It only made sense. Did you tell Woody?"

"We talked to him yesterday."

Andrew turned on his mixer, and I washed my hands then went into my office for my ballcap and apron; Ned followed me.

"Andrew said everybody knew. I didn't. Did you know?"

Ned kissed me. "I hoped."

I rolled my eyes. "Do you think anyone will be surprised?"

"Nope. I won't be gone long. Do me a favor and lock the door when I leave."

After I locked the door, I asked, "What's our plan for today?"

"Methodist Men at nine, like usual. One of the founding members' birthday is today, so they requested an older than dirt donut, and of course, we'll have our pink-sprinkled donut."

"How fun. Do you have any scone ideas?"

"Woody bought a huge supply of short, straight pretzels. He said you'd have an idea."

I squinted. "Wrinkles and bones. I'll think about it, but I'll come up with something, and Kim can make cranberry-orange scones."

I mixed my scones and rolled out a small batch thinner than usual then placed pretzels on one scone and covered the pretzels with a second thin scone. Colonel faced the front door and growled in a soft, low growl. I glanced at the window, and it was completely darkened by the shadows inside the shop. I squinted at what appeared to be a dark figure at the door, then the dark figure hurried away. I shrugged then slipped the pan with my four scones into the oven.

Andrew and I were so focused on our work, the tap on the door startled both of us. I smiled as I looked up then hurried to unlock the door for Ned.

"You two are definitely heads-down. What's the plan for today?"

"The Methodist Men are planning a birthday party," I said as Kim came into the shop.

"I'm making our older than dirt donut, and Miss Lady is making wrinkles and bones scones," Andrew said.

"Is there a recipe for wrinkles and bones?" Kim asked.

"There will be as soon as you taste the four I made and tell me what you think," I said.

"Ms. Kim, your assignment for today is to make cranberry-orange scones."

Kim nodded then hurried to the storeroom. When she joined us with her apron and ballcap, she said, "I've read the cranberry-orange recipe in the book, so I'll be fine, but I want to learn how to make wrinkles and bones."

"Can I tell Ms. Kim, Miss Lady?" Andrew asked.

Ned grinned, and I said, "Of course."

"Miss Lady and Mr. Ned are getting married just like we thought."

"That is wonderful news. We are really happy for both of you. Do you have any plans in place yet?" Kim asked.

"No," Ned said.

I smiled. "Our plan is to turn everything over to Barbara, Gee, and Darlene."

"Best plan ever, isn't it?" Andrew asked, and Kim smiled.

"How are your scones going?" Ned asked.

"I just pulled out the first four; how do they look?"

Ned frowned. "They look all wrinkly."

"Yes!" Andrew pumped his arm, and I giggled.

"Perfect, now the taste test."

Ned took a big bite. "I think I just broke something." He crunched as he chewed. "I think I'm breaking bones. Do I want to know what's in them?"

"Would you believe small, desiccated mammals?" I asked.

"Yes." Ned guffawed.

Andrew applauded and laughed. "That was a funny joke."

"It sure was." Kim frowned as she examined her scone then took a bite. "I just crunched a bone. Very well done, Donut Lady."

"Don't go thinking I'm being nice or anything, but what can I do to help?" Ned said.

"Wash your hands, and you can put the pretzels on top of the scones, then I'll put on the tops, and you can help me make wrinkles."

Ned grinned as he washed his hands. "Is that like growing old together?"

I smiled. "Exactly."

While Kim mixed her scones, I put our first large batch of scones into the oven.

While my second batch baked, I dusted the first batch of scones with a bit of powdered sugar.

"Your poor scones aren't just wrinkly, they look dried out and wrinkly," Kim said.

"Perfect," I said.

After I dusted the second batch, Ned asked, "Done?"

I nodded. "We would like to pick up our marriage license when Barbara and David arrive. They're meeting with Shirley then will be here."

"We can manage," Kim said.

"I'd worry about a snag with the offer at Shirley's office and that we would take longer than we thought. I'd rather wait," I said.

"As antsy as I am to get things done and not procrastinate, I agree," Ned added. "What else can I do?"

"Sit down and relax," Kim said. "If you continue pacing, you'll make me as nervous as you are, and I'm already married."

I poured Ned a cup of coffee, and he sat at the counter while I pushed the button on the large coffee machine.

The sheriff came into the shop, and Andrew put the sheriff's two donuts and a wrinkles and bones scone on a plate while Kim poured his coffee then returned to her scones.

The sheriff whispered to Ned, and Ned nodded.

"Karen, Emma wanted me to tell you how happy she is for you, and so am I. Congratulations to you both."

I felt my cheeks warm. "Thank you."

Ned grinned and winked, and my face felt like it was on fire.

"You made it worse," I hissed.

"We're really excited too." Kim smiled.

After Andrew set the sheriff's plate on the counter in front of him, the sheriff examined his donuts. "Monday's group is the Methodist Men, right? Is that the older than dirt donut? Haven't seen that in quite a while. What's the occasion?"

"Methodist Men are having a birthday party for one of their founding members," I said, and the sheriff chuckled.

"There's something wrong with my scone: it looks dried out and wrinkly." The sheriff squinted at his scone. "What did you call it?"

"Wrinkles and bones," I said.

"At least I have my pink-sprinkled donut." Sheriff bit into his scone. "Did I just bite into a bone? What's in this?"

Andrew laughed. "Miss Lady can tell you."

I smirked. "Small, desiccated mammals."

"That's disgusting," Sheriff said.

"Desiccated and disgusting. I like those words." Andrew snickered.

"Are you making cranberry orange scones, Kim?" Sheriff asked after he finished his scone.

"Unfortunately, I am. If we had gooey candies, I could call them blood and guts."

"Mama, I mean Ms. Kim, that is really smart," Andrew said.

After the sheriff left, Barbara and David came into the Donut Hole, and Roxie greeted David.

While he rubbed Roxie's face, David said, "We put in our offer; Shirley's actually a master negotiator. We have a great agent."

"We're ready to go, and Andrew and Kim know about our engagement," I said.

On our way to the courthouse, Ned said, "I talked to the sheriff earlier. There is no case against Richard, and the sheriff agreed to push for Richard to be released. The sheriff agreed with me that Richard was not a flight risk and expects him to be released today."

"I'm nervous about this." I peered at the courthouse, and my heart raced as Ned parked.

"I am too; if I faint at the counter, would you pick up my left hand and scribble where I'm supposed to sign?"

"Of course, I will, darling. I'm here for you." I giggled.

"Is darling a promotion?" he asked as we strolled into the courthouse together.

When we reached the county clerk's office, I paused and exhaled. "Okay, I'm ready."

Ned put his arm around me as we walked inside. A woman glanced up and smiled as she rose from her desk to meet us at the counter. "Were you hoping for a long line, Donut Lady?"

Ned smirked. "So much for sneaking off."

The woman giggled as she handed us a form. "This is the checklist of what we need, if you'd like to look it over; the process actually doesn't take very long if you have all the documentation."

After we left with our license in my new tote bag, Ned said, "I expected it to take much longer; I was really relieved we had all the paperwork."

"Amber's admin, Leah, pulled it all together when Amber was working on my appeal; otherwise, it would have taken me a week or two to request all the records from Ohio."

On our way to the Donut Hole, Ned said, "You might want to let the sheriff know we have our license."

I sent the sheriff a text, and he replied, "Expect entire town to know in five minutes."

My eyes widened, and I read the text to Ned. "Is that true?"

"Most likely. I didn't think about that, did you?"

I shook my head. *So much for keeping things quiet.*

As Ned passed the shop and searched for a parking spot, I said, "We're just in time for the Methodist Men."

"I think I'll join them," Ned said.

When we went into the shop, Barbara smiled. "Well?"

"It's probably public knowledge that we have a license," I said.

David's eyes twinkled. "Really?"

"Suppose I could join the Methodist Men today without upstaging the surprise?" Ned asked.

"You'd upstage the surprise more if you weren't in the room because somebody would have heard something on their way here, and they'd be whispering throughout the entire meeting. If you're there, we can announce your news at the beginning and still have our surprise," David said.

Ned glanced at me, and I nodded.

After the last two men hurried into the meeting room, David closed the door.

Barbara smiled. "Three, two, one."

The sound of applause and cheers erupted from the meeting room, and I giggled. "Better Ned than me. That's more attention than I could handle."

Barbara side-glanced Kim, and the two of them applauded, and Andrew cheered. The four customers who came into the shop applauded too. When a fifth customer came in, he joined in then asked, "Why are we clapping?"

One of the other customers shrugged, then Barbara whispered to the customer nearest the cash register, and he shouted over the cheers, "Donut Lady's getting married."

My face felt like fire as I sat at the counter, and Kim grinned as she poured me a cup of coffee. "Look at it this way. You won't have to worry about who knows and who doesn't."

"True." I pulled out my phone and sent the sheriff a text. "You were right."

"Before I forget," Kim added, "a mail carrier brought in a large envelope for you. It was registered mail or something, so I signed for it then put it in your top desk drawer."

David came out of the meeting room. "Karen, would you step in, please?"

I sighed.

"You can do this," Kim said. "Smile, nod, and thank them, then you can escape."

When I reached the door, David whispered, "Ned told them the two of you don't have a date yet."

As I walked in, the men applauded, and I smiled and nodded.

"Thank you so much for all the well wishes," I said. "Ned and I are very happy."

Ned beamed, and I continued to smile as they applauded and cheered; when I glanced at David, he opened the door. I fled the room with all the dignity I could muster, and David closed the door.

CHAPTER SEVENTEEN

I exhaled and hurried to the cash register as Shirley rushed into the shop with a poster in her hand.

"Woody made this sign yesterday. I forgot to give it to Barbara earlier."

After I set her to-go coffee on the counter, I read the sign and laughed.

Andrew handed Shirley her sack of pastries, and asked, "What does it say?"

I showed him as I read it. "Miss Donut Lady and Mr. Ned are getting married. Please celebrate with a donation to the Animal Shelter. It's signed Woody and Andrew."

Andrew grinned. "Can I put it in the window?"

"Absolutely. Shirley, please tell Woody how terrific his announcement is."

"I will. I called Alana at the shelter before I left my office, and she's bringing the large, ugly vase to collect any donations."

Alana came into the shop as Shirley dashed out.

"I got here as quickly as I could. Is on the reading table okay? We still have the donate sign Woody made for us."

She set the vase on the table then propped the sign against it and stood back. Colonel and Roxie trotted to the table and flopped down.

"Perfect, we even have security guards." Alana smiled.

"Coffee and a donut for the road?" Barbara asked.

"Of course, pink sprinkled for me, please. Make it a dozen donuts, so I can take some back with me to the shelter as a treat for our volunteers."

"My treat," I said.

"Got it," Barbara said.

As a steady stream of customers continued into the shop, I said, "I didn't expect so many customers today; I'll make vanilla scones."

"I can make a double batch of cinnamon and sugar cake donuts, Miss Lady." Andrew hurried to the storeroom for the ingredients.

"Kim and I can take care of our customers," Barbara said.

As the Methodist Men left the meeting room, they shook hands with Ned and waved at me. After they left the shop, a man pointed to the sign, and the men returned to drop money into the jar.

"Y'all are swamped," David said. "What do you need us to do?"

"Make more coffee and take over the dishwasher," Kim said.

"I'll take the dishwasher," Ned said.

David nodded and hurried to the storeroom for a second large coffee machine.

My phone buzzed a text from Richard, and I smiled when I read it. "Released thnx to sheriff and Ned. Good to have friends. Congrats to you and Ned."

I replied, "Yes, and thank you."

Toward the end of the morning, our crowd thinned.

"Does anyone have any idea how many people came into the shop?" Kim asked.

Before David went into the meeting room to clean, he strolled to the reading table. "Word really got around, didn't it? Did Alana bring the Animal Shelter jar? It's almost full; Ned and I will count the money, then Barbara and I can take it to the Animal Shelter after we close."

"We're leaving the sign and jar out all week, aren't we?" Kim asked.

"Yes," Andrew said.

Ned strode to the window and read the sign. "This is awesome. I'll help you clean the pink room, David."

After I cleaned the inside of the display case, I checked my phone. *Missed a call and a text from Francine.*

I opened the text and frowned.

"Something wrong?" Barbara asked.

"What's an updo?"

"A what?"

"I received a text from Francine earlier congratulating me, and she said she'd be happy to give me an updo for the wedding as a present from her, and she'll call me later to set up an appointment."

Barbara chuckled. "It's a fancy hairstyle with all your hair piled on top of your head. You don't want one for your wedding or anything else."

"Glad you knew what it was because I didn't, Barbara, and it definitely doesn't sound like Donut Lady's style," Kim said.

After I flipped the sign to closed, we finished cleaning, and David and Ned counted the money from the jar.

I hung up my apron and ballcap. When I opened my desk drawer, I found the envelope from the post office in its sealed, clear plastic bag and stuck it into my backpack before I headed to the front door.

"Before everyone leaves, Gee, Darlene, and I are planning an engagement party for Thursday," Barbara said. "Gee talked to the Methodist pastor yesterday, and Darlene will call the church office tomorrow because it's closed on Mondays. We're thinking the party can be from five thirty until eight, and we're planning on a light supper, which means nobody will leave hungry. I'll tell Darlene about the Animal Shelter because she might want to find another jar for them to have."

"I've been worried about your house, Miss Lady," Andrew said.

"I may be able to move some furniture into it on Thursday," I said.

"Good, so you'll be on vacation Thursday, Friday, and Saturday," Kim said.

"Yes," Andrew said.

"Yes," Ned echoed, and David chuckled.

"Unanimous," Barbara said.

I glared at them then sighed. "Okay, but I reserve the right to come in to work if I get bored."

"Granted," Ned said, "and I accept the challenge."

I giggled then cleared my throat. "I didn't mean to laugh; it sneaked past me."

"We'll lock up, Miss Lady," Andrew said.

Mia dashed to her carrier.

"You're really good at hiding, Mia." Ned zipped up her carrier, then Colonel and Roxie followed us to the truck.

On the way to the trailer, Ned asked, "Lunch at the trailer?"

"I'd love it."

Before we carried our lunch outside, I asked, "We're going to eat at the picnic table; anyone interested in going out with us?"

Colonel opened one eye then resumed his nap, and Roxie snuffled in her sleep.

"They had a busy morning," Ned said while we ate.

"Didn't we all? I didn't expect such a big commotion, but I guess I should have."

"I can't think of anyone I know in town that didn't show up," Ned said. "What's on the agenda for this afternoon? Feel like going for a ride?"

"That sounds nice. Where will we go?"

"I found a couple of cabins near a lake that isn't too far away from us; I thought we might enjoy driving around the lake then checking out the cabins."

"Are you giving up on your cabin in the mountains?"

"I'm more interested in a cabin that we'd be able to enjoy more often."

"You do owe me fishing lessons, and a cabin closer to us sounds much more convenient too. Lunch before we go?"

"Sounds great."

While I made sandwiches, Ned took Colonel and Roxie for a walk, and Mia hid in my bedroom with the shadows.

When they returned, Colonel stood at the trailer door, and when I opened it, he and Roxie came inside.

"Colonel thinks it's too hot out there, want to eat inside?" I asked.

Ned joined us in the trailer. "Colonel's not wrong. The humidity jumped up; I think our spring is trying to turn into summer."

After we ate, Ned asked, "We're going for a ride; are you going along?"

Colonel and Roxie rushed to the door.

"I didn't know if they'd go with us or not." Ned closed my door after he helped me into the truck.

"Colonel waited until you told him we were taking a ride," I said.

"Don't blame you, Colonel. It's getting too sticky and buggy for walks."

"Colonel and I walk to work before sunrise then walk home before the afternoon heat takes over. I've enjoyed the freedom of being outdoors."

"I've always thought that I wanted the freedom to travel with my trailer while I camped at one place after another, but now, I'm not so sure. The idea of having a cabin that we can call our own really appeals to me."

"I understand; I love the trailer, but a cabin really gives us more space, especially with the dogs and Mia. Are you sure you won't miss the travel?"

Ned chuckled. "The trailer gave me the freedom to avoid hotels when I was called to a town that needed my help with a wildlife problem. That has been the only traveling I've done. I've never had an itinerary to visit popular locations like a tourist who camps."

"When we were talking about a cabin, I was afraid you'd miss traveling, but I didn't realize you weren't so much traveling as working. So, if we have a cabin, would you still work as a wildlife consultant?"

"Probably like I do now: only when a friend calls, and that's only two or three times a year. I only came here because Sheriff and I go way back."

"I wouldn't mind doing that," I said. "We'd want to be sure our cabin has a place to park the trailer."

Ned nodded. "We could help an old friend if it sounded interesting or go fishing if it sounded boring."

As we traveled the country backroads, I leaned back and enjoyed the scenery. "Every time we go for a ride in the country, the corn looks taller."

When we reached the lake, Ned found a picnic area and parked.

Colonel and Roxie hopped out, then we walked a path that stayed close to the waterfront.

I pointed to the houses on the other side of the lake. "Those homes are beautiful, but they aren't cabins."

"No, they're close to the water for the view. Our view of the lake will be from our small fishing boat while we watch our lines for a tug. Have you ever cleaned a fish?"

I shook my head.

"Good. I've finally found something I can cook that you can't. I'll be in charge of cleaning and frying fish. Let's head back to the truck and see what we think about the cabins."

After we were in the truck, Ned handed me his phone. "That's the first cabin I found."

I read the listing and examined the pictures. "It has a large carport. It might be interesting to see whether it's big enough for the trailer and a boat."

"I've been thinking about my trailer. We might want to sell it; just a thought, but I can't pull a trailer and a boat."

"Makes sense to me."

My phone buzzed a text from the sheriff, and I smiled as I read it. "The sheriff said the investigators have released my house. I'll let Darlene know."

I texted Darlene, and she immediately replied, "On it."

Ned drove to the cabin. "What do you think?"

"The pictures didn't do it justice. I love how secluded it is in the woods, but it's not all that far from Asbury. What do you think about the carport?"

"Boat or trailer would fit nicely, but not both."

I read the listing again. "Two bedrooms and two baths, and the smaller bedroom would be a perfect office. There's plenty of room for the dogs."

"Let's look at the other one," Ned said.

When he pulled into the driveway then stopped, he handed me his phone with the listing.

"It's two bedrooms and two baths, but a little bigger than the other cabin. I think the great room may be bigger. We probably want to talk to Shirley about looking at them. What do you think?"

"I was hoping that would be what you'd say."

"I'll text the cabin addresses to Shirley."

Ned handed me his phone, and I sent the text to Shirley and included the addresses.

After we were back at the trailer, Shirley called me. "Both of those properties are vacant. We can see them anytime tomorrow, but I'd rather go in the morning, so we won't be rushed. Is that something you could do?"

"I think so, but I'll need to check with Kim and Barbara first. Can I call you back?"

"That's fine; just let me know what time." Shirley hung up, and I stared at my phone.

"What's wrong?" Ned asked.

"Shirley shifted to her business mode, and it was refreshing but a little scary. She wants us to see the cabins tomorrow morning."

Ned nodded. "I'd heard she's available for only morning appointments during the week, so she doesn't have to worry about picking up Woody from school on time. Weekends aren't a problem because Alfred and Woody have their time together."

"That's it. She's doubled up her business mode with mama mode. I'll check with Kim and Barbara; if either one of them is the least bit hesitant, I'll tell Shirley the weekend is better." I rolled my eyes. "Everything takes coordination around here, doesn't it?"

"I'll pour you a glass of sweet tea," Ned said. "Relax in your chair and make your calls." I sent separate texts to Kim and Barbara asking them to call me when they were available.

Barbara called first. *No surprise.*

"What's up? Did you already call nine-one-one?"

"There isn't an emergency. Ned and I looked at two cabins, and we can see them tomorrow morning, but it's not urgent. I wanted your opinion on whether I should leave the Donut Hole around ten or should we wait until the weekend?"

Ned waved as he went outside with Colonel and Roxie.

"Go. David and I don't have any conflict with being at the shop tomorrow at our usual time. If you wanted to leave at nine, that would be fine too, because the four of us can handle it."

After we hung up, Kim called. "We were in the barber shop. Are you okay?"

"Everything's fine." I told her about my conversation with Barbara. "What do you think?"

"I'll check with Andrew and call you right back."

Kim called back almost immediately. "There's only one group tomorrow. Andrew told me all the donuts and scones are made before seven thirty, and we don't see how we could be shorthanded, so go whenever you like."

"Thank you, I'll see you in the morning."

I called Shirley. "We can meet you at the cabins any time after nine."

"Good. We'll make it ten o'clock. I'll be at the one that is farthest from the state road. See you there."

When I went outside, Ned was sitting in his camp chair with Colonel at his feet, and Roxie was exploring under the grill in case Ned had dropped something for her.

"What's the verdict?" he asked.

"We'll meet Shirley at the cabin that's the farthest from the state road at ten. She's obviously already pulled their files."

"Sounds like it."

I sat in my camp chair that he'd placed closer to his. "I love the campground. If we don't find a cabin we like right off, I'd be perfectly content with the trailer here, and we could put our boat at the house." I smiled.

"That's definitely an excellent option." Ned reached for my hand and held it. "You know, we may find that a one-bedroom trailer suits us just fine, and we could even store the boat here. The campground has overflow parking where people store their boats."

I leaned my head on his shoulder. "I think seeing the cabins tomorrow will help us decide what we want to do."

"There is one thing we have to do tonight after supper."

"Oh no. I haven't even thought of supper."

"That's easy. I'll throw chicken on the grill, and you can make a pasta salad."

"Well that took away all my panic. Now, what's the one thing we have to do?"

"We need to talk about money. I'll show you my bank and tax records and go over my retirement income, then I'll explain my investment strategy."

I nodded. "I'll go over my bank statements and retirement income too and explain my original sources of income and the business records. This is really important for us to do before we are married; thank you for thinking of it."

He leaned close and kissed me. "I didn't want there to be any secrets between us, and money seems to be a sore subject with many couples."

"True." I jumped up. "I'm going to make the pasta salad, so it will be ready whenever we are."

After I put the pasta salad in the refrigerator, I headed toward the door to rejoin Ned outside and glanced at my backpack. *I forgot all about the envelope.* I took it out with me.

"What do you have there?" Ned asked.

"This came while we were getting our marriage license. A postal carrier delivered it, and Kim signed for it. I think it's the envelope that Giana told me she would send me. I'm hoping it's the records for the fourth bank."

"US Postal Service? Are you sure?" Ned asked.

"That's what she said."

He looked at the envelope in its sealed, clear plastic bag while I held it. "I don't see any stamps on it at all, much less anything that indicates it's from the US Postal Service."

I stared at it. "You're right. Just my name, Donut Hole, and the address of the shop. No return address, no bar codes, nothing."

"Don't open it," he growled. "In fact, set it on top of the cold grill top."

He picked up his phone. "Sheriff, Karen received a suspicious envelope at the shop today while we were at the courthouse. It's inside a clear, plastic bag. Kim signed for it then put it in Karen's desk."

He listened.

"Yes, it's still sealed; nope, Karen hasn't opened it. It's been in her backpack."

He narrowed his eyes. "Will do."

"Put your backpack in a plastic bag then go to the bath house and wash your hands then strip and put your clothes in a plastic bag and take a long shower. Be sure to shampoo your hair and rinse thoroughly. When you're out of the shower, give me a shout, and I'll bring in a clean towel and some fresh clothes for you."

"What?"

"We'll talk later. I'll get you two plastic bags. What else is in your backpack?"

"Only my flashlight you gave me; I had my records in my new tote bag along with my wallet."

"I'll give you another flashlight. Put your backpack in a plastic bag and put the bag next to the envelope."

After I put the plastic bag on the grill, Ned said, "Go. I'll bring in your shampoo and stuff after you put your clothes in the plastic bag, including your shoes; wash your hands then get into the shower and rinse off."

I hurried to the shower. *Ned's acting like I'm contaminated.*

I followed Ned's directions. As I stood stripped down in front of the sink, I sighed. *At least it isn't the middle of winter.*

I climbed into the shower and let the warm water flow over me.

"Are you rinsed?" Ned called from the door.

"Yes."

When he handed me the plastic bag with my shower things in it, I was relieved that he had turned his head.

I feel like a contaminated drowned rat.

I looked at my fingers and snorted. *Talk about wrinkled.*

I shampooed and rinsed twice then scrubbed myself with the shower gel and washcloth. When I felt thoroughly scrubbed and rinsed, I turned off the water.

Ned asked, "Ready for your towel?"

"Yes."

He handed me the towel. "Leave your shower things in the shower. Stay in the shower and dry off then let me know when you're ready for your clothes to wear back to the trailer."

"Clothes."

He handed me clothing piece by piece: underpants, shirt, and pants, then flip flops.

Is that it? I shrugged.

"Ready?"

"Yes."

"I'll walk with you."

When we left the bath house, two men who wore protective decontamination gear rushed into the women's shower then came out with the plastic bag of my clothes and the plastic bag with my shower things.

"The sheriff and I are very suspicious of that envelope, but you probably figured that out. A woman with the decontamination unit is at Kim's house, helping her to go through the same process as you. The good news is that the envelope is in a sealed plastic cover, which may have been to protect the courier. I'm really glad you had all your important records in that tote and not in the backpack with the envelope."

"What do you think is in the envelope?" I asked.

"I have no clue, and we may not hear officially for a quite a while. Sheriff is waiting at the trailer to talk to you."

As we walked to the trailer, Ned continued, "Speaking of unofficial, I understand Kim could not remember what the courier looked like at all; however, Andrew gave the investigators a detailed description. I have it on good authority that it wasn't Richard."

"Thank you."

"I'll tell you, hon, this whole thing scares me."

I frowned. "Alessandria called me on Giana's phone and told me a friend of hers would deliver some records from Giana, but now I remember that Papa told us they may leave the country and wouldn't take their phones."

"Did you recognize Alessandria's voice?"

"I never talked to Alessandria before. The voice was raspy, and Alessandria claimed she had a cold."

"It could have been anybody." Ned frowned.

"Not a man; the voice inflection and tone was definitely female."

"We're missing something."

"Yes, those additional mythical pages."

"So, what you have doesn't really prove anything?"

"Nothing, other than Sicily liked to move money around."

When we joined the sheriff, Ned said, "We probably want to go inside the trailer to talk."

When the sheriff glanced around, the nearby campers busied themselves, so they wouldn't appear as nosy as they had been before we joined the sheriff.

After we were inside, the sheriff asked, "What do you know, Karen?"

I told him about meeting with Giana and Papa, the bank records that Giana gave me, the phone call from someone who claimed to be Alessandria, and the extra records that a courier would deliver to the shop for me.

"Sounds like nothing out of the ordinary, although I don't understand why they didn't give the records to a professional to review," the sheriff said.

"Giana told me they hired a private investigator, and he provided most of the records that I have, but she needed someone who was familiar with their family to review the records. She told me their private investigator, a retired police detective, didn't find any evidence of criminal activity, and their lawyer didn't see anything illegal."

"So what were your conclusions?" Sheriff asked.

"I was convinced there was a fourth bank, and those records were missing."

"I don't see why that was worth…" Sheriff frowned. "Could the envelope be a prank or a hoax?"

I shook my head. "If it was a prank, it certainly backfired."

"I'll push for preliminary results by tomorrow." The sheriff rose. "I'd like to have a copy of the bank records."

"You can have them. I have my notes." I pulled out the bank records from my tote and handed them to the sheriff.

"We'll make copies, then I'll give them back to you in the morning. Thanks," the sheriff said.

After the sheriff left, Ned asked, "Do you think the sheriff will see anything you missed?"

"I doubt it, but he'll feel better reading them for himself."

Ned put his arm around me. "Now, I feel better too."

I leaned against him and sighed. "So do I."

My phone rang, and I glanced at it. "It's Kim."

Ned moved his arm, so I could reach for my phone that I'd set on the small table.

CHAPTER EIGHTEEN

When I answered, Kim's voice was shaky.

"Karen, did you have to shower?" she asked. "I was terrified that I'd brought home some horrible death powder or something, and the agent told me my shoes and clothes were fine, but she sacked them up and took them anyway; she did say that the fact that I washed my hands after I put the envelope in the desk drawer was good news. She went to the shop with Andrew and took all our aprons because I couldn't tell her which one I wore. They're going to burn all of them." Kim sobbed.

"I have more; we'll be fine."

"That helps." She sniffed.

"Can you describe the courier?"

"All I noticed was the courier wore driving gloves, a ball cap and a shirt with the US Postal Service logo, and dark blue slacks, but Andrew said the courier was taller than me, wore a brown toupee, and had a lumpy middle."

I frowned. "Lumpy? What did Andrew mean by that?"

"I'm not sure, but the courier might have been wearing padding."

After we hung up, Ned asked, "Is Kim okay?"

"She was upset because she was afraid she'd tracked something home, and the agent reassured her but still sacked up her clothes. The agent also took all the aprons that were hung on the pegs in the storeroom, but I have more."

"I'll fire up the grill."

After I fed Colonel, Roxie, and Mia, I made a dill dip then opened the door. When Colonel and Roxie went outside, I asked, "Care for any sweet tea, honey? I thought we'd enjoy a campground version of hors d'oeuvres while you grill."

"Sounds good to me."

I handed him the bowl of dip and the sack of corn tortilla chips then carried out two glasses of sweet tea.

The captain waved. "Glad you weren't hauled off to the pokey, Donut Lady. We've gotten used to seeing your pretty face around here."

I smiled when Ned said, "I've grown rather fond of her myself."

While we relaxed, Ned asked, "Am I pushing the cabin too hard?"

I stared at him. *I've never heard Ned be unsure of himself.*

I pulled my chair closer to his. "I think the cabin and being close to our friends is a great idea, if you're sure you can give up being a fulltime traveler."

Ned raised his eyebrows. "What if you hate fishing?"

"It depends; would you go without me?"

"Depends on whether that's okay with you and you'd have something to do, so you wouldn't be bored."

I giggled. "We could do this all day; If I don't go fishing, I'd read, garden, cook, and stroll to the lake with Colonel and Roxie as long as you are comfortable fishing alone."

Ned exhaled as he rose to put the chicken on the grill. "I love fishing. I've gone alone, and I've gone with friends."

"Good." I took the leftover dip and the half-eaten bag of chips into the trailer and set the table.

After we ate and washed dishes, Ned said, "I'd like to have our money talk now."

We sat together on the sofa while he reviewed his income from his retirement and investments then his bank statements. "My truck and trailer are paid off, so my only expenses I have are utilities, diesel for the truck, campground costs, medicine, insurance, and groceries."

After we reviewed my records of the Donut Hole then my personal investments, Ned said, "We have minimal expenses and no debt." Ned side-glanced me. "You're as cheap as I am."

I sniffed. "I prefer the term, 'frugal,' but cheap fits too. We're definitely a couple of old penny pinchers, aren't we? In fact, we could easily buy the cabin together, so neither one of us will have to dip very deeply into our investments."

After we put away all our paperwork, Ned sat in his chair to read.

I picked up my book then put it down. "I'm going to look at those surveillance photos the private investigator took. I spent so much time on the records, I never even glanced at them."

I spent an hour poring over the pictures then returned them to the folder.

"Anything interesting?" Ned asked.

"The only thing interesting is that there is not one picture of Sicily by herself. Francine is in most of them; I recognized her even though she was wearing wigs. Quinn is in almost half of them."

"Are you certain it's Quinn and not Richard?"

"I'm positive; Richard is not in any of them. The gun imprint on the jacket of the man in the photo is on the right side. Quinn's right handed, and Richard's left handed."

Ned raised his eyebrows. "I never noticed; you don't miss much, don't you?"

"I feel like I miss a lot and forget even more." I stifled a yawn.

"You're too hard on yourself, and I'm ready for bed too."

I kissed him goodnight, then he took Colonel and Roxie out while I changed clothes then climbed into bed.

When they came inside, Ned came to my bedside and kissed me. "Good night, hon."

Roxie followed him to the living room, and Colonel stretched out across the doorway.

"I love you," I mumbled.

"Love you too, donut warrior," Ned said as he turned off the lights in the living room.

Donut warrior? Wonder if my nightmares will decide it's time to fight donuts?

* * *

When I woke the next morning, the trailer was dark, but by the time I was dressed, the living room lights were on, and I heard the coffee pot gurgle.

"I'm going to the shower. If you take Colonel and Roxie out for a walk, your new flashlight is by the door, and you'll want a sweatshirt. Keep the dogs close to you. Captain's sitting in front of his trailer; he'll either come get me if anyone shows up or shoot them. He told me the sea pirates never bothered him after he dumped a few overboard."

I snickered as I hurried down the steps. "And I thought he was a sweet old man."

Ned snorted. "About as sweet as you are."

"I'm sweet, and don't make me toss you overboard," I growled, and Ned chuckled.

He opened the door, and the dogs rushed out. "We'll walk to the bath house with you," I said.

When I stepped outside, the captain had a citronella candle on his patio table, and the glow softened his deeply wrinkled brow and highlighted his ruddy, gaunt cheeks and bright eyes.

I said, "Good morning, Captain."

The captain saluted as Colonel, Roxie, and I accompanied Ned to the bath house. *I love my flashlight.*

After our walk, I fed Mia, Colonel, and Roxie and made my bed before Ned returned. When he came into the trailer, I was frying bacon.

I poured a cup of coffee and handed it to him. "Bacon, eggs, and toast sound okay this morning?"

"Perfect."

Ned folded up the sofa. "The captain wants to talk to me. Call me when breakfast is ready, or I'll be over there all morning."

Colonel and Roxie went with Ned, and Mia rubbed my leg and meowed for bacon.

"I have never given you bacon, and you haven't touched your food yet, so don't tell me you're starving," I said.

I put our eggs into the hot frying pan then opened the door and called, "Breakfast, honey."

"Be right there."

As I closed the door, the captain said, "You're a smart man, Ned; I'd hustle too if my woman had my breakfast ready."

Colonel and Roxie came inside with Ned, and I refilled Ned's cup after he put it down on the table.

By the time Ned washed his hands, the toaster popped, and I plated our eggs, bacon, and toast then set our food on the table.

While we ate, Ned said, "Captain wanted to give me advice on how to treat a woman. Do you need any jewels?"

I giggled. "Is that why we're getting a boat? Have you received your pirate training? Can you imagine me with jewels?"

Ned chuckled. "Tiara, maybe."

I nodded. "That would work, but not just any tiara."

"I was afraid of that." Ned wiggled his eyebrows.

"I was thinking about the trailer. I think we should keep it, and maybe even keep it here."

"I paid the annual campground fee in advance; it was cheaper than four months would have been," Ned said. "There's no rush to sell or move the trailer for a while."

"We have the option of selling the house and staying at the trailer during the week and spending weekends at the cabin. After I retire, we could live in the cabin and take short or long camping trips or just come to the campground for a change of scenery."

"I like the part where you're considering retiring. What would you do with the Donut Hole?"

"I haven't thought through that far." I smiled.

On our way to the shop, Ned asked, "Have you mentioned the idea of retiring to anyone?"

"Not really. Why?"

"Just curious. You might mention it to David and Kim sometime."

When Ned unzipped Mia's carrier, she dashed to Andrew, and the shadows waited near the front window.

"You found the aprons," I said. Andrew grinned. "Mama told me you said you had more, so I found them."

"That's great, thank you." I washed my hands. "We're going simple today, right? What's our group?"

"The Liar's Club. I told Mama you'd teach her how to do imaginary sprinkles."

I giggled. "Perfect. What else?"

"We'll put maple-sprinkled donuts and martini scones on the board."

"The martini scones are Kim's vanilla scones, right? What about the maple donuts?"

"Classic chocolate glazed, except I'll use milk chocolate instead of dark chocolate, and Mama can add the imaginary sprinkles. Woody and I planned on Saturday, and Mr. Alfred helped."

I chuckled. "You three are brilliant. I love it. Do I still make the cranberry-orange scones?"

"Yes because Mr. Alfred said the Liar's Club will be suspicious of everything, and it's good to keep them guessing."

"If there isn't anything I can do to help, I brought my book," Ned said.

"Right now's there nothing except for Andrew and me to get busy."

While Ned read, I mixed and baked scones, and Andrew mixed his second batch of dough then finished frying his first batch.

When Kim arrived, she smiled as she put on her new apron and ball cap then started her vanilla scones. I finished the drizzles on my scones then pushed the button for the large coffee machine and made coffee in our two smaller pots.

When the sheriff came into the shop, I poured two cups of coffee as Ned joined him at the counter.

Andrew plated two donuts and a vanilla scone for the sheriff and a cranberry-orange scone for Ned.

I poured myself a cup of coffee and stood behind the counter. "Our group today is the Liars' Club. Sheriff, you have what we're calling the maple donut, a martini scone, and your pink-sprinkled donut."

Sheriff narrowed his eyes as he examined his plate. "Are you sure this is maple?"

Andrew and Kim giggled.

"Would we tell a fib on the Liars' Club day?" I fluttered my eyelashes, and Ned spewed his coffee then coughed.

"Of course, you would." Sheriff rolled his eyes as he took a big bite. "Mmm. Milk chocolate. Excellent, Andrew. It definitely looks like maple to me."

"Will I have to put myself on administrative leave if I bite into the scone?"

"Only if you're looking for an excuse." Kim tittered.

Sheriff took a big bite. "This is good, Kim. It's your signature vanilla bean scone, isn't it?"

"Signature?" Kim's eyes widened.

"Yes, it's really good. Can I write the menu on the board?"

"It's your job, Sheriff," I said.

Kim marched to the sheriff. "Were you pulling my leg?"

"Not at all, but congratulations for becoming the Scone Lady. You fit right in here." The sheriff continued writing.

Kim beamed and sashayed to her scones then raised her arms. "I'm Scone Lady!"

We all applauded, and Kim bowed as Barbara and David came into the shop.

"What on earth?" Barbara asked.

"I'm Scone Lady," Kim squealed.

"Congratulations, Kim. Sorry we're late, everyone. We had to sign some more papers." David hurried to the pink room, and Andrew carried an apron for David as he joined him.

"Did you leave me anything to do?" Barbara asked.

"I haven't started the second batch of cranberry-orange scones."

"I'll show you where the aprons are, Barbara," Kim said.

"This place runs like clockwork, Karen. You've done a good job of training this crew." Sheriff hugged me before he left.

"Teach me how to throw the imaginary sprinkles, Karen," Kim said as she and Barbara came out of the storeroom.

"We need the clear fishbowl from the storeroom."

Kim lifted up the bowl. "Barbara told me. I've got it."

I smiled. "Set it on the counter, like it's horribly heavy."

Kim struggled as she carried the bowl with both hands then set it down hard on the counter.

"Whew." She wiped her brow.

"Excellent. Now reach in with one hand and scoop up all the sprinkles that you can. It takes concentration."

After Kim scooped up the imaginary sprinkles, she said, "Now what?"

I twirled my arm like I had a lasso then quickly flicked my wrist as I dropped the imaginary sprinkles.

Kim copied my motion; everyone cheered, and she curtseyed.

"You're a natural, Scone Lady," I said.

She grinned. "I love this job."

My eyes welled up, and I hurried to the storeroom. Ned followed me.

"What's wrong, hon?" he asked when we were in the storeroom.

Tears streamed down my face, and I brushed them away. "Kim told me she was bored to tears with working at the hardware store because she felt useless. The Donut Hole has been a huge boost for her."

Ned hugged me. "Add lifesaver to your resume, hon. Are you ready to look at some cabins?"

I smiled and hung up my apron and ball cap. "Yes."

When we walked out of the storeroom, I said, "We're on our way to look at cabins."

"We're ready," Kim said. "Take pictures."

"You're right, Kim; you're ready."

Ned stopped at the doorway. "Are you going with us, Mia?"

She darted into her carrier, and Ned zipped it up.

"Let's go." Ned picked up the carrier.

Colonel and Roxie trotted out and waited for us at the truck.

On the way to the cabins, Ned asked, "Are you okay?"

"I'm fine. I'm excited that Kim's found a career that's hers." I smiled. "And I've found a man that's mine."

Ned grinned. "You got that right, Cabin Lady."

"A promotion, wow." I kissed him on the cheek.

After Ned parked in the driveway, he said, "I like that they've cleared almost fifty feet between the trees and the cabin. The recommendation for our area is thirty feet. We'll hear Shirley drive up. Let's walk around."

"Is that cement board siding?"

"Yes, and it's definitely my preference."

"I like the gray; it blends in with the surroundings."

When we reached the back, I sighed. "That's a beautiful back porch. My rockers would fit there just fine."

As we headed back toward the truck, I said, "A car just turned in the driveway."

"Stand behind me until we're sure it's Shirley," Ned said.

When Shirley climbed out of her car, she wore her red jacket and high heels and carried a red folder.

I smiled and waved. *Only Shirley would wear high heels to show a cabin.*

After she unlocked the door, we went inside the great room.

Ned scanned the room. "I like the stone fireplace."

"These wooden floors are beautiful," I said.

"It has a dishwasher, a gas stove, and lots of cabinets." I pulled out our list and checked off items.

I opened the door next to the refrigerator. "Nice sized pantry."

"The utility room is here," Shirley said.

"It's larger than I expected. We could store our large bags of dog food in here."

Shirley checked the listing. "It has central air and heat."

After we checked the main bathroom and the guest bedroom, we walked into the master bedroom.

"Walk-in closet, hon."

"There is definitely enough space for us here." I looked in the master bathroom. "I love the tile they used in the bathrooms. The double sinks are a surprise." I opened the door between the standalone bathtub and the shower. "Linen closet."

"It doesn't have a garage, but I saw a shed in back for a lawnmower, a tool shed, and a wellhouse," Ned said. "How deep is the well, Shirley?"

"I have that right here." Shirley handed him a sheet of paper, and Ned nodded as he read it. "It's deep. It may be tapped into an artisan spring. Where's the septic field?"

Shirley handed him another sheet.

"Right where I thought it was."

"Is this the one with the partially finished attic?" I asked.

"I hope not," Ned said, "they are a hassle."

Shirley checked her folder. "No, that's the other one. Ready to look at the next house?"

"I need to take a few pictures." I snapped photos of the fireplace, the stove, and the master bedroom and bath then went out back and took a picture of the porch.

On our way to the second cabin, Ned followed Shirley. "What do you think?"

"I like it. I didn't know how I'd feel about a great room, but it gives us extra living space that is taken up by walls; we could have everybody over."

"Isn't this second house a little smaller?" Ned asked.

"Yes, but it's still bigger than my house. Do you think it's too far away from town?"

"I don't think so, but do you have any concerns about it?"

"It would be nice if it was fenced. I'm kind of spoiled at home because I can let Colonel and Roxie out back."

"We could make that a priority. How much would you want fenced?"

"I'd love to have the cleared space around the house fenced, so Colonel and Roxie would have room to run."

Ned nodded. "That's what I was thinking too, and there's some outdoor lighting I'd like to put in."

When Ned parked at the second house, he said, "I'll have some serious clearing to do, won't I? The trees are so close to the house that the limbs hang over the roof."

"Is that a dealbreaker?" I asked.

"No, there are good people that clear trees for a living."

When we went inside the cabin, Ned scanned the great room. "No fireplace; that's too bad."

I stared at the kitchen appliances. "Is that an electric stove?"

Shirley pulled the listing and frowned. "It clearly says gas stove."

Ned narrowed his eyes. "This stove is new." He pulled it away from the wall. "There's a gas line here that is capped off. I think they took their gas stove with them, not that I blame them, but I'm surprised their agent didn't update the listing. I'll check for a propane tank."

"Is that a dealbreaker?" Shirley asked.

"It's more of a strike one, although we'll have to ask Ned, but I think no fireplace might be strike two." I scanned the kitchen area. "Where's the pantry and utility?"

"I don't see a pantry. Here's the utility." Shirley opened bifold doors. "Maybe this used to be the pantry. Things aren't looking good are they?"

"Not really." I opened the back door; the porch was a covered step into the house. "I think no porch for my rockers might a dealbreaker."

Shirley peered out the door. "How much time do you spend outside?"

"Every chance I get."

"Well, then, I agree; this doesn't work for you."

Ned came in the front door. "I can see where the propane tank was, but it's gone. They love cooking with gas as much as you do, hon. We can buy a gas stove and a tank."

"There's no back porch, but maybe we could add one," I said.

"I suppose we could, but with all the other expenses to bring this cabin to the same level as the first one, that's a dealbreaker, unless the asking price is low enough to make it worthwhile. Shirley, can we go back to the first house again? There are a few more things I need to check," Ned said.

"The asking price for the first cabin is less than the second cabin, so you'd have to love this location more than the other one," Shirley said. "I'll lock up then meet you at the other one."

While we waited at the first cabin for Shirley, Ned strode around the corner then returned. "There is a propane tank here, and it's hooked up. I just wanted to check. There is also a tankless water heater, and it's gas. The heating and air conditioning unit is electric. I looked in the wellhouse, and the tank looks good, but we'll want an inspection by a professional."

When Shirley joined us, she asked, "Are you interested enough for me to work up an offer, or do you want to take some time to discuss? I can run some comps for you, and we can get back together this afternoon after I pick up Woody, if you like."

When I glanced at Ned, he said, "You're our business person. I like the cabin."

"Text me when you want us to come to your office," I said.

"Will do." Shirley locked up.

"What do you think?" Ned asked we headed back to the trailer.

"I loved the first cabin, but my frugal self is interested in seeing the comparable sales. We'll have to put in the fence right away."

Ned nodded.

After we reached the trailer, Ned took Mia inside and opened her carrier then his phone buzzed a text as we relaxed on our camp chairs. He glanced at it. "I'm going inside to return this with a call."

I nodded and watched Colonel and Roxie play. My phone rang. *Darlene.*

"Are you at work?"

"No, Ned and I looked at a couple of cabins near the lake this morning and really liked one of them."

"Are you breaking in that crew, so you can retire?"

CHAPTER NINETEEN

"Things are promising. Andrew, David, and Barbara are comfortable with their tasks, and Kim has really thrown herself into the business. Sheriff called her Scone Lady this morning, and she was thrilled. I didn't realize how bored she was at the hardware store."

"She has been for quite a while. Good for her on finding her niche where she can be successful, but I distracted myself. First, I talked to the church office, and the pastor forgot about a church function on Thursday; we can have our engagement celebration on Wednesday or Friday, but the office prefers Wednesday."

"Tomorrow? That's kind of up to you. Will you have enough time to prepare and get the word out?"

"I've alerted Barbara and Gee. Everything's taken care of, and Gee will be home this evening. She decided she didn't want to be left out, and I think she was driving Tiffany crazy."

"I think it's because they are so alike," I said.

"That's what I've always thought too. Second, the professional cleaners have cleaned up your house, but they want you to look over what they've pulled out to see if there is anything you'd like to salvage. After you've done that, they'll finish cleaning then haul away all the rubbish, and your house will be ready for you by the end of the day."

"That's exciting. When Ned gets off the phone, we'll go to the house."

"Pick up our lunch from Gus's. Gee's cousin left this morning, so you can catch me up on your news."

As I hung up, Ned came out of the trailer with a scowl. "Sheriff heard the preliminary results of that envelope. The fine powder inside it contained a high percentage of an illicitly manufactured street drug that drug dealers frequently used to cut other opioids because of its low cost and high potency. The street drug is fatal in small doses, and because it is in a fine powder, anyone could inadvertently inhale a fatal dose."

I shuddered. "If I'd opened it while I was at the Donut Hole…"

He put his arm around me. "You wouldn't have."

I sniffed back a tear. "You're right. I like to focus on Donut Hole business while I'm there; I would have waited until I got home. I'm glad your Wildlife Ruffian instincts kicked in."

Ned beamed. "I'm kind of useful to have around."

I smiled. "Yes, you are, honey, and I'm going to put you to work. Darlene called me, and the engagement party has been changed to tomorrow evening at the church."

"Really? Here's an idea, why don't I give the pastor a call, and we can be married forty-five minutes before the party starts. We'll have all the right people there."

"That's crazy," I said. "Tomorrow is Wednesday; we can't coordinate all those people in time."

"Not our job, hon, because you delegated all that to the Big Three; besides, when could you get everyone together again?"

"I don't know. Maybe."

"Give me a minute to call the pastor."

Ned stepped inside the trailer to make his call but wasn't gone very long.

"What did the pastor say?"

"He said it was the craziest thing he'd ever heard, and he wouldn't miss it for the world. He was still laughing when we hung up."

"See? What did I tell you?"

"You told me you'd marry me." Ned winked then smiled.

I giggled. "That I did."

"Time to get the pre-engagement party wedding plans in gear."

""Let me tell you what else Darlene said. The professional cleaners want me to see if there is anything I want to salvage before they take the rubbish to the dump. I'm sure there isn't, but they are waiting for me at the house."

"Let's go."

"Darlene wants us to pick up lunch at Gus's and eat with her."

"That's perfect because we can talk to her over lunch," Ned said. "Are you going to call in an order?"

I snickered. "It wouldn't do us any good. Darlene and Gus have a special relationship. I think she likes to call in orders and harass him. I'll text her now about the pre-engagement party plans."

I sent the text. "I told her we could talk more at lunch, but she's on board with the new plan and will get the word to the right people."

Ned chuckled. "Do you remember Darlene at school?"

I frowned. "No, I don't."

"She was just as feisty then as she is now. All of us younger boys were terrified of her; actually, I think every boy in school was afraid of her." He shook his head. "She certainly had a way with words. I'll call the pastor."

"Mia, we're going to check the house then visit Sandy and Mandy," I said.

Mia scooted into her carrier.

When Ned turned the truck onto my street, Colonel whined.

Ned parked and opened the back door of the truck, and Colonel and Roxie dashed to the front porch. When Ned picked up the carrier, Mia purred.

A woman opened the door. "Ms. O'Brien, we have everything in the back; the house is what they call broom clean right now, but we'll scrub all the surfaces and mop the floors, so you can move in anytime you like after three o'clock today."

Ned opened Mia's carrier, and she stalked the shadows who came in with me while Ned and I followed the woman to the back. Colonel and Roxie disappeared down the hallway as they investigated the house.

"This is everything," the woman said.

Ned and I walked around the rubble.

After a second time around, I said, "I don't really see anything to salvage."

Ned pointed. "There are a few pieces of wood that Vic would love. Do you mind if I pull them out? Won't take me long."

"Not at all," I said.

Ned pulled out five pieces of wood and set them on the back porch.

"That's it," he said.

"Great. Can you meet us here at three?" the woman asked. "We'd like for you to inspect the house then sign some paperwork, and we'll turn in our key to you, but we still recommend you change the locks. The locksmith installed new deadbolts on the front and back doors, but he gave those keys to Ms. Darlene."

"Thank you for everything," Ned said. "We'll see you at three."

"We're going to see Sandy," I said, and Mia dashed out of the pantry and into her carrier.

We waited in the truck while Ned picked up the order Darlene had called in. On our way to the thrift shop, his phone buzzed a text.

"We certainly are popular people today, aren't we?" I asked when my phone buzzed a text too.

I read my phone. "Shirley wants to know if we can meet her at her office at one-thirty."

"We should be able to do that," Ned said.

After he let the dogs out of the truck, Ned picked up the lunches, and I carried Mia as we followed Colonel and Roxie to the open thrift store door. I opened Mia's carrier, and she stalked the main aisle as she looked for Sandy, and the shadows floated behind her like a boat's wake.

"I set up one of the dining tables for us, so we can eat close to the door," Darlene said. "I made a quick list of who you might want to be at the wedding, and you can look it over while we eat."

Ned set our lunches on the table, and while I set my tote on the table then opened the sack and put the wrapped sandwiches and drinks on the table, Ned read his text.

"I've got another call to make. Go ahead and eat; don't wait for me."

He strode outside, and Darlene and I unwrapped our sandwiches.

"That's a nice tote. Where's your backpack?" Darlene asked.

"GBI has my backpack. Ned gave me the tote." I lifted out my flashlight and put it on the table. "He gave me a flashlight just like this one earlier, but it was in my backpack, so he gave me another one. I never thought how important a flashlight would be at a campground."

"Here's the list." Darlene handed it to me as I took a bite of my sandwich.

"You have Emma on here," I said.

"Sheriff called her, and she's coming home tonight for tomorrow's engagement party. Her mother's sister is going to stay with Emma's mother. It doesn't hurt for Emma to take a break."

"I don't see anyone missing."

Ned hurried inside. "There are a rash of coyote sightings being called in. The sheriff is skeptical, but he has to check them out. He doesn't have all the staff, though. One caller reported her neighbor trapped a coyote in her garage. Sheriff asked me to check that one."

Ned wolfed down his sandwich.

"I don't suppose you'd go with me. I told the sheriff I'd ask you, and he laughed."

"We've got three big dogs and two cranky cats," I said.

"And one crankier old woman," Darlene added.

"Keep the door locked. I won't be long," Ned growled while he hurried to his truck.

"We're not locking the door, are we?" I asked.

"No. I keep my phone in my lap and my pistol in the side pocket on my wheelchair. We'll be fine."

I nodded and took another bite as a car parked in front of the store.

"Who's that?" Darlene squinted at the driver. "I can't think of any redheads we've seen around here, but she looks familiar. Is she wearing a wig? That's a good quality one if she is."

Wig? I rose from my chair and set my flashlight on the seat.

The woman walked into the shop. "I'm looking for a small figurine of a mother and child. Do you have any?"

It's Francine.

Darlene put on her customer smile. "I have two on a shelf in the back. I'll get them."

As Darlene wheeled herself to the backroom, I said, "We have coffee. Do you care for any, Francine?"

Francine's nostrils flared as her eyes flashed her hatred. "You've always been so high and mighty. Shirley was my best friend until you showed up; she told me everything until you stole her from me."

Colonel growled, then he stepped between me and Francine; Roxie stood between Francine and the door, and Mandy assumed a position in the aisle to guard the back room.

While the shadows swirled over Francine's head, flecks of spittle sprayed from her mouth as she ranted. "Everybody in town thinks you're so great, but you're just a meddling prison convict. I got rid of that obnoxious Sissy and that wimpy boyfriend of hers; they cramped my style and tried to blackmail me. Parasites."

She hissed. "I've waited a long time to see you dead. Call off your dog, or he's first."

Mia and Sandy raced down the aisle and hissed at Francine.

Roxie stepped closer to Francine and growled, then Mandy stalked Francine with a snarling growl.

"What's wrong with these animals? Call them off."

When Mia swiped at Francine's leg with her claws, Francine screamed then kicked at Mia, but Mia jumped to the side. Francine's voice struck a maniacal pitch. "You never fooled me, you witch. I knew you wanted to snatch away everything I had for yourself. It's time for your last haircut."

She whipped out a pair of long, slender scissors then lunged toward me. Colonel snarled and leapt up, and I used both hands as I swung the flashlight and slammed it against the side of her head, and her wig went flying. She dropped to the ground and didn't move as the snarling dogs stood over her.

"I called nine-one-one when she said, 'high and mighty'." Darlene wheeled out from behind a bookcase. "I couldn't get a clear shot."

I glanced away from Francine and stared at the parking lot as Ned slid to a stop then jumped out of his truck followed by the sheriff and Benjamin in their cruisers.

"Oh lord, I'm in trouble." I shook my head.

"Just look all bridey," Darlene said.

I snorted. "Bridey?"

Ned snatched me off my feet and carried me away from Francine.

"Good boy, Colonel. Leave it. I've got her," Sheriff said.

Colonel barked, then he, Roxie, and Mandy backed away; Mia and Sandy held their tails high in triumph as they marched down the aisle to the back.

"Do I call for an ambulance?" Benjamin asked.

"Are you okay, Karen?" Sheriff asked.

I mumbled, then Ned loosened his hold on me, so I could talk. "I'm fine."

"Go ahead. I'll call the crime scene investigators," Sheriff said.

As the sheriff returned from making his call, the ambulance loaded the still-unconscious Francine into the back of the rig then pulled away from the parking lot with flashing lights and a piercing siren.

"Does this mean we have to close the shop?" Darlene's woeful expression on her face twitched as it shifted into her wicked smile.

Sheriff sighed. "Yes, and the chief crime scene investigator wants to know if you're going to retire, Karen, or do they open a regional office in Asbury."

"She's going to retire, aren't you, hon?" Ned asked.

"Yes, I'm ready to retire."

After I told the sheriff what happened while Benjamin took notes, I gave the surveillance photos to the sheriff. "I don't have any idea how useful these are, but the private investigator took them, and Giana gave them to me."

Darlene wheeled to her desk and checked her messages on her computer. "Your wedding dress will be ready tomorrow at two, and you can pick up the tuxedo any time after one thirty."

"Western boots for both of us," Ned whispered, and I nodded.

On our way to Shirley's office, Ned asked, "You're retiring from the Donut Hole, right?"

"Exactly, and thanks for covering for me."

Ned laughed. "Anytime, hon. I knew that was what you meant, so what's your name going to be tomorrow? Whatever you want is fine with me; I think Shirley will want to know for the offer. Are you going to stick with O'Brien, or will you be Mrs. Burke?"

"Well, I can't see you as Mr. O'Brien, so I think I'll be Mrs. Burke."

"Yes!" Ned pumped his arm, and I giggled.

"So, what are we doing after we sign papers at Shirley's office?" he asked.

"We buy appropriately gaudy Western boots for both of us and a fishing pole for me then go to a combined bachelor and bachelorette party that Barbara is hosting as soon as I tell her about it. I'll text her."

Ned laughed as he parked in front of Shirley's office, then we trooped into Shirley's office with our two brave dogs and our fearless cat.

ACKNOWLEDGMENTS

Thanks to my husband for his amazing patience, support, and being relatively willing to listen to my latest plot dilemma. Thanks to my editor for her encouragement and determination to stamp out bad grammar beginning with my random commas.

Thank you for reading. You keep reading; I'll keep writing!

Tell a friend how much you love Donut Lady and a leave a short review with your favorite bookseller. Authors can always use a few sparkles to brighten the gloomiest days.

PRO TIP: Post a five-star rating or recommend a book: both count the same as reviews!

Ready for news about what's next? Subscribe to my not-your-typical newsletter via my website: https://judithabarrett.com

ABOUT THE AUTHOR

Judith A. Barrett, award-winning author, lives on a farm in Georgia with her husband, two dogs, and chickens. She writes series for her readers: thriller, post-apocalyptic science fiction, and cozy mystery novels. Stories with a twist: not your typical characters from not your typical author!

Her motto: *You keep reading; I'll keep writing!*

When she isn't writing, Judith is working on farm chores, hiking or camping with her husband and dogs, or rocking on her front porch while she watches the sunset.

Follow Judith on Bookbub or your favorite bookseller for news of her latest release!

Let's keep in touch!

www.ingramcontent.com/pod-product-compliance
Lightning Source LLC
Chambersburg PA
CBHW031958060726
47497CB00015B/301